TRAPPED

Jack raised his M-16 and shot the huge man. He stumbled backward, a growing red stain on the front of his shirt. Jack and Bert knelt by the girl's side and looked at her torn and bloody bare feet. "What's your name?" Bert asked.

"Lindsey Marlowe. They killed my mother."

"How many of them are there, Lindsey?"

She shook her head. "I don't know. Twenty-five or thirty, at least." She cut her eyes to the fallen man. "Is he dead?" When Jack nodded, she went on, "They have men waiting for you at both ends of the valley. The convicts . . . they'll never let any of you out alive. Especially the leader, Karl something or other . . ."

"Karl Parsons," Bert muttered. "He's from this area. He was born no good."

"The woman with the convicts is his sister, I think," Lindsey said, shuddering. Then she added, almost in a whisper, "It's disgusting, they're. . . ." She stopped, unable to go on.

"Kathy?" Bert asked. "Is her husband's name Dave?" Lindsey nodded.

"Kathy is the last relative Karl has around here," Bert said. "They're half brother and sister. Now things are beginning to make some sense."

"She helped her brother in the breakout?" Jack asked, astonished.

"Yeah, but there's no way she could get her hands on all those automatic weapons. Others are involved. Did you hear any other names, Lindsey?"

"I'm sure I did." She looked at both men. "What are we going to do?" she asked.

"Try to stay alive," Jack replied.

BOOK YOUR PLACE ON OUR WEBSITE AND MAKE THE READING CONNECTION!

We've created a customized website just for our very special readers, where you can get the inside scoop on everything that's going on with Zebra, Pinnacle and Kensington books.

When you come online, you'll have the exciting opportunity to:

- View covers of upcoming books
- Read sample chapters
- Learn about our future publishing schedule (listed by publication month *and author*)
- Find out when your favorite authors will be visiting a city near you
- Search for and order backlist books from our online catalog
- Check out author bios and background information
- Send e-mail to your favorite authors
- Meet the Kensington staff online
- Join us in weekly chats with authors, readers and other guests
- Get writing guidelines
- AND MUCH MORE!

**Visit our website at
http://www.pinnaclebooks.com**

ORDEAL

William W. Johnstone

Pinnacle Books
Kensington Publishing Corp.
http://www.williamjohnstone.com

In war there is no second prize for the runner-up.
Omar Bradley

Prologue

"You old farts have a good time in the wilderness," she told her husband.

"We always do, Baby," he replied, reaching out and patting her butt.

She laughed and playfully slapped his hand away.

"You sure you don't want me to take you to the airport?"

"No. The taxi will be here shortly."

He carried her suitcases outside for her and together they sat on the front steps, waiting for the taxi.

"Real estate agent upped the price again on the house," Jack said. "I told him I'd talk to you about it, but I felt the answer would be the same."

"It is. We don't need the money, Jack. And where would we go if we sold?"

"I don't want to sell either, Honey. I'm going to tell him to stop wasting our time . . . and his."

"Good. There's the taxi."

Jack carried her bags to curbside and kissed his wife of

thirty-five years good-bye. He stood for a moment watching the cab round the corner and move out of sight. She would be gone for a month, on a long cruise with friends: the wives of the men Jack was going camping in the wilderness with.

He walked back to the house to resume his own packing. He was driving out to Montana and would meet his buddies there. Harry was driving his Explorer out from St. Louis, and the two vehicles would hold all their gear. They would drive as far as the roads would allow and meet up with the guide, who would take them deep into the wilderness.

Jack fixed a pot of coffee and stood by the counter waiting for it to drip. Hard to believe it had been forty-five years since he and his friends had first met in Korea. Just kids, all of them, in 1953. Then the war (the Police Action, as it was called for a long time) was over, and they didn't see each other again until they were all recalled as advisors early in the Vietnam mess. They still weren't much older than kids even then. But that war sobered them and matured them.

Now they were all retired and living comfortably and getting together every year for a camping/fishing trip while their wives went on a cruise.

Jack fixed his mug of coffee and walked through the house to the bedroom. He finished his packing and carried the bags out to the garage, stowing them in the back of his Explorer with the gear he'd already packed for the trip: tent, sleeping bag, and other camping equipment.

Jack Bailey hesitated for a moment, deep in thought, then walked back into the house and opened the top drawer of his dresser. He took out a Beretta 9mm pistol, model 92S, in a leather military style flap holster, and two boxes of ammunition. He walked back to the garage and stowed the weapon in one of his suitcases.

Then he set about securing the house for his departure.

Jack was due to pull out in the morning. He was really looking forward to this camping trip.

Ted Dawson sat in the den of his home just outside Chicago and stared at his oldest son. Father and son just didn't like each other. They were stuck with each other on this camping trip and neither one—at least for the moment—was going to budge an inch toward any sort of reconciliation.

The elder Dawson's wife had left that morning on an early flight for New York City, her daughter-in-law with her. The two women got along great. It was father and son who couldn't stay in the same room for ten minutes without getting into a fuss.

"You want me to look over your camping gear, Andy?" Ted asked.

"I'm perfectly capable of packing for a camping trip."

"I didn't say you weren't, Son."

"Fine. Let's just leave it at that."

Ted sighed. What a delightful vacation this was going to be.

"I still say the best thing for me to do is stay here," Andy said. "Mom will never know I didn't go along."

"Of course she'd know. There'll be four cameras on this trip, and your mother will want to look at all the pictures. If you're not in any of them ..." The father shrugged his shoulders. "She'd put that together in a hurry."

"I guess you guys are going to yak about the wars you fought in," Andy remarked.

"I'm sure the subject will come up."

"That's why I packed a dozen paperbacks. I can always go off in the bushes and read when the four of you start talking about your wartime heroics."

Ted sighed with the patience of a father. He did love his son; he just didn't like him. Andy was a jerk, and had been since he was barely in his teens. A liberal, left-wing rabble-rousing jerk.

Ted was a solid, law and order, very conservative member of the Republican Party . . . and so were his friends. As a matter of fact, Ted didn't have any friends who supported liberal causes. Not a single one.

"Let's make the best of this trip, Son. How about it?"

"I'll try, Dad. For Mom's sake."

"Thank you," Ted said drily. "For that much."

Andy stared at his father for a moment, then shrugged his shoulders. Andy hated everything even remotely connected with camping.

Dennis Jackson walked through the empty house, giving it a final check. He was really looking forward to this trip. Retired not quite a year, he found the inactivity was driving him crazy. The offer to buy his business had been just too good to let pass. Not that he and his wife needed the money, for they didn't. As a matter of fact, all the guys going on this trip had been wildly successful in business.

And now they were all retired. A bunch of guys in their early sixties with nothing to do.

Dennis turned out the lights in the kitchen and stepped out into the garage, locking the door behind him. "See you in a month," he said to the empty house, then got in his car and backed out.

Harry Michaels put St. Louis behind him as he pointed the nose of his vehicle westward. The interstate stretched out before him. It would be good to see all the guys again. Harry knew that they all looked forward to these camping and fishing trips . . . much more so now that they were all retired with time on their hands.

Harry thought about the pistol he'd tucked away in his luggage at the last moment, and wondered why he'd felt such a strong urgency to take it. He hadn't fired a gun in years.

He shrugged off that thought and clicked on the radio, punching buttons until he found a station playing music that was at least comprehensible to older ears. He was really looking forward to this trip. They were all going to have a good time. Well, except probably for Andy. That jerk.

"This is going to be fun, Sandy."

The woman looked at her husband and smiled. She tried not to make the smile dutiful. Spending several weeks in the wilderness was definitely not real high on her list of favorite things to do, but she was determined to make the best of it. Both of them needed this vacation in the worst way—Ed certainly needed to get away and have some fun.

"Right, Sandy?" he pressed.

"Right," she replied. She looked around the den. Sure was quiet with the kids gone.

As if reading her mind, Ed touched her shoulder. "The kids are having the time of their lives, Sandy," he said. "They're not even giving us the first thought."

"I'm sure you're right."

He laughed at the expression on her face. "Camp will be fun for them. It sure was for me—after that first day, anyway."

She looked at her watch. Her new watch. Ed had bought it for her—a sportsman's model guaranteed to be shock-proof, waterproof, dust-proof, and every other kind of proof. Problem was, there were so many dials and numbers and buttons and gizmos on the thing it took her half a day to figure out how to tell the time. "We'd better get moving."

"We're off to see the wizard!" Ed shouted.

She laughed at his childlike excitement and took his hand. "First let's get to the airport on time."

Laughing, they made one final check of the house, locked it up, and headed for the airport.

I really hate this outdoorsy crap! Abby thought.

"I think this is what we both need," her husband said.

Right, Abby thought. *My God, Shawn—the marriage is over. It's finished. Let's just sweep the pieces into a dustpan, dump them in the trash, and be done with it.*

"This will probably do it for us, Abby," her husband said.

I'm sure of that, she mused.

"I think in the wilderness we'll both see where we've made mistakes and how to correct them."

Abby said nothing. *Maybe if we'd had kids that might have helped,* she thought, but she knew in her heart that wouldn't have made any difference. She and Shawn had been all wrong for each other from the start. She had wished a thousand times she had listened to her parents about Shawn and not been so mulish.

She lifted her eyes to her husband of ten years but he had turned away. *Oh, Shawn, I don't mean to hurt you. But we've got to end it now before we end up saying terrible things and hating each other.*

Shawn turned back to his wife. She could see hurt in his eyes, brought there, she knew, by her continued silence about their vacation trip. "I guess I'll make one more check of the house," he said.

"You do that, Shawn." *One more check is right*, Abby thought. *Because I won't be coming back here.*

Abby Hayes had no way of knowing how prophetic her thoughts were.

One

Thirty miles from the nearest town, the brand new ultra-maximum security penitentiary was a showcase of technology. Built to house the most brutal of criminals, it was escape-proof, the engineers boasted. The guards and technicians had been in training for months, learning all about the equipment and all the latest techniques in dealing with hard-core criminals.

Prisoners had begun arriving several months before: the most vicious criminals in America. There was Jans Pendley, mass murderer. Oscar Mansford, kidnapper and murderer. Scott Craig, a homicidal killer who preyed on young girls—he'd killed a dozen before being caught. Tony Gorman, a syndicate hit man—he'd killed at least ten people, and was suspected of killing at least that many more. Randy O'Donnell, bomber for some shadowy group in Ireland—he was responsible for the deaths of several dozen people: men, women, and children. Randy had been caught by the FBI after a bombing in America in which a dozen civilians had been killed. Barry Randall, murderer. Newton Holmes, rapist, killer. Dozens of other hardened criminals, tried and convicted of the most heinous crimes. The worst of them all was Karl Perry, real name: Parsons. Karl had turned rotten at fourteen and never looked back. During his years on the outside, Karl had—in addition to stealing anything he could get his hands on—raped and killed and tortured and terrorized his way from New York to California.

The men in the maximum security lockup were serving multiple life sentences for their crimes. After their heavily guarded trip from various jails and penitentiaries around the nation, the only way any of them would ever again leave the walls of the prison was to die and be carried outside for burial.

That was what the designers of the prison said. The prisoners, however, had other ideas about freedom. Most had begun working on escape plans from the first moment of their arrival.

Especially Karl.

The prison would not be full for several more months; the authorities were being very careful in the transporting of prisoners. They did not want any of this scum ever again to be allowed to mix with the law-abiding general public.

Because the prison was nowhere near capacity, the guards were not as diligent as they should have been. It was easy to keep tabs on a couple of hundred men, and so far the prisoners' behavior had been exemplary.

The behavior thus far was something that had been carefully planned in advance . . . by a dozen of the prisoners. Everything on the outside was almost ready. Only a few more days to go.

* * *

"Beautiful," Beth Post said, sitting her horse and looking out over the terrain. "Isn't it, Max?"

"Yeah," her seventeen-year-old son mumbled sarcastically. "Beautiful. Right, Judy?"

"I think it is," his sister said brightly.

Max looked at his sister. What the hell did a fifteen-year-old know anyway? Judy wasn't anything but a suck-up. Always had been.

The guide looked up at his charges over the small camp-fire and smiled. *Pretty good bunch this time,* he thought. *Seem like real nice people. With the exception of the two teenage boys: the Post kid and the Fisher kid; both of them were shitheads.* Harden's smile faded. And troublemakers, he silently added. Both of them. He knew the type all too well. He'd been guiding tourists into the wilderness for more than twenty-five years. *Never lost one yet,* he thought, a tiny smile returning to his lips.

"God!" Walt Fisher exclaimed, slapping his chest. "This air is so pure it's scaring my lungs."

The others laughed at the man's antics. Walt was a cutup, always smiling, never complaining seriously about anything. He was going to be a lot of fun.

"How's your rear end holding up, Walt?" Roger Chambers asked, a smile on his lips.

"Numb, Roger."

None of them were experienced riders, and most hadn't been on a horse in years—since childhood, if then. They were city folks from various locales around the nation. They had all flown into Montana for the vacation of a lifetime. Several weeks in the pristine wilderness, camping and eating food prepared over an open fire and seeing the wildlife up close, maybe doing some fishing. Relaxing.

Harden looked over at Claude, his partner in the guide business, and smiled. He knew that Claude felt this was a pretty good bunch, too. Claude never said much, but Harden could tell the man liked this crew. With the exception of the two teenage boys. Claude didn't care for them, either. The boys were going to have to be watched closely. They were types who just might try to pull something real stupid and get everybody in trouble.

And out here, pulling something foolish was dangerous. Doctors were a long way off, over some of the wildest terrain in America.

"Come get it, folks," Harden said. "Grub's ready." City folks liked to hear the guides use words like 'grub' and 'cayuse' and phrases like that.

"Shit, I hate beans!" Max Post said with a grimace.

Yep, Harden thought. *The punk is going to be trouble. Sure as hell is hot he's going to screw up real bad before this trip is over.*

Harden lifted his eyes and looked at his partner. Claude was frowning. Harden hated to see that, for Claude was not a frowner. That meant he had really taken a dislike to the young man. And that took some doing for Claude was one of the most easygoing men Harden had ever met.

Damn! Harden thought. *The trip hasn't even gotten started good and one customer has pissed off my partner.*

"Now it starts gettin' rough," the guide told the four old friends. "Let's take us a break and rest for a few minutes. I'm not kiddin,' boys—it's wild from here on in."

"How far in are we going, Bert?" Jack Bailey asked.

"Three days. As the crow flies." He shrugged. "Thirty-five miles. But it's rugged in there. Wild and beautiful country. You're going to see it the way it was when my granddaddy come out here."

"And we won't see another living soul, right?" Ted Dawson asked.

"Well," the guide drawled out, "I won't say that. It's certainly possible, but we might run across some other people. I know from talkin' around town there are two, three, other trips goin' on right now." He smiled. "But don't worry, Boys. If it's solitude you're cravin,' you'll get plenty of that."

All the men had taken an instant liking to their guide. He was about their age, and from the brief conversations they had before starting out from town, shared most of their philosophy about life, government, and especially the IRS. When the subject of crime was mentioned, Bert's eyes narrowed to slits, and everyone around him knew they'd touched a sore spot.

"You take a life, you give a life," Bert said. "It's costin' taxpayers millions of dollars a year to keep mass murderers locked up. They get three good meals a day, TV and radio to watch and listen to, books to read, medical care. That's wrong. I'm not sayin' they should be mistreated, 'cause they shouldn't be. Just hang 'em and have done with it."

"I think we're gonna get along just fine, Bert," Harry said.

The men rested for a time, then once more swung into the saddles and were off at a leisurely pace, the guide letting the horses set their own gait. They would do about twelve miles that day before stopping and making camp.

South of them, another group of tourists were on their way to the same general area Jack and his friends were heading for. About twenty miles north, another group was riding in to spend several weeks in the wilderness.

To the east of them, just on the edge of the wilderness area, sat the ultra-modern, brand new maximum security prison. Escape-proof, the builders boasted.

The prisoners were about to prove the builders wrong.

Two

"How does that new prison look, Sheriff?" one of his deputies asked.

"Impressive," the sheriff replied. "And it'd better be. Some of the meanest bastards in the nation will be housed there."

Sheriff Hawkins had just returned from a daylong visit to the prison. The visit had been arranged by the Federal Bureau of Prisons in an attempt to soothe any misgivings or apprehensions that might remain from local sheriffs in the area.

"Well, it's a long way from us, Sheriff," the deputy reminded the man.

"Not far enough," the sheriff responded. "I wish to hell the damn thing was a thousand miles away." He sat down behind his desk and picked up the mug of coffee the deputy had just placed there. He took a sip. "Good coffee, Willis." He smiled. "For a change."

The deputy grinned. "You'll be happy to learn that absolutely nothing happened while you were gone."

"Town's full of tourists. Give it time. Something will pop. It always does."

"I saw Dave and Kathy headin' out yesterday morning early. Had them eight or ten happy campers."

"You talk to them?"

The deputy shook his head. "No. But judging from all the supplies they had, they was goin' to be gone several weeks."

"Do we know where they've gone?"

"I don't. They might have told somebody, but it wasn't me."

Sheriff Hawkins cussed. Shook his head. Both Dave and Kathy knew better than to go off into rough country without telling the sheriff's office where they'd be. They'd worked that out a long time ago. Goddamnit! "That isn't like them."

"No, sir, it isn't. Oh, one more thing—"

Sheriff Hawkins lifted his eyes.

"They had them several spare horses."

Sheriff Hawkins blinked at that. "Why?" he asked after a few seconds' pause.

Willis shrugged his shoulders. "I don't know. It just seemed odd to me."

Hawkins leaned back in his chair. It was odd. Damned odd. He shrugged it off and put it out of his mind. That was Dave and Kathy's business. They must have had their reasons.

But the sheriff didn't like it. If something were to happen, a broken leg, snakebite, a serious fall, *anything*, the emergency people would have no way of knowing where Dave and Kathy and the tourists might be.

Unless Dave and Kathy took a radio with them, a transceiver . . . which was very doubtful.

Well, no point in worrying about it now. No telling where they might be. By now they'd be a good fifteen/twenty miles in. Deputy Willis wandered out of the office and Sheriff Hawkins sipped his coffee and thought about the new prison. It was many miles away, in another county as a matter of fact, but as far as he was concerned that was still too close. Hawkins had heard about every man that was pointed out to him during the visit. Pendley, Mansford, Craig, Gorman, O'Donnell, Randall, Holmes . . . two dozen others. And especially about Karl Parsons: that no-count miserable piece of shit. Parsons was the worst one of the whole bunch. There wasn't anything evil that bastard hadn't had a hand in. Why in the hell the courts just didn't go on and execute people like that was something that Hawkins just could not understand. Every inmate in that prison was a murderer, every one of them, several times over. Why spend thousands of taxpayer dollars a year, per prisoner, to keep them alive?

The sheriff lit a cigarette and smoked and sipped coffee while his thoughts rambled, touching on this and that, but always returning to Dave and Kathy. The husband and wife team had been back country guides for fifteen years, and damn good ones, too. Started in business about two years before they got married. Never had a real serious incident in the rough country.

"Well," the sheriff muttered, "I just hope you folks don't run into any trouble in there. 'Cause I don't have the vaguest idea where in the hell you are."

"You folks have any kids?" Walt asked the two couples.

"Three," Roger Chambers replied. "Two boys and a girl. They're with their grandparents."

"Two," Janet Stinson said. "They're staying with friends back in the city."

Walt looked across the camp at Beth. "Wonder where Mister Post is." he whispered.

"They're divorced," Anne Chambers told him. "It was just final a few weeks ago. She told me back at the motel."

"That seems to be happening a lot nowadays," Walt said. "Doris and me been married twenty years. We've had our share of problems, but always managed to work them out."

"Same here," Don Stinson said. "Nobody ever said it was going to be easy."

They would camp here for a few days, take pictures, hike, explore, and then move on to another locale.

The guides would work them in a large circle, ending back at town in several weeks. The people would be trail-worn and most of them saddle-sore when the trip was over, but they would have seen some of the wildest and most beautiful country in America; memories to last them a lifetime.

"Harden said there were other hikers and campers out here," Roger said. "But odds were we wouldn't see them."

"I guess not," Don replied. "Man, this is hundreds and hundreds of square miles of wilderness."

"And I don't have the foggiest notion where I am!" Walt said with a grin.

"If something were to happen," Doris said, her expression serious, "Harden said to travel west, just follow the sun. We'd get to a road. Or let the horses have their heads and they'll go back home . . . hopefully."

"Relax, folks," Claude said, walking up with an armload of firewood. "Nothin' bad's gonna happen to any of you."

"But it is a bit, well, overwhelming out here," Walt told the guide. "I can't speak for the others, but I've never seen anything like it."

"It's so . . . *empty,*" Doris said. She looked around her and rolled her eyes.

"Not really," Claude told them, a smile on his lips. "There's game everywhere. You'll see planes goin' overhead. You might even hear the forest service workin' chain saws. You're not alone. It just seems that way." He pointed. "Over yonder a few miles there's a bunch of campers." He pointed in another direction. "Over there is yet another group. There's folks all over the place."

"Somehow just that knowledge makes me feel a lot better," Walt said.

Claude smiled at the man. He liked Walt. Walt had no pretense about him when it came to the wilderness: he didn't know a thing about it, and would readily admit it. Walt's wife, Doris, was also a likeable sort, but she never had a whole lot to say. Claude got the impression that Doris was the boss in that family. Their kid, Phil . . . well, he was a shithead and would more than likely grow up to be an older shithead. Someone needed to clean that kid's clock—that might straighten him out some.

Roger and Anne Chambers were likeable people. About thirty-five-years-old, both of them, Claude guessed. City folks; professional people, he'd heard them say. Insurance, or something like that.

Don and Janet Stinson were good people, too. Both of them easy-going and not prone to complaining. Lord, he'd guided some people who bitched and moaned about everything, day and night, never shutting up. Both Don and Janet had something to do with education on the college level.

Claude felt sorry for Beth Post. The woman had a real sad look in her eyes. He guessed her recent divorce had really rattled her world pretty hard. And her boy sure as hell wasn't helping matters any. Max was a craphead just like young Phil, only more so. Claude knew all the signs. He had spent some time on the sheriff's department back in his younger days. He knew something about punks. Judy

Post was a good kid, real likeable. Sort of quiet and shy, well-mannered. She acted as though she had plenty of common sense for a fifteen-year-old. A really pretty and shapely girl.

All in all, this was a good bunch.

Bert looked at the four older men he was guiding on this trip. He liked every one of them. They were all about his age, and that gave them a lot in common right there. Bert was ex-military, too, having pulled a hitch in the navy back in the mid-fifties. And, like Bert, all these guys had been happily married for years and all had grown kids.

Bert cut his eyes to Andy Dawson. Now there was a study. The younger man and his father obviously did not get along worth a damn. And neither man was trying very hard to settle whatever it was between them. They just didn't like each other. There was love between them, Bert felt sure of that; he could sense that emotion. But nothing that came close to *like*. Bert figured he'd know what the problem was long before this camping trip was over. The wilderness had a way of bringing that out.

The older men had spent time in the back country: they knew how to set up a camp and do all the little things that had to be done. Andy didn't know crap about the outdoors, and didn't seem all that interested in learning.

Oh, well, Bert mused, *it's only for a few weeks.* Bert hid a smile and thought: *If Andy doesn't fall off his horse and bust his ass, it will all work out.*

Dave cut his eyes to his wife as she worked over the fire fixing lunch. Something was wrong but Kathy wasn't sharing the problem . . . at least, not yet. Dave knew all the signs. After fifteen years of marriage, partners learn the signals.

Dave turned his gaze from his wife to the group they were guiding in. Ed and Sandy Monroe seemed like two pretty squared away people. Ed was much happier about this trip than his wife, though. Didn't take a genius to figure that out. But they would be all right.

Shawn and Abby Hayes were another story. They were just going through the motions of marriage. Dave had seen that before. This trip would finish them, he would bet on that. They were polite with each other, but Abby's politeness was tinged with a coldness. Well, that was *their* problem.

Dick and Joan Jamison were the oldest of this group. They were both in their mid-fifties: calm and steady and very secure in their marriage, comfortable with each other. Bert could tell that by their actions. Neither one of them would be a problem on this trip.

Henry and Christine Matthews seemed like nice people with no problems. Their twins, Patti and Paul, were good kids, well-behaved.

Dave gazed back at his wife. He sure wished he could figure out what was eating at her. Whatever it was, it was weighing heavily on her mind. Maybe in time she'd share it with him. That always helped.

"We go in two days," Karl Parsons mumbled to Randy O'Donnell. He spoke as only experienced cons can: with almost no lip movement.

"My people are ready and in place," Randy replied.

Karl nodded and walked on. He had not changed his expression during the brief exchange.

Of all the prisoners who would make the breakout, only eight would know the exact time it was going down. And of the eight, only two would know all the particulars: Karl Parsons and Randy O'Donnell. Karl because he knew the country and had friends on the outside and it was his plan from the outset; Randy because his outside contacts were creating the diversion and planting the explosives, and supplying the weapons . . . among other things.

Karl walked back to his cell and stepped inside. Only then did he allow a smile to touch his lips. He had to struggle to keep from laughing. This was going to be a piece of cake. And once he was out, he would never allow any man to put him back behind bars. Never again.

There would be people killed during this breakout; that was almost a dead-bang certainty: a few inmates, and some guards. Karl and Randy and some of the others would be looking at the gas chamber if they were captured, so that just wasn't going to happen. And while the subject had not been discussed at length among the other prisoners, Karl knew they all felt the same way about it. None of them had anything to lose. They were all facing spending the rest of their lives behind bars, in hard lockup. So what the hell? Why not go for the brass ring?

Karl sat down on his bunk and thought about the outside, just as he knew Randy was. They were both thinking of the same thing: women. Karl felt he would explode if he didn't have a woman very soon. And he wanted a woman that would fight him. He liked it that way. He loved to rip the clothing from them and slap them around and then take them hard and fast while they struggled and cried and screamed in fright and pain and humiliation.

Karl forced the thought of women from his mind. There would be plenty of time for all that in a few days. He had to keep his mind clear until then. Keep all thoughts of pussy for later. Later, there would be plenty of time for women and the one thing any of them were good for.

Karl really hated women. All women. Except for his

sister. He loved his sister. He used to fuck her when they were kids. She had some good snatch, too.

He pushed the thought of his sister away and concentrated on the breakout. Two more days. Forty-eight hours to freedom. Just the thought put a good taste in Karl's mouth.

Randy O'Donnell sat in his cell and thought of revenge against those who had put him in this goddamn place. He would kill them all. Slowly. He would kill their wives and kids and mothers and fathers. Wipe them from the face of the earth. He would do all that after he had a woman. That was the first thing Randy wanted once he was free of these bars: a woman. Then he would start his program of retribution against those who had put him in prison. Bet on it!

Scott Craig knew the breakout was near. He could feel it. He rubbed his crotch and thought of young girls . . . the younger the better. He liked them about ten or eleven years old, all smooth and ready for fucking. Scott was scared of real women; they intimidated him. But not young girls. He had the power over them. He liked the look of fear in their eyes.

Scott could hardly wait for his freedom.

Oscar Mansford knew the breakout was near. He could sense it. Just the thought of it got him all giddy.

Tony Gorman thought solely of revenge. He dreamed of killing those responsible for putting him in prison.

* * *

Barry Randall liked to kill. He got off by killing. He dreamed of killing; it was always on his mind. He didn't give a damn, really, who he killed, but he did especially enjoy killing older people. He liked the look of fear in their eyes just before they died.

Newton Holmes dreamed of two things he would have in his life after he was free of the prison: women and killing. In that order. He planned to get his share of both.

There were other inmates who sensed the breakout was close. They had their dreams as well, almost to a person about women. But most also dreamed of killing guards, the administration people in the offices, the warden—anyone in a position of authority—for these men all hated authority. Some of them would get their killing wish.
   Soon.

Three

Jack and Dennis smelled the coffee and crawled out of their sleeping bags, leaving Andy, Ted, and Harry to sleep. After a very quick wash in the cold waters of a tiny stream, they joined Bert by the fire. No one had much to say until midway through the first cup of coffee.

"Hell of an argument Ted and Andy had last night," Jack said. "Did anybody ever figure out what it was all about?"

"Politics," Dennis replied. "I think that started it. It sort of went downhill after that."

Jack looked at Bert and smiled. "Jump right in with your opinions, Bert. You're part of this group for the next few weeks. Don't feel like an outsider."

"None of my business," Bert said, after taking a slug of coffee.

Jack and Dennis chuckled at that. Dennis said, "If you have to listen to it that makes it your business, Bert."

Bert smiled. "I thought your friend was gonna slap the piss out of his son 'fore it was over."

"I think he came close to doing just that," Jack said. "Those two haven't gotten along since the boy was just a kid. It just keeps getting worse between them."

"The boy don't have his head screwed on straight," the guide remarked. "I never heard so many silly ass comments in my life. Especially comin' from a grown man."

Jack and Dennis looked at each other and laughed softly. "Bert," Dennis said. "I thought you were going to swallow your coffee cup when Andy said we should tear down all the prisons."

The guide shook his head. "What the hell does he plan on doin' with all the rapists and murderers and hard core criminals and the like?"

"Loving them," Jack said, pouring another cup of coffee from the big pot.

Bert drained his coffee cup, looked at the two men, and said, "Horseshit!"

Jack and Dennis laughed at the expression on the man's face. Dennis said, "Andy is far too young to have been a part of the anti-war movement of the sixties, but if he'd been old enough he would have sure been involved in it."

"Sad time for America," Bert said, refilling his coffee cup and lighting a cigarette.

"Were you in 'Nam, Bert?" Jack asked.

The guide shook his head. "No. I missed it and I'm glad of it. I was in the navy back in the fifties. I was just a kid. You boys?"

The two men nodded. "Yes," Dennis said. "All of us. We met in Korea and hooked up again during the early days of 'Nam."

"Advisors?" Bert asked softly.

Both men laughed. "That's what the government called us," Jack said. "Other folks called us officially sanctioned mercenaries. I guess the truth lies somewhere between the two.''

"Anyway, it was a long time ago," Dennis said. "It's just misty memories now."

"What is?" Harry asked, walking up, tucking his shirttail into his jeans. He spied the coffee pot and smiled. "Pour me a cup, boys. While I go shake the dew off my flower."

"Be sure you grab your dick and not a hair," Jack told him. "I know they're about the same size. I'd hate for you to piss down your pants 'fore we ever got to wet a hook in that lake over yonder."

"I seem to recall that little gal in Saigon thought I was too big," Harry called over his shoulder.

"Yeah, but she was a midget," Dennis told him.

"Big woman, little pussy, little woman, all pussy," Harry called.

Bert smiled at the antics of the men. He correctly guessed they didn't talk this way at home, and were just letting their hair down while away from their wives.

Bert watched as Andy left his tent and stood for a moment, stretching. *Not a happy camper,* he thought. *Doesn't like to fish or hike or camp, doesn't know one end of a horse from another. He doesn't really like any of his father's friends. Probably his mother urged him to come on this trip, in the hopes that would bring the son and the father closer together.*

Sure no signs of that yet, Bert mused. And after last night, there probably wouldn't be. That was a hell of an argument, with both men saying some things they probably wished now they hadn't said.

Bert had to take the elder Dawson's side all the way, for there just wasn't very much in Andy's liberal philosophy that Bert could stomach.

Ted came out of the tent and stretched, smelled the coffee, and smiled, walking over to the fire. It was not yet seven o'clock in the morning and the dawning was cold.

"Morning, troops," Ted said.

Andy gave the man a dirty look and Bert wondered why. Then, after a few heartbeats, he guessed the younger man probably did not like to be referred to as 'troops.' *Andy sure hates the military,* Bert thought as he poured a couple of cups of coffee and placed then on the circle of rocks around the fire.

"Did anybody bring a radio?" Andy asked, squatting down and picking up his cup. He put it down very quickly, for the cup was metal and it was hot.

"Shit!" Andy mouthed the word.

Bert was careful to hide his smile at that.

"No radios, Andy," Jack said.

"What about news?" the younger man asked.

"What about it?" Dennis asked.

"How will we know what's going on in the United States, the world?"

"Who cares?" Jack asked. "The anchors are all liberal to the core, and so are the reporters. The stories they report always have a liberal spin. Who gives a shit what they say?"

Ted returned and sat down on the ground, picking up his cup of coffee and taking a sip. "Ahhh, good. Gets the old motor started."

"How can you say things like that, Jack?" Andy asked. "And mean them. And I know you do."

Andy's father lifted his cup, hiding his smile. His son was on his own in this crowd.

"Because they're true, Andy. For the most part. No one here means to imply that every liberal cause is wrong, because it isn't. There are some that are needed. It's the liberal philosophy in general that we take exception to."

"Compassion and care and hope, you mean?"

Jack smiled. "Typical liberal response, Andy. I expected it. Take everything to the extreme. To the absurd. You've known me since there was a you. And you sure as hell know that I give a lot of money to various charities and causes. But I don't just throw it at them in hopes that some of the money will reach those who need it."

"And we do?"

"I think the record speaks for itself on that."

Andy picked up his coffee cup and walked back to the tent, his back stiff.

"Shore don't take much to piss him off," Bert remarked. "I've never seen such a touchy fellow."

"He feels he's in the midst of the enemy," Andy's father said. "He feels overwhelmed. Surrounded. And he's angry because he's here. But we all felt it would help. I guess we were wrong about that."

"Well, he's here," Harry said. "And he's going to be here for several weeks. If he doesn't square himself away and get with the program, he's going to be a very lonely man."

"He won't come around," Ted predicted. "He'll just stay to himself and pout. He's done it since he was a little boy." Ted sighed heavily. "I stopped worrying about that years ago, guys. Doesn't do any good. It would take something drastic to change him now."

"That can happen out here," Bert said, pausing and looking up from his slicing bacon from the slab. "I'm not sayin' it will. Just that it can."

Harden and Claude settled their bunch in about eight miles from where Bert had camped his people. Dave and Kathy had camped their people further east, some ten miles away, much deeper into the wilderness. When Kathy had told her husband she'd found a much better spot, he didn't argue, but he did wonder about it. There were a lot of things Dave had been wondering about the past several months, but every time he brought up the subject Kathy almost took his head off. He finally just tried to ignore her sometimes strange behavior. Then, a couple of weeks back, quite abruptly, she'd become all sweetness and light and lovey dovey toward him. Dave didn't understand what in the world was going on, but he was certainly grateful for the change. It made his life a whole lot easier. There was such a change in Kathy that Dave forgot all about her several months of strange behavior. But now she was all uptight again. He had talked to a buddy of his about it and he thought Kathy was probably going through the change of life.

"Damn near caused a divorce in my house," his buddy told him. "I couldn't do nothin' right. If I'd say good morning, she'd look out the window to check. It was awful. I think that's what Kathy's going through. I feel sorry for you."

"But it will pass, won't it?" Dave asked.

"Oh, yeah. Eventually. Might last a damn year, though."

"Jesus Christ!"

"Just hang in there, Dave. That's all you can do. Except just try to stay the hell out of her way."

"She's about to drive me crazy."

"It'll get worse 'fore it gets any better. I can promise you that."

"I don't know whether to thank you or hit you," Dave told his friend.

His friend laughed at him. "It'll get better, ole' buddy. It always does."

The three groups of campers settled in for several weeks of hiking, fishing, exploring, and relaxing.

At the prison, the administration was happy with the smoothness with which the new facility was running. The prisoners seemed relaxed. The guards had completed their training, and another shipment of prisoners was scheduled to arrive in about a week.

But in less than thirty-six hours, one of the largest and deadliest prison breaks in modern American history would take place.

The breakout would plunge the pristine wilderness into a terror filled hell for the campers caught up in the mass escape, and would pit the rusty skills of four men against dozens of desperate murderers.

Four

In case of a power failure, the prison would automatically switch over to emergency power, unless of course, someone inside the prison blocked the switch-over. That was to be done by a guard named R. G. Laine. R. G. had no choice in the matter—none whatsoever. Not if he wanted to see his kids again. R. G. had three daughters ages ten, fourteen, and sixteen, and one twelve-year-old son. He had already been informed, quite bluntly, what would happen to those girls if he didn't cooperate. R. G. Laine would no longer have a family if he screwed up. And just to show him the threats were very real, his fourteen-year-old daughter had been raped repeatedly by several men the night before . . . while R. G. was forced to watch and listen. Then his young son had been stripped naked in front of his family, and R. G. had been told what would happen to him if R. G. didn't do exactly what he was told to do.

R. G. didn't have a choice in the matter. He would do as he was ordered.

With the backup power system inoperable, the electrically charged fences would be nothing more than chainlink fences: they could easily be cut through.

Since the prison was located in a very isolated area, miles from the nearest town and accessible only by one road, it would normally take twenty to thirty minutes to make the trip. However, if the bridge over the river was out that would delay matters quite a bit. And the bridge over the river was definitely going to be out. The explosives that were to take down the bridge had already been placed and were ready to blow.

Food, clothing, and weapons for the escapees had been secretly moved into position, at night, just a few miles from the prison.

Everything was set. The clock was ticking, the hands edging slowly toward Go.

Inside the prison, the inmates were behaving as usual, with no change in their limited and highly structured routine. In a matter of a few hours, they would be free. No one was going to do anything to jeopardize that now.

Karl Parsons and Randy O'Donnell and the others who were aware of the breakout sat in their cells, their thoughts busy with dreams of the outside ... and women and revenge. They would occasionally cut their eyes to clocks or watches and check the time. The hands or the numbers seemed to be moving very slowly.

Hours later, Sheriff Hawkins sat straight up in bed, sweat dripping from his body, soaking his pajamas. He had almost screamed upon awakening. What a horrible nightmare he had just experienced. He slipped from bed, being careful not to wake his wife, and padded into the kitchen. He looked at the clock. Four in the morning. No point in trying to get back to sleep now.

He made a pot of coffee and sat at the breakfast nook, waiting for it to drip. He understood the nightmare: he'd been having the same one every night since returning from visiting the new prison.

Breakout.

The damn government had stuck the nation's worst criminals in his backyard and Hawkins was worried about it, so worried he was having nightmares.

He fixed a mug of coffee and sat back down, opening a pack of cigarettes. He had made up his mind a couple of days back to try to quit smoking. Now, he decided, was definitely not the time for it.

Dave and Kathy and the campers had been all mixed up in his nightmares. It was horrible. Torture and rape and killings, with the escapees all over the wilderness, dozens of them, with all sorts of exotic weapons at their disposal. Jesus H. Christ, what a terrible nightmare!

Hawkins—Hawk, as his friends called him—lit another smoke and leaned back in the booth.

He hoped that this was the last of the nightmares; it had damn sure been the worst of the lot. Goddamn the government for putting that friggin' prison in his backyard.

Hawk had a huge county to patrol and not nearly enough deputies to adequately do the job . . . and no chance of getting more deputies.

His wife wandered into the kitchen, yawning. She at first gave her husband a dirty look. Then that vanished and she smiled at him.

"Nightmares again, Honey?" Viv asked.

"The worst ones yet. Sorry I woke you up."

"School's out, Hawk. I can go back to bed after you go to work. Don't worry about it. The coffee smells good."

"It is. For once I made a decent pot." He started to rise from the booth. "Let me get you a cup."

She waved him back. "Sit still. I'll get it."

Seated across from him in the booth, Viv said, "I thought this prison was state-of-the-art? Escape-proof?"

"Oh, it is state-of-the-art. All sorts of bells and whistles and fancy electronic gizmos. But there is no such thing as an escape-proof prison. And the men housed there, while the worst in the nation, are not dummies. Like so many criminals, many of them are very intelligent. If there's a way to bust out, they'll find it. Bet on that."

"And you think the prison has a flaw?"

"Oh, I don't know, Viv. I doubt it. It was designed and built by the leading prison experts in the nation. It's just when I close my eyes to sleep, my imagination is running wild. These are the worst criminals in the nation—murderers, rapists, child molesters, hired killers. You name something evil, those men have done it. the damn government sticks them all together in my backyard."

His wife of more than twenty years touched his hand. "You have this one last term in office, Hawk. You'll still be a young man when you retire. Think about that."

"Oh, I do, Baby. I do. I can't wait to hang up this badge and start my own little guide service. Two more years and that's it." He smiled at her. "Young man, Viv? Well . . . not quite. But I'll have a few good years left in me, for a fact."

"Young man," she persisted.

Hawk laughed at the expression on her face. "Because you're getting older right along with me, huh, Viv?"

"I'm not getting older, Hawk. I stopped having birthdays, remember?"

Hawk sipped his coffee and stared across the table at his wife. Viv sure didn't look her age, for a fact. Seeing three kids go from babies to adulthood had scarcely touched her. *Of course,* he thought with a smile, *we did marry young.*

"What are you thinking, Hawk?" she asked.

His smile widened.

"At four o'clock in the morning!"

He nodded his head.

Her eyes softened. "Well . . ."

He took her hand and together they rose from the breakfast nook and without another word walked into their bedroom. Out of long habit, even though their kids were grown and gone, Hawk closed the door.

Five

The front gates to the prison dissolved in a mass of twisted, torn metal. A second later, rockets knocked holes in the fences and destroyed part of the administration building. The cells could not be locked, except manually, due to the loss of electric power. The guard towers came under heavy machine gun fire from men who had moved into place under the darkness of night. Randy O'Donnell's people were experts at this sort of thing, as were their grandfathers back in the old country.

A section of the bridge over the river was blown. It would be hours before crews could lay down a temporary floor that would allow light traffic to use the bridge.

In the prison, R. G. Laine would never have to worry about facing a judge and jury for his part in the escape. He lay dead in a utility closet, his throat cut.

Technicians immediately hit the switch that was supposed to throw emergency equipment to banks of batteries. The move didn't work. Wires had been cut, and the only thing that happened was a shower of sparks and more panic.

The guards in the towers were either dead or badly wounded.

A call was sent out by radio and it was received. Help was on the way. But it would take precious minutes to arrive. By the time the radio call went out—and it was sent within seconds of the first explosion—a dozen prisoners had reached the outer fence and were gone, several dozen more only a couple of minutes behind them, the men running hard for their freedom.

The breakout shouldn't have succeeded. All the odds were against the prisoners making it out of the prison compound. But it did work, and dozens of prisoners had gained their freedom.

Sheriff Hawkins received the call minutes after the breakout. He listened for a moment, then slowly hung up the phone. "Son of a bitch!" he cussed. "Those weren't dreams I had, those were premonitions. Oh, shit!"

"What the hell's goin' on, Sheriff?" a deputy asked from the doorway.

"That multi-million dollar, brand new, super-duper prison that just opened?"

"Yes, sir. What about it?"

"Mass breakout."

"You've got to be kidding!"

"I wish I was." Hawk stood up from his desk. "Everybody in, Joe. All time off canceled for the duration. Call in the reserves—all of them. Get in touch with the mayor and tell him I want to meet with him and the city council ASAP. We've got to make plans and warn the public. Go!" He reached for the phone. "I've got to find out what happened over there."

Deputy Willis had been reading flashes over the teletype

and walked into the office. "People are going to be shooting at shadows, Sheriff."

Hawk nodded his head. "Don't I know it. Willis, some of those bad ones will probably be coming through here on the way to Canada. We've got a few hours to get ready. We can't waste a minute of it . . ." He stilled the sudden and incessant ringing of the phone and listened for a few seconds. His face paled and he blurted, "Two hundred! That's every fucking inmate that was housed there!"

Hawk listened for a moment more and then slammed down the phone. Half a dozen deputies were crowded around the door to his office. He looked at the men and women. "Almost the entire prison population made it out. Only a few were captured. A lot of guards are dead and others are badly wounded. FBI and ATF teams are on the way in. The warden's dead. He was beaten to death and his head cut off."

"Nice people," a deputy muttered.

"Yeah," Hawk said. "Just lovely."

"Have you found out what exactly happened over there?" another deputy asked.

"Not yet. It's all confusion and panic. But there was a lot of outside help involved." He held up a hand. "No more questions, people. I don't know the answers to them. Not yet. You'll know just as soon as I do. Get geared up. The escapees are going to be heavily armed, and they've got nothing to lose now. Betty, call the local radio station and advise them of the situation. Urge people to stay in their homes. Lock the doors and don't open them unless they know the person. I'll have a lot more to say when all the reserves get here. Move!"

Sheriff Hawkins sat back down and placed both hands on his desk top. He quietly began cussing, the words softly offered but with considerable heat behind them.

Another deputy interrupted Hawk's cussing. "People

from the TV station on the horn, Sheriff. They want a statement.''

"I bet they do," Hawk muttered. "Tell them I'll have a statement for them just as soon as I find out exactly what the hell happened over there. Right now, they probably know as much as I do about the situation . . . maybe more.''

"Yes, sir.''

Every line on the sheriff's phone suddenly lit up. Hawk looked at the flashing lights. "Shit Shit Shit!'' he cussed.

"You want me to get that, Hawk?'' Betty, the department's bookkeeper who doubled as the sheriff's secretary asked from the doorway.

Hawk shook his head. "No. It's for me, Betty. And it's gonna be ringing off the hook for days to come.''

"I called my husband. Told him to lay out the guns and load them up full.''

Hawk nodded his head in agreement. "Just don't wound anybody, Betty.''

She smiled, knowing exactly what he meant. Shoot to kill. If some citizen wounded one of the escaped convicts, in all probability they would face a civil lawsuit . . . and some lawyer would be more than happy to take the case.

Dead men don't testify against you.

Only a handful of prisoners had failed to make their way to freedom. The rest, over two hundred of them, were on the loose.

The deputy warden had taken over, and would be in charge for the duration. The warden's head had been found, and the head and body bagged for removal. Several civilian workers had been killed during the breakout, and three women had been taken by the prisoners. No one held out much hope of ever seeing them alive again. The women would be raped repeatedly and then killed and tossed aside like yesterday's garbage.

Federal investigators began swarming all over the prison in a matter of hours, looking to place blame on somebody. R. G. Laine would be targeted, of course, but as the investigation went deeper it would be found that he played only a small part in the breakout: it would have succeeded even without his cooperation.

Sheriff Hawkins had some of the answers within a few hours . . . but he knew they were lies. He also knew he would probably never know what really happened.

"The in-ground sensor equipment was down for maintenance," the sheriff was told by a prison employee who was a longtime friend of his. "That's why the assault team was able to get close to the fences and towers."

"Horseshit!" Hawk blurted. "You and I both know that's pure crap. No one would have allowed that to happen."

"That's the story, Sheriff. There were other factors involved, but that's part of it."

"Whitewash."

His friend's silence told Hawk he had touched on the truth. Hawk also realized he would probably never know what actually happened at the prison.

Hawk's friend broke his silence. "We've captured a dozen already."

"Wonderful," Sheriff Hawkins said. "Only two hundred or so to go. God help us all. See you, Sam. Good luck."

There were no large cities close to the prison, but there were lots of small towns where some of the escapees were sure to go in their wild bid for freedom. Those towns were placed on high alert by police. For all practical purposes, they were shut down after dark. Checkpoints were set up on all roads in a huge circle around the wilderness area, running north to south from just south of the Canadian border down to just north of Butte, from west to east from the Montana border almost all the way to Great Falls. National Guard units were mobilized to assist, and police from half a dozen states were called in to help out in the massive search.

Sheriff Hawkins and half a dozen other sheriffs around the area sat in their offices and drank coffee and smoked cigarettes and quietly fumed at what had happened.

There was little else they could do.

Deep in the wilderness area, the campers knew nothing of the breakout. They hiked, they fished, they explored, they marveled at the beauty of nature, unaware of the danger that was moving toward them. The campers got lost in the shuffle by the authorities.

"Five more cons were just captured," Sheriff Hawkins was informed. "They stole a car and tried to run a road-block."

"I don't even want to know how many that leaves out there," Hawk replied.

"Too many," the deputy responded.

"The majority of the cons avoided the wilderness area," a government 'expert' announced to a roomful of experienced cops who had gathered for a briefing. "Those who did enter rough country will probably stay on the fringes rather than go deeper."

The sheriffs and chiefs of police exchanged glances and kept their silence. They all knew that was a crock of shit a foot deep. Some of the escaped prisoners were from this area, and knew the wilderness, having hunted and fished in it before landing in the bucket.

"We have found many articles of clothing," the government expert droned on. "Most of the escapees are now in civilian clothing. The clothing we've found leaves us a clear trail, telling us the majority of men headed east. The vast majority."

"But some surely went into the wilderness?" a state cop questioned.

"We believe a few did," the federal 'expert' replied. "No more than a handful. We believe the clothing trail clearly points the way east. And that is the direction most of the escapees took."

"How many headed into the wilderness area?" Sheriff Hawkins asked.

"We don't know as yet. But we think no more than a dozen headed west."

The articles of clothing the government 'expert' talked about were carefully left for the authorities to find . . . deliberately left by the convicts.

"What happened to the tracking dogs that were brought in?" a chief of police asked.

The government 'expert' looked embarrassed. Cleared his throat. "Well, ah, it appears there were quite a number of people involved on the outside in this escape. Several kilos of a substance were scattered about behind the escaping convicts." He shrugged his shoulders. "Probably was cocaine. We don't have the lab results back yet. Of course, when the dogs sniffed that it ruined their sense of smell for hours. Then it began raining, and that's holding us up further."

It wasn't just raining, it was pouring down. A summer storm was pounding the area.

"How many kilos of coke were used?" a sheriff asked.

"Ah . . . we estimate about a dozen kilos were scattered about."

"Doesn't that tell you anything?" the sheriff persisted.

"I don't know what you mean." The government 'expert' turned a tad huffy.

"A lot of money and a big organization behind the breakout. Perhaps organized crime."

"We rejected the organized crime theory. But there definitely was organization behind the breakout. It was very well planned," he added grimly. "We just don't know what organization."

Hawk let his attention wander as the government 'expert' started droning on about cooperation among local, county, state, and federal law enforcement agencies.

There was no way on God's Green Earth they were going to flush a dozen or so hardened and tough as hell cons out of thousands and thousands of acres of wilderness . . . much of it damn near inaccessible.

Hawk did his best to pull his attention back to the speaker. But his thoughts kept drifting back to those campers in the wilderness. If the cons ran up on them . . .

Six

It had been less than twelve hours since the mass breakout from the federal prison. About forty of the escapees had been captured and were being held in various jails around the area . . . under very heavy guard. Some of those had been captured within five miles of the prison. A half a dozen more had been shot and killed . . . all of them by citizens. Another half dozen or so had been shot and wounded and recaptured . . . again, by local citizens.

But nearly a hundred and fifty desperate and extremely dangerous criminals were still on the loose, and many of them were beginning to live up to their reputation for evil and mindless violence.

A rural family—father, mother, and teenage daughter—had been terrorized by four escapees. They had been found by a neighbor who became worried and drove over to check on them. The father had been savagely beaten, the mother and daughter beaten and repeatedly raped and sodomized. The women had then been beaten unconscious and left in the locked basement with the nearly dead husband and father.

A group of local citizens formed a posse and went after the escaped convicts—against the advice of the authorities, mostly federal. But telling fourth or fifth generation rural westerners they can't do something is like shoving a cold bit in a horse's mouth: expect resistance.

The locals told the feds to go right straight to hell and keep out of their way. They would handle this little problem.

The citizens cornered the four escapees and a very brief gun battle ensued. After the shooting was over, the locals told the feds they could have the bodies.

But most of the citizens the escapees came in contact with were not that lucky. Several locals in the area were killed, and others were wounded or badly beaten. A dozen women were reported raped.

But Sheriff Hawkins had to admit that the federal 'expert' who had briefed them was right: it appeared that the vast majority of the escapees were indeed heading east. They would take their chances in more settled areas rather than face a very uncertain future in the wilderness.

And Sheriff Hawkins breathed a huge sigh of relief when the news came over the teletype: Karl Parsons had been spotted in the company of several other cons . . . heading east.

"That's good news," Hawk muttered.

But it wasn't Karl Parsons who had been spotted. It was someone who looked a lot like him. That person had been given a wad of money by Karl and Randy's friends on the outside, and told to take off east.

Sheriff Hawkins began to breathe a lot easier when the word came over the wire that Randy O'Donnell and Jans Pendley and half a dozen of the worst of the bunch had been spotted a hundred miles away from Hawk's county, and heading east.

"Thank God," Hawk said.

But it wasn't Randy or Jans who had been spotted. Randy and Jans and two dozen more were in the wilderness, moving cautiously and slowly deeper into the primitive area. They had located the cache of supplies and weapons left by Randy's friends on the outside, and were now well-equipped. They were heading in the direction of the three groups of tourists. The campers knew nothing of the break-out and the dozens of escaped convicts. They had not heard any news for several days. There was not a single radio among any of the groups.

The escapees who had headed west were very well-armed. Also, among the cache of supplies had been warm clothing, packs filled with emergency gear, food, maps, and compasses, the best route through the rugged country clearly highlighted on the maps.

Helicopters flew low and slowly over the wilderness, working a search pattern, but the cons avoided open meadows and fields, staying in the timber and brush. Their clothing was camouflage. Karl Parsons and several of the others were experienced woodsmen; they knew how to avoid being spotted, and they brought that knowledge into play.

Three days after the breakout the search helicopters had moved to another grid, far south of the route the escaped convicts were taking as they made their way west through the wilderness. To the east, dozens of escapees had been recaptured as they attempted to slip past the roadblocks and barricades set up by law enforcement groups and civilians.

The original hysteria and panic over the breakout had calmed. Many of the nighttime curfews had been lifted, and conditions in the area were slowly returning to normal.

Tourists were being allowed into the western sections of the wilderness area to camp and hike and explore. Summer is short-lived in the mountains, and those whose livelihood depend on tourists have to make it during the summer months, or not at all.

"It's too soon," Sheriff Hawkins told his wife over supper. "Those tourists should not be allowed into the wilderness. There are dozens of escapees still wandering around in there."

"You tried your best to keep the curfew on for a few more days, Hawk," his wife reminded him. "What else could you do?"

Hawk fiddled with his coffee mug. "I could have tried harder, Viv."

"You were going up against the city council and the county commission. Even some of the other sheriffs agreed to let the tourists back into the western sections."

"And chasing that almighty dollar is going to get some people killed," Hawk said. "The problem is I don't know where Dave and Kathy have taken their bunch. The copters didn't see a trace of them. I know where they *usually* take their people, but they've changed camping locations for some reason."

"You're going to worry yourself into a bad case of heartburn, Hawk. There is nothing you can do about the campers. Nothing at all. They're camped deep in the back country having a wonderful time. They don't even know about the breakout."

"Yeah, Viv. That's what worries me."

"That was a shot, Bert," Jack said, sitting up and looking all around him. "I think."

"Yeah, I think I heard a shot, too," Dennis said. "Poachers, maybe?"

"Could be," Bert replied. "But I don't know if that *was* a shot. It was a long way off."

"What else could it have been?" Ted asked.

"I hate guns," his son piped up. "All they're good for is killing and injuring innocent people."

Harry sighed and looked heavenward.

Ted ignored his son and said, "It *was* a shot, Bert. I'd bet on that."

Bert poured him a cup of coffee. "It was a long way off, boys. Might have been the rangers havin' to put a wounded critter out of its misery."

"Probably wounded by some damn hunter," Andy said. Andy was also very much opposed to hunting. His children could not have toy guns to play with. They had never played soldier or outlaws and bad men or cowboys and Indians . . . the latter being politically incorrect, anyway, and a no-no in Andy Dawson's family.

"Not in here, and not this time of the year," Bert told him. "Unless it was a poacher."

"Are you going to go investigate?" Andy asked him.

Bert looked at him and smiled. "No."

"Why not?"

" 'Cause for one reason, it ain't my place to do so. And if it is a poacher, I don't want to get myself shot messin' around his kill."

"But it's illegal here, right?" Andy persisted.

"Yeah, it's illegal. Still goes on," Bert told him.

Jack stood up and looked in the direction of the faint shot. For some reason he could not explain, the shot worried him, but he decided to say no more about it. "Oh, to hell with it," he muttered, and put the incident out of his mind.

* * *

The shot had been fired as a warning, and it worked. The tourists froze where they stood and put their hands in the air.

"That's better," Randy O'Donnell said, grinning at Anne Chambers, his eyes flicking over her body. "You do what we tell you to do, nobody gets hurt."

Barry Randall laughed at that.

"What do you boys want?" Claude asked. "If you want the horses, take them."

"Shut up," Randy told him. "Get somebody to cooking something to eat. We're hungry." He again looked at Anne. "You, Baby. Get your ass moving and fix us something to eat."

Before he gave his predicament any thought, Roger blurted, "Don't speak to my wife in such a manner!"

Newton Holmes stepped forward and hit the husband in the mouth with his big fist, knocking the man flat on the ground. "You shut your blowhole and keep it shut, candy ass," Newton warned him. "That goes for all of you."

Anne knelt down beside her husband, who had a bloody mouth and a dazed look in his eyes.

Roger sat up and put a hand to his lips. He looked at his bloody fingertips. He opened his mouth to speak and his wife softly shushed him. Roger got the message and closed his mouth.

"Now you people listen to me," Randy said. "We're gonna be together for a few days. Sorry, but that's the way it is. You do what we tell you to do, we're all gonna get along just fine. Any of you gets out of line, you get hurt or dead. Does everybody understand that?"

"We understand," Harden said. "We'll give you no trouble."

"That's just ducky," Randy said with a smile. "That's what we want to hear." He again looked at Anne. "You, Baby, get away from sweetheart there and get busy fixing us something to eat. Right now."

Barry Randall looked at young Judy Post and licked his suddenly dry lips. She filled out her jeans just right, and had her some nice titties, too. The next two or three days should be fun. Barry felt himself getting an erection. He grinned at the girl.

Karl had split the men up into two teams of eight each. That was eight more people than he and Randy had figured on, but for now it couldn't be helped. He'd kill the others when the time came. For now he wanted things smooth and quiet, and for everybody to stay calm.

Karl had heard the shot and had cursed under his breath. But Randy had a mind of his own, and nobody was going to tell him what to do.

Karl had wished he could kill Randy when he whacked the others. But Randy's group, while not large, had world-wide connections and a lot of money behind it . . . much of that money coming from sympathizers right here in America. Karl would never have a moment's peace if he wasted Randy and his people ever learned he did it.

Karl looked at Abby Hayes and licked his lips. Now there was a prime piece of ass if ever he'd seen one. And she liked to fuck, too. Karl could sense that, or at least he thought he could. Yeah, Abby would be a wild ride, for a fact. Nice set of tits on her, too.

Karl looked over at Dave. The stupid bastard was standing there not knowing what to believe. When Karl and Kathy had embraced and kissed, Ole' Dave almost had a stroke. He still couldn't get it through his thick skull that

Karl and Kathy were brother and sister, and his darlin' wife was up to her ass in this escape. It was really funny.

Jans Pendley walked over to Karl and whispered, "I want the blonde girl. That one." He cut his eyes to Patti Matthews.

"You can have her," Karl said. "Just tape her mouth before you run that horse cock of yours up in her. Big as you are, she's gonna scream her head off first couple of times."

Jans smiled. "I like it when they scream and struggle. Makes me get rock hard and stay that way."

Karl nodded his head. "Have fun, Jans."

"I will."

Jans walked off and Karl once more looked over the group, carefully eyeballing each man and woman. He could see no one that might give them any trouble. The men all looked as scared as the women. Dave, now, might be another story. Karl could tell by the look in the man's eyes he was plenty pissed.

Scott Craig walked over to stand by Karl. "No guns in camp, Karl."

"Good. Hunting knives, pocket knives?"

"We gathered them all up."

"Okay. Tie up the men. Hands behind their backs. Do it right, Scott."

"Will do."

Karl knew if any man had big enough balls to cause trouble, he would do it when they learned they were going to be tied. But none of the men offered any resistance; none of them said anything. Karl smiled with satisfaction. Everything was going smooth as glass.

Karl again cut his eyes to Abby. What a fine looking honey she was. He did a little fast arithmetic: Four women, one teenage girl, and one old broad who looked to be in her mid-fifties. Well, that was all right. She still had a pussy.

Eight men in his group. And Karl didn't want any trouble with his people about who was going to fuck who and when. They would all get their turn.

Karl knew he'd have to hump his sister at least once, for old-times' sake. But that was all right. They were only half brother and sister. Wasn't like they were full blood kin. And Karl remembered that Kathy had some pretty good snatch.

"The men are all tied up, Karl," Scott reported. "They ain't goin' anywhere."

"All right. Now let's have some fun and relax some." He cut his eyes to Jans and the big man grinned.

A few minutes later, fifteen-year-old Patti Matthews started screaming.

Seven

Randy O'Donnell stepped out of the tent and zipped up his pants. Behind him, on the sleeping bags, Anne Chambers lay naked. She had not fought Randy's attack. She sensed that to fight these men would mean death. She tolerated Randy's grunting and snorting stoically at first. But then he hit her twice, really hard, open-handed, and told her she'd better start moving her ass some and telling him how much she liked the fucking or she was going to get hurt. Anne knew the man meant every word and did her best to comply with his wishes. She did not want to die.

In the tent next to where Anne lay, Judy Post had stopped her near hysterical sobbing and endured the rape . . . but only after she'd been struck several times. Now a second man had mounted the girl and was taking his turn with her. It was going to be a very long, oftentimes painful, and always degrading afternoon for the women in camp.

The convicts had taken all the women in the camp and

raped them repeatedly: From Judy Post, fifteen-years-old, to Doris Fisher, in her mid-fifties. They spared none of the women. When Walt Fisher objected to their dragging his screaming wife off, several of the escapees beat him unconscious. Walt was not seriously hurt, just humiliated and sick over what had happened to the women. The men lay silently, hands tied tightly behind their backs.

"Take the horses," Randy ordered. "I want them guarded all the time. One man to guard the horses, another to watch the men."

"The men ain't gonna do nothin,' " Dick Gordon told him. Dick had been serving life for multiple murders. "They're all a bunch of candy asses."

"I wanna fuck the kid," John Wilson said, staring at Phil Fisher. "He's got a nice ass on him." John was serving life for rape, torture, and murder. He had been in prison for so long, fucking punks, that women held little attraction for him. But then, John had always liked boys.

"Just shut up and do what I tell you to do," Randy told the escapees who had unexpectedly linked up with the main bunch. "And I don't care if you brown dick the kid, if it'll make you happy. Fuck him all you want."

Randy walked away and sat down. He began field-stripping his weapon and cleaning it. The weapons that had been cached for the escapees were new: M-16's and Uzis with a huge supply of ammunition for the weapons. Also in the massive caches of supplies were grenades. The convicts now had enough firepower to make one hell of a stand against just about anything the authorities could throw against them.

They also had radios, and they could listen to newscasts and pick up police band transmissions to get the real truth about what was going on in the hunt for them.

As Randy O'Donnell had put it, "Anything done halfway

won't cut it. I don't do anything halfway, and I won't allow
my people to do sloppy work."

Karl knew that Randy's people had worked hard on the
breakout plans—hard, but very fast. He both marveled
and was impressed at the efficiency of Randy's group. And
Karl was not easily impressed, by anything or anybody.

In the bushes around the camp, young Phil Fisher began
screaming as John Wilson stripped him naked and
mounted him. Walt began weeping silently as the sounds
of his son's painful shrieking echoed around the camp.
Walt did not know if his wife was aware of what was going
on. She was being repeatedly raped in one of the tents.
Sexual gruntings and vivid profanity from all around the
camp filled the air.

Walt guessed it was only going to get worse as time
passed. Then the convicts would kill all the hostages. It
did not take a genius to figure that out.

The campers in both camps had all heard the newscasts
about the mass prison break on the cons' radios. The news
commentators had been quite blunt in explaining that
these men were among the nation's most brutal and dangerous. The escaped convicts had grinned at the hostages
when the newscasters said that.

The hostages got the grim message, loud and clear in
its silence.

Jack Bailey and Dennis Johnson set out to do a bit of
exploring. Jack had taken their bearings with his compass,
and also a bit of kidding from Dennis.

"You sure you still know how to read a compass, Jack?"
his friend had ribbed him.

"I got my team out of North Vietnam that time, didn't
I?"

"Hell, that's easy. Turn left and keep walking."

"You're losing faith in your fellow man, Dennis."

"No, just you, you old goat."

"I seem to recall that you are several months older than me, you old fart."

"But I can still see without goggles. Where do you have to go to get your glasses, a binocular shop?"

"These are only mild bifocals."

"Look like goggles to me. Me, now, I still have perfect vision."

"Oh, yeah? Then what are you doing carrying around that glasses case?"

"Those are merely reading glasses, my old, half-blind friend. I don't even use them most of the time."

"You don't *read* most of the time, either. I always said I believed you to be nearly illiterate. And on the plus side, I still have my hair, baldy."

"I suffered hair loss because of too much sex," Dennis fired back. "When's the last time you had a piece?"

"The night before I came up here. Which will probably prove to be a great mistake on my part. My coming up here, that is. Not making love to my wife."

"Hah! If you'd have gotten any pussy before we left you wouldn't be able to walk for a week."

"I refuse to discuss my wonderful sex life with a cretinous barbarian such as you."

"Cretinous? Me? Hell, you haven't read a newspaper in so many years you still think Ronnie is president."

"I wish to hell he was."

Both men laughed and kept on walking.

They walked for nearly an hour, taking their time and enjoying the scenery. They rested for a few minutes and then started out again, walking for another hour through the quiet and beautiful wilderness.

Suddenly, Jack held up a hand and said in a low voice, "Easy, Denny. Don't say a word and don't move."

"What the hell's the matter?" Dennis whispered.

"Man with a rifle. Cut your eyes to the left. Over by that little clearing. See him?"

A few seconds later Dennis said, "Yeah. He's dressed in military cammies, and I think he's looking right at us."

"I don't think he can see us. Our clothing is earth-colored, and we're in the trees. Just don't move."

"You think he's a poacher?"

"I don't know what he is. But I suddenly got a very bad feeling in my guts."

"Do you have to fart?"

"No, you big dummy. That old feeling of danger. You do recall that feeling, don't you?"

"Oh, yes. I do remember that sensation. Hell, Jack. The guy may be with the forest service."

"With an M-sixteen? I don't think so. He's turned his head away from us. Back up, slowly. Get some more trees between us. That's good. Now kneel down."

"Yes, Sergeant. Whatever you say, Sergeant. Damn, Jack, this is ridiculous."

"I don't think so, Buddy. I really don't think so."

Dennis uncased his binoculars and held them up, questions in his eyes.

"Yeah, go ahead and take a look. But it's not mid-morning yet and we're facing northeast, so be careful the sun doesn't reflect off the lenses."

"You're really serious about this, aren't you?"

"Very. That old feeling is getting stronger."

Dennis gave the man with the M-16 a long look, then lowered the binoculars. "Jesus, what a hard looking guy. Here," he held out the long lenses, "you take a good look and tell me what you think."

Jack gave the man a once-over through the binoculars, then lowered them. "That's no forest service guy, Denny. Not with that goatee and haircut."

"A poacher?"

"Maybe. But whoever or whatever he is, he's sure a rough lookin' hombre."

"Look!" Dennis grabbed Jack's arm. "Another man joined the first one."

Jack lifted the binoculars and looked for a moment. "Now I know they're not forest service people. The second one is armed with some sort of machine gun. An Uzi, I think."

"An Uzi? Good God, Gertie! Well, that lets poaching out, too."

The two old friends looked at each other in silence for a moment. Jack said, "They may be dopers, Denny. Does marijuana grow in this part of the country?"

"You're asking me? Hell, I don't know. But dopers would be more dangerous to strangers than poachers."

"Yeah. I think you're right. But how about this: they may be part of some local militia or survivalist group."

"I hadn't thought of that. Could be. But I still don't believe showing ourselves at this time would be a good idea."

"No. Let's get the hell back to camp and tell Bert about this."

"I think that's the best idea you've had all day."

Eight

Bert was silent for a moment after Jack and Dennis told him what they'd seen. The guide's brow was furrowed in thought. "I don't know of any militia or survival groups who meet around here," he finally said. "And the forest service damn sure doesn't pack Uzis. You're sure it was an Uzi?"

Both Jack and Dennis nodded their heads. Ted, Harry, and Andy had gathered around, listening.

"Militia and survivalist people are all crazy, anyway," Andy said. "They think they're above the law. The laws that apply to decent people don't apply to them . . . so they believe. They may be prowling around in here and you don't know it."

Bert looked at the younger man and smiled gently. "You know lots of militia people, huh?"

"Well," Andy replied. "No. Not really. Actually, I don't know any. But I read the newspapers and listen to the news on television. I know the types who join those groups."

"Do you now?" Bert asked softly, pouring himself a cup of coffee. "That's very interesting, Son."

"Yes," Andy continued, determined to stick one foot in his mouth and the other one up his ass. "Most of them are losers. Poorly educated and unhappy with their station in life. And they're racists, too."

"Is that right?" Bert said, taking a sip of coffee. "By all means, Son, go on. Tell me more about the people who join militia and survival groups."

"Well," Andy said, wriggling around on the ground in an attempt to get his butt in a more comfortable position. "Those types don't like authority. . . ."

Andy's father had a disgusted look on his face as he listened to his son rattle on. Ted knew his son did not really know the first thing about militia or survival groups. Everything he thought he knew he had learned from the press, and Ted also knew that most members of militia or survival groups would not give a member of the press the time of day because they didn't trust them . . . for good reason, most of the time.

"They aren't compassionate toward the needy, and most are homophobic—"

"They're what?" Bert asked.

"They don't like homosexuals."

"Oh. In other words they believe God created Adam and Eve, not Adam and Steve?"

A pained look crossed Andy's face. "That's one way of putting it, I suppose."

"Go on, Son," Bert urged. "Sorry for interrupting you."

"That's all right. Well, they're all gun nuts. They own dozens, perhaps hundreds, of guns. Nearly all of them own various types of assault rifles." Andy paused to take a sip of water.

Bert said, "You mean fully automatic weapons, Son?"

"Well, not necessarily. But any weapon which can hold

a large magazine, the magazine capable of containing twenty or thirty rounds, is an assault rifle.''

"Is that right?''

"Oh, yes,'' Andy said. "And those weapons are useless for any legitimate hunting purpose. They're good for killing and maiming other human beings, and that's all.''

"Oh. I see,'' Bert said. "How about self-protection? Those types of weapons are no good for that?''

"That's why we have laws and the police to enforce them, Bert. I don't own any type of gun, and neither I or any member of my family have ever been bothered by anyone with criminal intent.''

"That's good, Son,'' the guide said. "I hope you never are. Anything else about these wacky militia types you think I need to know?''

"Don't get involved with any of them. They're all crazy.''

Bert smiled. "Well, Andy, I have a problem with that. You see, two very close friends of mine are militia members. . . .''

Andy's face reddened and he suddenly looked very uncomfortable.

"Both of them good family men,'' Bert continued. "Both of them big church workers, and sincere in their belief in God. They both give to charity, and for years served on various non-paying civic boards. I don't think they're crazy at all.''

Andy rose stiffly to his feet and walked off, his face set in anger.

Bert smiled at Ted. "He's not a bad fellow, Ted. But your son sure has some strange ideas.''

"Believe me, I've been listening to them for years, Bert. And I gave up trying to change his opinions when he was just a boy.''

"You belong to a militia group, Bert?'' Jack asked.

Bert shook his head. "No. I'm too damn old for all that

business. But I certainly support most of what the legitimate militias believe."

"What about the guys with the automatic weapons Jack and Denny saw, Bert?" Harry asked.

"I don't know what to do about them." Bert admitted. "They may be poachers. I don't think they're dopers, though. Short growin' season up in this country."

"We'll just stay away from that part of the area," Harry suggested.

"That might be the best thing we can do, for the time being," Bert said. "When we get back, I'll report it to the sheriff."

"You brought a rifle, Bert," Dennis remarked. "That's a .thirty-thirty, isn't it?"

"Yep. Had it for years. I always bring it along, just in case."

"Ever had to use it out here?" Ted asked.

"Several times. 'Bout five years ago I come face to snout with a bear some damn poacher had shot and wounded. That bear was hurtin' and pissed off, and wantin' real bad to tear me to pieces. My old rifle is a good one, but when it comes to killin' bears you'd better make your shot count. Lucky for me, I did. It shook me up, and I'm not ashamed to admit it."

"I damn sure would have been. Did the authorities catch the poacher?" Harry asked.

Bert shook his head. "I don't know. I doubt it. There aren't enough forest service people to really take care of this area. The government pisses away billions of dollars a year on crap, but don't do shit in a lot of places where the money is really needed. We'll have us a good discussion about the government later on, boys. You get me started and I'll bend your ears for hours about those sorry bastards in Washington. Especially the goddamn liberals."

"I heard that!" Andy called from his tent. He stepped out.

"Oh, shit," his father muttered. "Here we go."

"Naw." The voice came from the brush surrounding the camp. "You people ain't goin' nowhere."

Many of the escaped convicts had been captured, some picked up several hundred miles from the prison. Nearly a dozen had been shot and wounded or killed by citizens when they tried to run various police roadblocks in stolen cars. Captured federal prisoners were being held in several dozen jails from Canada to Louisiana.

There were reports that Randy O'Donnell and Karl Parsons had left the country and were now in South America, and also that they had been spotted in Europe and Mexico. Federal authorities were getting spread thin chasing down all the rumors.

Several of the escaped prisoners had died in fiery automobile accidents, crashing after lengthy high speed chases, what was left of their bodies burned to a blackened, unrecognizable crispness. It would take weeks for the forensic people to ID the charred remains. Some authorities believed two of the burned and dead bodies were the remains of Karl Parsons and Randy O'Donnell.

There was no way Karl and Randy could have planned the fiery crashes, but they certainly worked out well for them.

The helicopter search flights over the wilderness had all but ceased. The search for the escapees had now moved nearly one hundred percent to the east. Things were definitely looking up for the escaped convicts.

But things were looking decidedly grim for the campers.

* * *

"You're the guys we saw earlier today," Dennis blurted before he thought.

"Yeah, that's right," one of the convicts said. "We seen you at the edge of the timber and followed you old bastards over here."

"Who are you and what do you want?" Bert asked, his tone anything but friendly.

"I don't like that one," the second con said. "He's got a smart mouth on him."

"I've got the horses!" a third voice added. "I'm gonna need some help gettin' 'em saddled."

The first con that spoke waved a hand. "Go help him, Lucas."

"You're welcome to the horses," Bert said. "Take them and leave us alone."

"Bossy bastard, ain't you?" the con said with a nasty smile. Without waiting for Bert to reply, he added, "I got some advice for you, old man. If you want to stay healthy, shut your goddamn mouth and keep it closed."

"Easy, Bert," Jack said. "We can walk out of here."

"In about a week," Bert told him.

"But we'll be alive," Harry said.

"Listen to your buddies, old man," the con said. "They're tellin' you straight."

"I can't wait to get back to camp," one of the cons helping saddle the horses called from the makeshift corral. "That woman I been humpin's got some fine pussy on her. 'Course her husband's a little pissed off about it."

"Shut up, Big Un," said the con standing guard over the campers.

"Huh?" Big Un said. "Oh. Yeah. I got you. Sorry 'bout that, Pauly."

The campers and their guide exchanged glances, worry

in all eyes. At least five of them suddenly felt they were very close to death, and getting closer with each passing moment.

"You remember that time we were captured by the Cong, Ted?" Jack asked.

"Ahh . . . yeah! Hell, how could I forget it?"

"You old farts was in Vietnam?" the con asked. "Stupid war. My old man was in the paratroopers over there. Got his dumb ass all shot up. Couldn't work. Laid around the house and drank hisself to death. Dumb. I wouldn't do nothin' for this fuckin' country. It stinks."

The campers and guide sat on the ground and looked at the escaped convict.

"What about the time you was captured by the Slopes?" the con asked.

"Just making conversation," Jack said.

"Yeah? Well, you put your conversation on the back burner and shut up."

"All right. Whatever you say."

"Hold still, you goddamn nag!" Lucas hollered.

"Don't shout at the horses," Pauly called. "You'll get 'em spooked and it'll take half an hour to calm 'em down. Talk to 'em gentle like."

"Son of a bitch is stupid!" Lucas said.

"They ain't very smart, for a fact," Pauly told him. "Just take it easy. We got the time."

"Why are you doing this?" Andy asked. "We haven't done you any harm."

His father sighed. Now was not the time for dumb questions.

Pauly looked at Andy and smiled. "We don't like prison, fancy pants. We were part of the breakout."

"What breakout?" Dennis asked.

Pauly shifted his gaze and stared at the man for a moment. "You folks don't have radios, do you?"

Dennis shook his head. "No."

Pauly laughed. "Well, I'll be damned."

"The horses is saddled and ready to go, Pauly," Big Un called.

Pauly smiled and lifted his M-16. "Sorry, boys. But I can't afford to let none of you live. That's the way it is." He cut his eyes toward the corral for a couple of seconds.

Ted threw the handful of dirt and rocks he had furtively gathered while the others talked, and Jack lunged at Pauly. Before the much younger man could react, Jack was all over him, riding him to the ground. He slammed the knife edge of his hand down on the man's throat and brought his knee up into Pauly's groin. Jack tore the M-16 from the man's hands and tossed it aside, tearing the pistol from Pauly's belt. Jack wasn't all that familiar with the M-16. It had been years since he'd handled the earlier models.

"Let's get out of here, Big Un!" Lucas shouted. "Them old bastards done downed Pauly. Ride, boy, ride! Take them horses with you. Go, Go."

Jack ran to the corral just as Lucas was trying to get into the saddle of the spooked horse. Jack lifted the pistol and shot the man in the side, knocking him to one side. Lucas dropped his M-16 but managed to recover his balance. He got into the saddle, grabbed up the reins of two other horses, and galloped off, a few hundred yards behind Big Un.

"Damn!" Jack said.

"This man is dying over here!" Andy called. "You killed him, Jack. I think his throat is crushed."

"Good," Jack said, walking back to the camp. " 'Cause he damn sure was going to kill us." Jack tucked the 9mm autoloader behind his belt and squatted down by the fire, pouring a cup of coffee. He looked down at the shaking cup. The incident had shaken him up, for a fact. Just like the old days in Korea and 'Nam: Jack was never scared until after it was all over.

"The horses are gone!" Bert called. "The bastards took my horse. I'm gonna kill me a son of a bitch for that!"

Lucas was jerking and kicking and thrashing around on the ground, unable to breathe. His throat was crushed. He would be dead in another minute.

"Good?" Andy shouted. "A man is dying horribly here, a man you savaged with your bare hands, and you *shot* another. All you have to say is *good?*"

Jack wished Andy would shut his damn mouth. He took a sip of coffee and noted with some satisfaction that his hands had stopped trembling.

"Son," Ted said, "that man was going to kill us all. Can't you get that through your head? Jack had absolutely no choice in the matter. My God, what in the hell is the matter with you?"

Lucas made several horrible noises and expired.

"Boys, we've got to get the hell gone from here," Bert said. "Whoever those bastards were, they'll probably be back with their friends."

"We walk out?" Harry asked.

"Got no choice in the matter," the guide told him. "Douse that fire and let's hurry up and break camp. It's gonna take us some time to pack up some gear. We've got to get gone from here."

"What about the dead man?" Andy asked.

Jack looked at the younger man, open disgust in his eyes. "Fuck him!"

"I couldn't have said it any better," Dennis said.

Nine

Breaking camp took longer than anticipated. The men were going to have to walk out of the wilderness—several days' march, without incident—and they had to rig makeshift backpacks for the trek out. Jack smiled, and Andy almost had a hissy fit when all the men produced pistols from their gear.

"Those are *guns!*" Andy blurted.

"Very astute of you, Son," Ted said. "Your formal education was not a total waste."

Andy gave his father a very dirty look. "I know your men won't take the time to bury that hoodlum, but don't you think we should say some words over him?"

"How about bon voyage?" Harry suggested.

"Or, have a really miserable time in hell, you son of a bitch?" Jack added.

Bert pointed a finger at Andy. "Boy, we're in a run for our lives. And you heard the one called Big Un say something about women I guess they're rapin.' Campers, probably. And when they get done with the women, they'll kill them. Just like they was gonna do us. If we was lucky enough to kill every damn one of the escapees—I guess that's what they are—we'd be doin' the world a big favor. Now pick up that damn pack, shut your fuckin' mouth, and *walk!*"

Andy took a long silent look at Bert. The man was in his early sixties, but tough as wang leather, no unnecessary fat on his lean frame, just muscle and gristle and bone. Andy picked up his pack and struggled into the straps.

"Let's go," Bert told his charges. "We've got a damn long walk ahead of us."

"We've got to find those men and kill them," Karl said. "If they get out of here, we've had it. This place will be swarming with cops."

Randy O'Donnell and his bunch had linked up with Karl and his people just that morning, preparing for the march out and to freedom. The terrorist had been studying a map. He looked up at Karl's words and nodded his head. "Agreed, Karl. Look here." He laid a very detailed map of the area flat on the ground. "We're here." He jabbed a finger at the map. "The old men are there." He pointed. "Say it took them an hour to pack up some gear and get ready to walk out. They're either just leaving, or haven't been gone long." He traced a long route with his finger. "This is the shortest way out. I say we let them take it. It leads right into this valley. The valley is miles long with mountains on either side of it. Longest valley in the range . . . says so here on the side of the map. If we can get there before they do, we'll have them trapped."

"I know that valley." Karl spoke in a low voice, but the alarm and irritation he felt was clearly evident. "At least I remember it. And you're right on every point. Let's make certain the men are tied securely, pick some guards we know will stay alert, and get moving.''

"It's your show from now on, Karl," Randy said. "This is your country.''

"Well . . . there is someone who knows it a hell of a lot better than I do.''

Randy looked at him for a moment, then smiled and nodded his head. "Yes. Quite. Your sister. She certainly would know the country. But does she know if she helps us do this she'll be facing some heavy charges if we're caught?''

"She doesn't give a damn anymore. And I believe her when she says that. Her husband can't fuck worth a shit. She told me all about it. He sticks it in, hunches twice, and blows his rocks.''

"One of those," Randy said.

"According to Kathy, yes. She's with us a hundred percent. And I remember once she commits she goes ahead, no matter what.''

"All right." Randy punched a finger on the map. "I'll take some boys out with her to block this end of the valley.''

"Yeah," Karl agreed. "Once we get that end plugged, we can relax some. You want me at the other end?''

"Right.''

"Let's get rolling.''

None of the escapees paid any attention to the pained, wracking sobs of Phil Fisher, who lay nearly naked under a blanket. As soon as the two groups of escaped convicts had linked up at the new camp site John Wilson had taken the boy again, and Phil's anus felt as though it was on fire. John had forced Phil's mother and father to watch the assault, grinning at them as he raped their son. There was nothing either parent could do: they were both tied securely. Before he mounted Phil this last time, John had forced the boy to commit oral sex, warning him if he didn't comply he would kill the boy's mother . . . after he sodomized and tortured her.

Karl had watched in disgust, whispering to Randy, "I've had just about all I can take of Wilson."

Randy grinned nastily. "So has the kid!"

Both men had enjoyed a good laugh at that.

"How far have we come?" Harry asked, sitting down on the ground with a sigh of contentment.

"Maybe two miles, at the most," Bert told him.

"How far do we have to go?" Andy asked.

"About thirty-five or forty miles," the guide replied, taking a sip of water.

"Dear God," Ted muttered.

"There is a thin line of smoke over there," Dennis said, pointing.

"It's miles away," Bert told him. "And in the wrong direction."

"Campers?" Jack asked.

"Probably," Bert replied.

"Those helicopters we heard and saw in a distance a couple of days ago," Andy said. "They were the authorities looking for the convicts?"

"I'm sure they were," Bert told him. "But for some reason they haven't returned to this area. If they do, we can signal them with a small, controlled burn."

"I wish they'd return," Andy said.

"I thought you didn't like cops," Bert remarked. "That's what you said. Something about the police having too much power."

Andy took another sip of water and said nothing in rebuttal.

Andy had gotten sideways with Bert, and the guide wasn't about to let up.

Jack had opened a map as soon as he sat down, and now he looked up. "We're approaching the longest valley in this range. Has several natural springs and a pretty good size creek in it."

"Yeah," Bert said. "It's one of the prettiest places God ever created. Indians trapped some people in there a hundred and fifty or so years ago and killed them all. Two ways in—north end and south end. Neither one is a picnic."

"So if a person were to get trapped in there?" Ted let that trail off.

Bert shook his head. "If you're talkin' about us, well, that valley is twenty or so miles long. Widens out to four or five miles at several points. Lots of timber and rocks, dozens of caves on both sides, many of the entrances covered with brush. I doubt all the caves have been found to this day. Lots of places to hide. Those pioneers just ran out of luck, I reckon."

"Or shot and powder," Harry said.

"Yeah," Bert agreed. "Or shot and powder." The guide looked at Andy. The younger man had a very worried expression on his face. Bert hoped the seriousness of the situation was finally beginning to sink in, but he wasn't ready to take any bets on that . . . not just yet.

"You beginning to realize just how much trouble we might be in, Son?" Ted asked.

"I guess so, Dad. It's just . . . well, I've never come face to face with anything like this. I've never seen real violence before."

"You ever had a fight, Andy?" Bert asked gently, no hostility in his tone.

Andy looked puzzled at the question. "A fight? As in a fistfight?" He shook his head. "Ah . . . no. Never. Well . . . kid stuff, sure, when I was in grade school. First and second grades. Why do you ask, Bert?"

"Oh, just curious. Forget it, Son. It's none of my business, anyway."

"I'm not a coward, Bert," Andy said.

"I never said you were. Didn't mean for you to take it that way."

"At least I don't think I am," Andy added softly. "I really don't know, I guess."

"I don't believe you're a coward, Andy," Jack said. "And I don't think anyone here does. You've just never been tested, that's all."

"But I'm about to be, right?"

"I think we all are," Dennis said. "We're in a hell of a lot more trouble than any of us yet realize."

"But we've got several hours head start on the criminals, right?" Andy asked.

"Not really," Bert told him. "We're all afoot and they've got horses. It all depends on how many of them we're up against. If they know anything about this country—and I've got a hunch at least one of them does—they could cut around and block the south end of the valley. If that happens . . . well, yeah, we'd be in big trouble."

"Well, let's look on the bright side," Jack said. "We've got our pistols and two M-sixteens. Bert has his .thirty-thirty. We don't have a lot of ammo, but we've got enough to do some damage. I think we're in pretty good shape."

"We've damn sure been in worse shape," Ted said. He smiled. "Of course, that was forty years ago."

"If they trap us somewhere," Harry said, "we fight. We lived through Korea and the early days of Vietnam, through dozens of fire fights. All of us know how to fight, and we've killed our share of the enemy."

"More than our share," Dennis said softly, his eyes cloudy with memories.

"That's sure a fact," Jack agreed.

"I think I got this weapon figured out," Harry said.

"Little switch here on the side sets the fire. But I'm not real thrilled about these sights."

"We've got to remember that they don't have the range of our old M-ones," Jack said. He held up a 5.56 round. "Sure is a little bitsy thing, isn't it?"

Bert stood up. "Let's go, boys. We've got a long walk ahead of us."

"Oh, my achin' tootsies," Dennis said.

"We walked thirty miles in Korea one time," Harry said. "Carrying a lot of gear."

Jack smiled. "Yeah, but that was before we all had arthritis!"

Chuckling, the men moved out, toward the valley that the press would later call The Valley of Death.

Ten

By mid-afternoon the men were ready to call it a day. They were just about all pooped out. To a man they collapsed on the ground and lay there for a time, not speaking. Even Andy was showing signs of fatigue. It had been a tough hike over some very rough country.

"Lie to me, Bert," Dennis said. "Tell me we're almost back to home base."

Bert smiled as he rubbed his own aching feet. "Can't do it, Dennis. That'd be a whopper. I figure 'bout four more days. Unless we get spotted by helicopters and rescued."

The bullet slammed into a tree by Jack's head, knocking off bits of bark.

"Shit!" Jack hollered, rolling away and getting behind cover. "Where the hell did that come from?"

"There was no noise," Bert said, bellied down on the ground.

"Sound suppressor," Harry told him from his newly

acquired position behind a tree. "And a damn good one, too."

Another bullet silently ripped the air, knocking a small chunk out of the side of the tree Dennis was crouched behind.

"Damn!" Dennis said. He had pulled his pistol from his holster for comfort, for just knowing he was armed. The pistol was no good against a rifleman several hundred yards away.

"Bastards beat us here," Bert said. "I was afraid they would. Damn!"

"Why don't you use your rifle, Bert?" Andy asked, from his place behind a jumble of large rocks.

"I don't know where the rifleman is, Son," the guide told him. "And this .thirty-thirty doesn't have the range of that weapon being used against us."

"My ignorance of weapons," Andy said. "I thought all rifles were the same."

"Not quite," Bert replied, his tone very dry, but holding no hostility or sarcasm.

Another round quietly tore through the air and screamed off the rocks in front of Andy. Andy pressed himself against the earth and softly cursed the rifleman, ending with, "You rotten, no good son of a bitch!"

Ted chuckled despite the desperate situation. "Now you're getting into the spirit of matters, Son."

Andy cut his eyes to his father. "I see nothing amusing about this, Dad." Then he smiled despite himself.

Father and son suddenly found themselves drawn much closer, emotionally. The closeness would not last long.

Ted winked at his son.

"He's on that ridge to our right," Jack informed the pinned down group. "I spotted movement just a few seconds ago. And I've got an idea."

"Would you like to share it?" Harry asked. "I'm certainly

open to suggestions on how to get my ass out of here . . . in one piece, preferably.''

"Yeah," Jack said. "Start scrooching around until you're facing that ridge, Harry. Lock and load your weapon—"

"It's locked and loaded, Buddy." Then Harry frowned as he looked down at the unfamiliar weapon. "I think," he added.

"I seem to recall, Ole' Buddy," Ted called from his position, "that you were the weapons expert when we were in 'Nam."

"I also seem to recall that we carried Thompsons, M Two carbines, and M-ones," Harry came right back.

"What's your plan, Jack?" Dennis asked just as the hidden sniper fired again, the bullet ricocheting off rocks and whining away.

"At my signal, Harry and me will open fire on the sniper's position. When we do that, the rest of you run like hell toward the timber to the south. It looks like maybe fifty yards at the most. When you start your run, give it all you got, boys."

"We have to do something," Ted said. "We can't stay here. Sooner or later he'll nail one of us. Your plan's okay with me, Jack."

"Yeah, let's do it," Bert said. "How about you, Dennis? You for it?"

"We don't have a choice in the matter. All right, boys. I'm game. Let's do it."

"But, Jack, what about you guys?" Andy asked. "You'll be stuck over here."

Jack shook his head. "When you people get to safety, then Harry and me will go one at a time, with the other giving cover fire. You ready to spray some lead around, Harry?"

"Ready as I'll ever be with this weapon. What the hell is this thing on the end of the barrel, Jack?"

"I think it's a flash suppressor. I'm really not sure."

Bert had to smile. "You guys haven't fired a weapon in some time, have you?"

"Oh, it's been about thirty years, I guess," Jack said. "For most of us. We're all rusty as hell with guns. You guys ready to make the run?"

The men were as ready as they would ever be. To a person they were scared, but they were ready.

Jack and Harry lifted their rifles. "Now!" Jack called.

The plan was a simple one, and like most simple plans it worked. Those running for better cover made it without taking a bullet in the back. Then Jack laid down cover fire for Harry, and when Harry reached the timber, he laid down fire for his old friend. The gunman on the ridge had to hug the ground or risk catching a bullet in the head.

"Now what, Bert?" Jack asked after his breathing had returned to normal after the run.

"We head for the valley and get ourselves lost in the timber and brush. We make cold camps and hope to God we're not spotted by those bastards." He looked up at the sky. Clouds were moving in. "It's gonna start raining in a few hours. Once we get to a secure place, we can't move around. We'd leave tracks that a child could follow."

Jack held out the pistol he'd taken from Pauly. "You want this pistol, Andy?"

The younger man shook his head. "I've never fired a gun in my life, Jack. I'd probably shoot myself in the foot, or one of you guys."

"I have a suggestion for you, Andy," Bert said. "Once we get out of this mess, that is."

"What's that, Bert?"

"Join the National Rifle Association."

* * *

"They're trapped in the valley," Karl said. "They can't get out."

"Max should have killed at least a couple of them," Randy replied, a sour look on his face.

"It's been almost ten years since Max fired a weapon," Karl reminded his friend.

Randy cut his eyes to the bigger man. Nodded his head. "Yeah? Ten years," he said softly. "I can't imagine ten years behind bars. Three years almost drove me crazy."

Karl didn't immediately respond to that. He was pretty sure Randy had been totally bonkers before he was sentenced to spend the rest of his life in prison.

Randy broke the few seconds of silence. "Everyone in place?"

"Everyone is in place and knows what to do."

Randy cut his eyes to Anne Chambers. He couldn't get enough of the woman. She had some of the best pussy he'd ever pumped. And she couldn't fool him: she liked to bump. He felt himself getting hard again, and with an effort he pushed Anne out of his mind for a moment. "Everybody knows who relieves who on guard?"

"Relax, Randy. Everything is A Okay, and all the men are in place."

"They've stopped the search in the wilderness," the man monitoring the radio called. "And the cops are sure those guys killed in that car crash were you and Randy, Karl."

"Couldn't have worked out better if we'd planned it," Karl said with a satisfied smile.

Randy nodded in agreement. They just might make it, he thought. If they could get rid of these old men, they had better than a fifty-fifty chance. The more he thought about it, the better he felt. Hell, the men they were pursuing were old, probably a bunch of near-retirement, fatass executive types. Pauly getting killed by these old farts was a fluke, nothing more than that. Nothing like that would happen again.

"Get rid of them," Randy said. "Kill them, get done with it, and let's get the hell out of here."

Jack and his friends made a cold camp deep in the brush, all of them, including Andy, collapsing wearily on the ground. No one said anything for a few minutes. Jack finally sat up with a barely suppressed groan and gave each of the men a long look, his gaze settling on Bert.

"We're in deep shit, aren't we, Bert?"

"I been in better situations," the guide admitted.

"But have you been in worse ones?" Andy asked.

"Truthfully, I got to say no."

"We all have," Ted said, sitting up. "But it was forty years ago."

"It seems incredible to me that there are only two ways out of this valley," Andy remarked. "But I'm a city boy. I know nothing about the wilderness."

"There are dozens of ways out, Son," Bert replied. "But all except two require some rock climbing and rapelling. We don't have the gear for it."

"Or the muscle and stamina," Dennis added.

"Yeah, we're all in pitiful physical shape," Harry said. "Sucking up martinis Monday through Friday evenings, having two hour lunches, and playing golf on the weekends for decades won't keep a guy in the best of condition."

"I wish I *had* a martini," Jack said. "A great big pitcher of them."

"Icy cold," Ted added. "A pitcher of vodka martinis and a chilled glass filled with ice. With huge olives. Ahhh, shit! Might as well wish for the Eighty-second Airborne to drop in.''

''I wish I had a cigarette to go with those martinis,'' Dennis said. ''About a foot and a half long.''

''And Ingrid Bergman to light that cigarette and share the martinis with me,'' Bert surprised them all by saying. Bert did not look the martini type. ''The most beautiful woman that ever lived.''

''She sure was,'' Jack agreed.

''I prefer the Courteney Cox type,'' Andy said.

The five older men looked at him and said simultaneously, ''Who?''

''They're opening up more areas for tourists, Sheriff,'' a deputy said, sticking his head into the office.

''Shit!'' Sheriff Hawkins said, looking up from the seemingly neverending paperwork associated with his job and hurling his pen on the desk. ''Who opened it up?''

''A bunch of mayors and town councils petitioned the forest service, and the President, and God only knows who else to open it up. Said they were losing a lot of money and couldn't take the economic losses.''

''They'll be sorry they did that when they start losing *people,*''Hawk said. ''My God! The government had admitted there are probably escaped cons all over the area.''

''It's a big area, Sheriff. Maybe the tourists will get lucky.''

Sheriff Hawkins got up and walked to one of the windows in his office. He stood for a moment, staring out. He turned and faced the deputy. ''I've got a real bad feeling about letting those tourists back in, Nate.'' He sighed. ''But it's out of my hands. Nobody asked for my opinion.''

''All we can do is hope for the best, Sheriff.''

''I guess so. That's about it.''

Hawk sat down and drummed his fingertips on his desk

for a moment. Then he stilled the jangling of the phone. His private line. "Sheriff Hawkins."

"Hawk? Sheriff Osborne. Just thought you'd want to know the body of a camper was found late yesterday on the eastern edge of the wilderness."

"Shot?"

"Her neck was broken. A woman. She was naked. She'd been used pretty badly. From both ends," Sheriff Osborne added drily. "These are some real nice guys runnin' from the law."

"Yeah. Just a bunch of little darlings. If they could tell that immediately—that she'd been raped, I mean, and sodomized—then the body was not badly decomposed."

"No. And the animals hadn't gotten to it yet, either. She had photo ID in a folder in the back pocket of her jeans. Which were found about fifty feet from the body. Her family was notified. But her sixteen-year-old daughter is missing . . ."

"Son of a bitch!" Hawk said.

"Yeah. The feds think the escaped cons are keeping her alive for entertainment."

"That's one way of putting it, I suppose. You in on the search?"

"No. Signs show the cons made a half circle and left the wilderness, heading east."

"What do you think, Ossie?"

"I think they headed west, deeper into the wilderness, and took the kid with them. But I'm just a country sheriff. What do I know about anything?"

"Yeah, well, don't feel too bad. The feds didn't ask for my advice, either."

"I think we've got a bunch of hardass cons heading west, Hawk. I think when they get tired of dragging that poor girl along, they'll kill her with just about as much emotion as stepping on a roach."

"Yeah. And more tourists are being allowed in."

"Some of the packers are refusing to take people in until all escaped cons are caught."

"And some are looking at the dollar and heading in."

"But the word I get is they're armed," Sheriff Osborne said very sarcastically.

"Oh, yes. Absolutely," Hawk replied, an equal amount of disgust in his words. "But what can we do about it?"

"Nothing. Just sit back and wait for the blood to start flowing."

"And then go in with body bags."

"That's it. The feds are in charge. They have everything under control."

"They know it all."

"Sure they do."

"Shit!"

Sheriff Osborne's laugh held no mirth. He sighed and said, "Just wanted to yak for a minute or two, Hawk. You have a good day, my friend."

"Same to you, Ossie."

Hawk sat at his desk for several moments after hanging up. He felt deep in his guts there was going to be a major disaster in the back country, and there wasn't a damn thing he could do about it. The feds weren't at all happy with him, and hadn't been for a long time. Sheriff Hawkins had a habit of voicing his opinion about crime and criminals, and he didn't particularly give a damn whether the person or group listening liked it or not. And he'd been voicing his opinion about the federal government for years . . . not much of it good. He'd gotten into a very heated shouting match with several federal officials in Washington during the national sheriff's meeting a few years back, and to date Sheriff Hawkins had not been asked to return. Not that he gave a damn, for he certainly didn't.

Hawk swiveled in his chair and stared out the window

for a moment. "There's gonna be a bloodbath in the back country," he muttered. "Bet on it."

He could hear Betty's voice in the outer office. "Yes, Mrs. Miller. Right. I agree with you, Mrs. Miller." His phone rang and Hawk answered it. "Sheriff, Mrs. Miller out on Little Creek Road called—again. Her neighbor's dog got loose—again—and is shittin' in Mrs. Miller's yard—again. She wants you to come right out and have a long talk with her neighbor—again."

Hawk sighed deeply. About fifty of the nation's most dangerous escaped cons were running around loose in his backyard—so to speak—and the best he could do was deal with crabby old Mrs. Miller's dogshit in her front yard.

"Tell her I'll send someone out just as soon as possible, Betty."

"She wants to see you personally, Sheriff."

"Doesn't she always? Oh, hell, why not? Tell her I'm on my way."

"That will make her very happy, Sheriff."

"I'm glad somebody can find something to be happy about," he muttered, and reached for his hat.

Walking to his car, Hawk stepped in a big wad of bubble gum some damn asshole punk kid had tossed aside. Sitting in his car, the door open, Hawk scraped the bubble gum from his boot. "I suppose it's better than stepping in shit," he mumbled.

Eleven

"We've got to make some plans," Jack said. "We can't just wander around with no firm plan."

"I've got a real bad taste in my mouth about running away and leaving the campers in the hands of those thugs," Ted added.

"I've been thinking about that myself," Dennis said. "Seems like to me we've turned into a bunch of chicken-shits."

"I agree," Harry said. "But we don't know where they're being held, we don't know how many people we're up against, and we don't even know if what that convict said was the truth. But if there is just one person being held against their will, and being abused, well . . ." He paused for a few seconds. "I think we should do something."

Andy said nothing.

Bert had been rubbing his feet. He laced his boots back up and looked at the men, giving each one a hard look.

Finally he shrugged his shoulders. "Whatever you guys decide to do, I'll go along with it."

"What about you, Andy?" Ted asked his son.

The son looked at the father for a moment. "Well, you know until I changed majors I was going to be a doctor. I still remember most of it, I suppose. So I have some limited medical training I can put to use if anybody gets hurt. That's about all I can contribute to the plan . . . if we decide to stay and try to help those who were taken hostage."

Ted smiled at his son and nodded his head.

"What do you have in mind, Jack?" Dennis asked.

"Three men stay in camp. Two of us reconnoiter the, ah, situation."

"That would be you and me, Jack," Harry said.

"Yeah. That's the way I figure it."

"You guys don't know this country," Bert said. "You better give that some thought."

"It won't take us long to learn what we have to know. We didn't know Korea or Vietnam," he countered. "But we all made it out alive. Besides, the escaped cons don't know this country, either."

"All right," Bert said. "I'll give you that. And I want you all to know I'm with you in doing something for those people being held hostage. But let's plan it carefully, and don't do nothing real stupid."

"Agreed," Harry said.

"We have two M-sixteens, one .thirty-thirty rifle, and four pistols. All the weapons with a limited amount of ammo," Harry said. "Once Bert runs out of ammo for his .thirty-thirty, it's doubtful there will be any more. So we have to get more weapons and as much ammo as possible."

"I don't know anything about guns," Andy said. "I'd be less than useless with a gun."

"You point it in the general direction of the enemy and pull the trigger," Jack told the younger man. "You might not hit anything, but when the lead starts flying, you'll damn sure keep their heads down."

Andy shrugged his shoulders. "I don't have much choice in the matter, do I?"

"None at all, Son," his father told him. "Not if you want to stay alive."

The men all looked up at the sound of a very faint cry that seemed to come from the east of their location.

"What the hell was that?" Dennis asked.

The pleading cry was heard again.

"It's a girl," Bert said. He pointed. "Coming from over yonder. A long way off, sounds like to me."

Jack stood up. "Come on, Bert. You and I'll check it out. The rest of you stay in camp and keep your eyes open."

Bert picked up his rifle and the pair moved out, slowly and cautiously leaving the brush. The cries became louder.

"We're on the right track," Jack whispered.

"If it isn't a trap," Bert said.

They walked on through the timber for another twenty-five yards. Jack suddenly touched Bert's arm. "Hold it," he whispered. "To our right about thirty yards."

Bert stared intently for a moment. "I see her. It's a young girl."

"Not her," Jack said. "That big bastard to her left."

Bert and sucked in air audibly. "Shit!" he whispered. "Now I see him. That's a big son of a bitch."

"Thought you could run away from ole' Cliff, did you, you little cunt? Well, guess what? Ole' Cliff found you. Now stop all that whimperin' and squealin' and peel them jeans off. Let me see that fine lookin' bush of yours. Ole' Cliff wants some of that pussy."

"Get away from me!" the girl screamed.

"Not likely, Baby," Cliff said, unhooking his ammo belt

and laying his M-16 aside. "But you go right ahead and scream. There ain't nobody can hear you squallin.' We're all alone out here. Just you and me. Now if I have to tell you again to shuck them jeans, I'm gonna kick the shit outta you. You understand all that, pretty girl?"

"Leave me alone, you monster!"

Cliff drew back one boot and gave the teenage girl a vicious kick on her butt. The girl yelped in pain. "Git outta them jeans, bitch, and spread them legs. I'm fixin' to give you some hard cock. Hell, you like it. I know you do. I never seen a bitch yet that didn't like to fuck."

Jack raised his M-16 and shot the huge man. Cliff stumbled backward and sat down hard on the ground, a growing red stain appearing on the front of his shirt. He remained upright in a sitting position for a long moment.

"Goddamnit!" Cliff finally said, then fell over onto his side.

Jack and Bert moved as fast as they could. Bert knelt by the girl's side and looked at her torn and bloody bare feet while Jack grabbed the ammo belt and Cliff's M-16. He cut his eyes to Cliff. The big man was still breathing. But, Jack thought, he's damn sure out of the game for a while. Then Jack had an idea and removed the man's boots and socks, leaving him barefooted. It would take him five times as long to get back to his camp.

"Good move," Bert said, then turned his attentions back to the girl. "What's your name, Girl?"

"Lindsey Marlowe. They killed my mother."

"Damn!" Jack said. "How many of them are there, Lindsey?"

She shook her head. "I don't know. I'd guess twenty-five or thirty, at least. Maybe more than that. Probably more than that. They're all in little groups of four and five. My feet hurt really bad."

"I know they do, Dear," Bert said. "But you're going to have to walk. We can't carry you, but you can lean on us. We'll get you away from here and then see about those feet."

"I can walk slowly," the girl said. "I'd walk across hot coals to get away from those escaped convicts." She cut her eyes to Cliff. "Is he dead?"

"He's still breathing. But he's wounded and out of it for a time," Jack told her.

The girl, showing a lot of smarts and spunk for her age, knelt down and took off the sheath knife from Cliff's belt. She straightened up and said, "I've never fired a gun, but I bet you I can sure cut someone if they try to mess with me again."

Jack and Bert smiled, both thinking: *This girl will do. She's got sand in her.*

With Lindsey leaning on Bert, limping painfully along, Jack carrying the wounded man's M-16 and ammo pouch—which held ten fully loaded twenty round magazines—the trio made their way slowly out of the timber, across a small meadow, and into the thick brush. It was not yet nine o'clock in the morning.

"The criminals have men waiting for you at both ends of the valley," Lindsey said. "That is, if you're the men who escaped from some guys named Big Un and Lucas and Pauly."

"We're the men," Bert said, stopping for a short rest.

Lindsey sat down on the ground with a sigh. Her feet were in bad shape. "The thugs will never let any of you leave this valley alive. They're determined to kill all of you. Especially one of the leaders—Karl something or another. He seems to know this country really well."

Bert looked at the girl. "This Karl have a last name?"

Lindsey frowned. "Persons, or Pearson, or something like that."

"Could it be Parsons?"

"Yes! That's it. Karl Parsons."

"Karl Parsons," Bert muttered. "Well, I'll be damned."

"You know this Karl Parsons?" Jack asked.

Bert shook his head. "No. But I've heard of him. He's from this area and he's a bad one. He was born no good. Started getting in trouble with the law when he was just a little kid. His name isn't really Karl Parsons. I'm trying to think of his real name—can't pull it up out of my mind. All his family moved away from around here years ago."

"One didn't," Lindsey said. "The woman with the escaped convicts is related to him. Sister, I think. It's disgusting. They're sleeping together. He feels around on her all the time. Karl keeps the woman's husband tied up. They're both guides, or something like that."

"Kathy?" Bert asked, a startled expression on his face. "Is her husband's name Dave?"

"Yes. It sure it."

"Well, I'll just be double damned," Bert whispered. "Yeah. Now it's comin' back to me. Kathy is the last relative Karl has around here. They're half brother and sister. Now things are beginnin' to make some sense."

"She helped her brother in the breakout?" Jack asked.

"She was probably one of them helpin,' for sure. But there's no way she could get her hands on all these automatic weapons. There has to be others involved. Did you hear any other names, Lindsey?"

"I'm . . . sure I did, but I don't immediately recall any of them. More names will come to me in time, probably." She looked at both men. "What are we going to do?"

"Try to stay alive," Jack told her.

* * *

"Cliff's hit hard," Karl and Randy were told. "The girl's gone. Whoever shot him took his M-sixteen and ammo belt. I don't think Cliff's gonna make it."

"It's those old men," Karl said. "Has to be. Damn those old bastards!"

"We have no choice in the matter now," Randy said. "Not that we had much from the start. We've got to kill those old men, and we've got to do it quickly."

"We've got more people comin' in, Karl," one of Karl's men told him. "Nathan's leadin' them. He's from this area originally."

"Nathan?" Karl asked, looking at the man. "He's from around here?"

"Yeah. Says he just forgot to tell us. He went to school in some little town on the west side of the wilderness. Says he used to poach game in this part of the back country."

"Interesting," Karl said. "We can use another man who knows the back country."

"How many people do we have now?" Randy asked sourly.

"I don't know for sure. 'Bout forty or so, I guess. And some of them are bitchin' pretty hard about cold camps, no fires, and no coffee."

Randy opened his mouth to cuss and Karl held up a hand. "Let's keep the men split up into groups of five or six. Put someone we can trust in charge of each group. We'll keep the hostages in that cave we found on the east side of the slope. It'll be a lot easier keeping track of them there. Okay, Randy?"

The Irishman nodded his head. "All right. Sounds good to me. Let's get it done and the hostages moved."

"And then we've got to deal with those old men," Karl said. "We've got them trapped. They can't get out of this valley. Now we've got to find them and kill them."

"And after we do that?" another con asked.

"We fuck the bitches one more time, and then kill everybody and leave them in the cave," Karl replied very matter of factly.

"Sounds good to me," Randy said.

Twelve

The cloudy skies darkened that afternoon and a cold rain began falling. Jack and his friends and Lindsey huddled under hastily strung shelter halves and tried to stay warm and dry—both losing propositions.

They all took some consolation in the fact that the rain was helping to erase, any tracks they might have left, at least to some degree. It was also helping to keep them from the eyes of their searchers.

They all were cold and damp and miserable, and all longed for a warm fire and a hot cup of coffee.

"At least those damn cons are in the same fix we are," Jack said. "We can take some grim satisfaction in that."

"I'd rather have a cup of coffee," Dennis replied.

Andy had cleaned and put Mercurochrome on the cuts and then carefully bandaged Lindsey's feet. The girl had no shoes, and none of the camp moccasins the men had brought with them would fit her. Finally Jack took a torn shirt and ripped off pieces of it and stuffed them into the moccasins. Now Lindsey had something to wear on her feet, but the footwear was so large she walked around like a circus clown.

"Feels great to me," the girl said. "You guys are all right. I never had anything much to do with, ah, older people."

"Old farts like us?" Ted said with a gentle smile.

Lindsey laughed. "Man, you guys aren't old. Not the way you came to my rescue and are sitting around thinking up ways to make war against those crummy guys."

"We don't have a choice in the matter, girl," Jack told her. "We're not the bravest men in the world."

"You are to me," she said simply.

None of the five men had anything at all to add to that. Andy smiled at his father, who was looking clearly embarrassed. "They are to me, too, Lindsey," Andy said.

Harry cleared his throat a couple of times. "Well, that's enough of that. We'll all be strutting around like a bunch of John Waynes here in a minute."

"Yeah," Dennis said. He looked at Jack. "You've been quiet for over an hour, man. You got something working in that head of yours?"

"We take the fight to them," Jack said. "I don't see that we have any other option."

Harry stared at his nearly lifelong friend for a moment. "Man, are you crazy?"

"Yeah," Ted said. "That was my question."

The other men said nothing.

"We're trapped in this valley," Jack replied. "The way I see it, we don't have but two options, and the first one isn't worth shit."

"We sit around with our thumbs up our asses and wait for those escaped killers to find us and kill us," Bert said.

"That's right," Jack said. "Or we can find our balls— excuse me, Lindsey—and take the fight to them. Now what do the rest of you guys want to do?"

"You're the boss, Jack," Harry said. "You had the stripe in Korea, and you had the stripes in 'Nam. We followed you then, and we'll do it now."

The other men slowly nodded. Dennis said, "I guess when all the cards are laid out we don't have a choice in the matter. Okay. I say we fight."

"The Over-The-Hill-Gang rides again," Harry said. "Or limps along, as the case may be."

"Let's show those bastards we can still bite," Ted said. "And draw blood when we do."

Dennis smiled and then chuckled. "I'll go along with that. But let's all make sure of one thing before we do."

"What's that?" Bert asked.

"We all have our dentures firmly anchored in before we try!"

The shot caused a con with the strange nickname of Doober to hurl himself to one side, a panicked look on his face. The slug from Harry's rifle had hit a rock beside Doober and splattered his face with rock fragments, bloodying his face. Doober thought he was more severely wounded than he really was, and was hollering about not wanting to die.

"Oh, shut up, goddamnit!" Nathan called to him. "You're not gonna die. You ain't even hardly bleedin.'"

"I'm wounded!" Doober yelled.

"Asshole!" Nathan muttered, then hit the dirt as another round came dangerously close to his own head.

"I missed and you missed," Jack said, disgust in his voice.

"I wish I had my old M-One," Harry replied. "I could really shoot with that rifle."

"I wish I had a platoon from the Eighty-second Airborne," Jack came right back.

"Let's get the hell out of here," Harry suggested. "Since neither one of us can hit the side of a barn."

The two men eased back into deeper cover, then ran for about fifty yards before they had to stop and take a rest break. Both of them collapsed on the ground and lay still for a moment, panting to catch their breath.

"Damn, but I'm in lousy shape," Harry bitched.

"Both of us, pal," Jack said a half minute later, after he'd caught his breath.

"Well, I guess we gave that bunch something to think about."

"Yeah? What?"

Harry thought for a moment. He sighed and shook his head. "You're right. We didn't accomplish crap. We've sure got to do better than this."

Jack sat up and looked at his friend. "That bunch we just fired at will be hot after us, right?"

"I 'magine so."

"And we've got supplies for two days, right?"

"Yeah. The other boys don't expect us back for a couple of days. What do you have in mind?"

"We circle around and come in from the opposite direction, try to steal some ammo from the camp."

Harry smiled. "And Lindsey said they had grenades, too. Said she saw them."

"I'd sure like to have a rucksack filled with some of those pineapples."

"So let's do it!"

The men began a long, slow circling of the area they'd just left, being very careful not to leave tracks or any other sign of their passing. The memory of the hard and intensive training they'd received years back was slowly returning to them. They broke no small branches, uprooted no plants, and did their best to avoid tearing off any leaf or vine. It was slow going, but when the circle was complete and they were behind the enemy camp, they knew that only an expert tracker could detect their trail.

Both men now referred to the escaped convicts as the enemy. The two aging veterans of two wars were on a search and destroy mission, and they were on the prowl—to kill.

They reached a spot where they could catch a glimpse of the enemy camp. It appeared to be deserted, but neither man believed that. Both men thought that the escapees were surely not that stupid.

Then they caught a quick sighting of movement and a man walked into view. The man poured a cup of water from a canvas bag and sat down on the ground, his back to Jack and Harry.

On their bellies some several dozen yards away, Jack pulled out his hunting knife from its sheath and held it up so Harry could see. His friend's lips tightened and after a moment, he slowly nodded. It had been almost four decades since either man had used a knife on another human being in a silent op, but they both knew they had no other option. They couldn't use their rifles or pistols: the shot could be heard for several miles, and would bring the man's buddies back on the run.

This kill would have to be silent and up close.

Shooting a man with a rifle is usually very impersonal. You can't look into the target's eyes from several hundred yards away. You don't get sprayed with his blood. You can't smell him. You can't see or sense the fear as life leaves him.

Using a knife is very personal, and even highly trained soldiers sometimes balk at doing it.

Without another word, two old friends moved silently through the brush toward the camp.

Jack reached the guard a few seconds before Harry. The escapee sensed someone behind him and turned just in time to receive the long blade of the hunting knife in his throat. The man's eyes widened in pain and shock. He opened his mouth to speak, but no words could push through his destroyed throat. Blood sprayed from his mouth and splattered Jack's shirt.

Jack jerked the knife out and slashed at the man, the heavy blade making a deep cut in his neck. The guard fell over on his side as life began to slowly leave him.

"Die, you son of a bitch!" Jack panted the words. He was sickened by the sight and was fighting to keep from puking. He fought back the sickness and stood over the dying man.

"I remember it being a hell of a lot easier nearly forty years ago," Harry remarked.

"I hope I don't have to do anything like this again," Jack said.

The dying man's legs trembled and kicked spasmodically as death crept up and laid a cold hand on his savaged body. He grunted several times, then started making really disgusting noises as his hands clawed at the ground.

"Shit!" Jack said, unable to take his eyes off the man.

"I'll start gathering up stuff we need," Harry said, turning away from the awful scene and looking around the campsite.

"Yeah," Jack said in a low voice. He cleared his throat and spoke in a normal voice. "Yeah, we'll both do that. This guy's had it."

"We'd better get moving," Harry suggested.

Jack nodded his head affirmatively.

"You wanna wipe the gore off that blade, Jack?" Harry asked in gentle tones. "It's dripping on your boot."

"Damn," Jack said, holding out the blade and staring at it for a few seconds. He then looked down at his blood-splattered boot. He knelt down and wiped the blade clean on the dying man's dirty shirt.

"You gonna be all right?" Harry asked.

"Yeah," Jack said, standing up and facing his friend. "It's okay. We've been peaceful for too many years, Harry. But you never forget the rough times. They're coming back to me in rushes."

"I know. Me, too."

"Come on. Let's grab what we need and get gone from here. Will you get the guard's pistol and ammo belt?"

"Sure."

Another 9mm pistol and four full magazines were added to the campers' growing arsenal. Harry looked around and spotted the guard's M-16 propped up against a tree trunk. He retrieved that and a rucksack filled with full magazines.

"We're rackin' up," Harry said.

"We'll need everything we can carry off," Jack said. "And then some." He was looking into a full duffle bag. "What the hell is this stuff?"

"Beats me."

Jack pulled out one of the packages and studied it for a moment. "Meals Ready to Eat," he read. "MRE's."

"Whatever happened to C-rats?" his friend asked.

"Damned if I know. Wonder if these things are any good?"

"Well, they couldn't be any worse."

"You have a point."

Jack looked around and found a rucksack filled with grenades. Now the game was going to get really interesting. "Come on, Harry. Let's get out of here."

The guard was dead, his body cooling. There was blood all over the ground around his body. Both men paused for a moment to stare at the dead man.

"I wonder what he did to get sent to prison?" Harry asked.

"Whatever he did, the taxpayers won't have to worry about footing the bill for him anymore."

Harry cut his eyes to his friend. Jack had changed,

reverting back to a warrior role. He had wondered briefly, after Jack's killing of the guard, when this metamorphosis would take place . . . but he had known it would. It always did. He'd seen it in Korea when Jack got his second stripe at age eighteen, before the others did. Then when they all stayed in the Guard, Jack had advanced quickly. He'd seen it in 'Nam, when Jack showed outstanding leadership qualities in the field. Jack could be mad dog mean when he got riled up. It always took him a while to reach that point, but from that point on, Jack was the boss.

Which suited Harry and the other two friends just fine.

"Let's go," Jack said, and shouldered his heavy load of gear.

Both men were carrying quite a weight, and they had to rest often. During one of the breaks Harry asked, "What were you doing back there, with that dead guy's body, Jack?"

"Leaving a present for the others," Jack replied.

"A present?"

Jack smiled. But it was not a pleasant smile. "Yeah. A pineapple present."

"Oh. Now I get it. Did you really do that?"

"I really did, Harry. That bother you?"

"Ah . . . no. Just bothers me that I didn't think of it. But that's why you were always a couple of stripes ahead of us." Harry grinned. "I hope the whole bunch is standing around the body when they move it."

Jack looked at him and returned the grin. "Me, too!"

Thirteen

Crain looked at the body of the dead guard and cursed. He had no way of knowing it, but he and two others in his group were soon going to join the dead man on the short, very warm walk to Hell.

Six men were gathered around the body when Crain said, "Looks like his throat was cut. Took somebody with some know-how to do that. Roll him over."

Five seconds later the grenades that had been carefully placed under the body, the body weight holding the spoons down, roared into life.

Crain was hurled backward, minus his face. He would linger for several hours, blind and in intense pain, before death took him in his bony arms. Another man was killed instantly, and yet another would die in a couple of days, his chest and belly riddled with shrapnel.

Several others in the group would receive minor injuries. Another man would become so panicked he ran off, wandering for several miles, becoming hopelessly lost in the back country—until he found Bert.

"Put your damn hands in the air and stand still, you rotten bastard." Bert's cold voice stopped the man in his tracks. "If you do anything I don't like, I'll do the world a favor and kill you where you stand."

"Don't shoot!" the escaped con blurted. "I ain't gonna do nothin,' Man. I'm loose as a goose."

"Turn around," Bert ordered.

The man slowly turned.

Dennis walked up to stand beside Bert. "I don't like this at all, Bert. What in the hell are we going to do with him?" he whispered.

"Get some information," Bert returned the whisper. "After that, I don't know and I don't care."

Both men knew they were going to have to switch camps as soon as Jack and Harry returned, so they would take the prisoner back to their camp. Bert said, "Drop your gunbelt. Kick it away from you."

That done, Dennis picked up the web belt, complete with four full magazines and 9mm pistol in a holster, and carefully backed away. Bert motioned to the escaped con with the muzzle of his rifle. "Move." He pointed. "That way."

"That's one of the men who raped me!" Lindsey blurted when the men walked into camp with their prisoner, his hands tied behind his back with heavy cord that Dennis had in his jacket pocket.

"Bitch!" the prisoner flared.

Bert popped the man not too gently on the back of the head with the butt of his rifle. The prisoner grunted and sank to his knees on the ground, his head filled with flashing stars.

"Watch your filthy mouth," Bert warned him. "It

wouldn't take much for me to put a bullet in you and leave you for the varmints to eat."

"You guys ain't real," the con muttered. "I ain't believin' none of this."

"You can believe it," Ted told him. He looked at Bert and Dennis. "You find out what that explosion was?"

"Sturgis here told us on the way in," Dennis said. "Tell them all about it, Sturgis."

"Man," the escaped con named Sturgis said, "I don't know really what happened. I guess somebody planted a couple of grenades under Parman's body. When they turned him over, the damn grenades blew. I know that Crain and one other guy is dead. They couldn't have lived through that. One other is bad hurt. That's all I know. I run off and got myself lost. Until this mean old man here," he cut his eyes to Bert, "found me. I wish to hell I was still lost."

"You're lost in more ways than you know," Ted told him.

"Huh?" Sturgis asked.

"Never mind," Ted replied.

A moment later, Jack and Harry came staggering in with their heavy loads. They dropped their burdens and stood for a moment, panting and looking at Sturgis.

"Found him wanderin' around, lost," Bert said. "Couldn't take a chance on him blunderin' into camp."

Jack caught his breath and walked over to Sturgis. The escaped con crawled backward for a few feet. He did not like the look in the older man's eyes.

"That's one of the men who raped Lindsey," Ted said. "She told us."

"Bitch didn't have to fight us," Sturgis blurted. "She could have give up that pussy easy."

A look of pure disgust crossed Jack's face. He stood for a moment, struggling to hold onto his rising temper. "You tell us everything you know about what's going on, mister. And if we think you're truthful, you can live. If I think you're lying to us, I'll kill you."

"Now see here!" Andy blurted. "This has gone far enough. You're not going to kill that prisoner, Jack. We're all decent men here."

"All but one of us," Jack told the younger man. "And nobody asked for your opinion."

Andy wouldn't shut up. "Some type of rules and law have to apply here. We have to behave as civilized men."

"Yeah, that's right!" Sturgis said. "You tell 'em, boy."

The five older men looked at Andy. Even Andy's father had an open expression of disgust on his face.

"If we allow our baser instincts to take over, we're no better than the men who escaped from that prison."

"You damn right, boy," Sturgis said.

"Oh, shut up, Sturgis," Dennis told the prisoner. "You don't even know what in the hell he said."

"Sounded good," Sturgis replied.

"Andy," Ted said, "go over there at the edge of the clearing and sit down and take some deep breaths. Get your head screwed on straight. You're spouting crap."

"Dad—"

"We're locked in a fight for our lives, Boy. Damn you, can't you understand that? We could all be dead in the next few heartbeats, and you're spouting nonsense. Just shut up, Son. Be quiet. You don't know what in the hell you're talking about."

Andy opened his mouth to protest and his father held up a hand. "I mean it, boy. Close your mouth. Shut up. Stay out of this."

There was a note in Ted's voice that caused Andy to pause for a moment and stare at his father. The younger man finally turned and walked off a few yards and sat down.

Jack turned to Sturgis. "Now then, mister. You start at the beginning and tell the whole story. Don't leave anything out. If I sense you're lying," he paused and picked up a large stick from the ground, "I'll beat your goddamn head in. You understand?"

Sturgis nodded his head. "I get you. Okay. It was Karl Parson's plan, him and Randy O'Donnell. . . ."

"Let's pack up and get the hell out of here," one of Randy's men suggested after viewing the bloody carnage caused by the two grenades.

"Where would we go?" Randy countered.

Karl tried to settle that growing debate before it got started. "We stay in the back country. We got thousands of cops looking for us outside of this area, and no one looking for us here."

"Then who killed these guys?" a con named Ray asked, pointing to the freshly dug graves. "The hell we don't have people looking for us in here. 'Cause we sure do. I'd rather take my chances in St. Louis, or L.A., or Chicago, or New Orleans—any damn place but here."

"You think you can find your way out?" Randy asked, looking at Ray, a grim expression on his face.

"I can try."

"You'd be turned around and hopelessly lost in an hour," Karl told him. He had joined the group only moments before. "You're a city boy, Ray. You get lost in a five acre park. Right now, we've got something else to worry about—where the hell is Sturgis?"

"I think them old bastards took him," a con said.

"Why would they do that?" Randy asked. "He doesn't know anything. Sturgis is as dumb as a brick."

"But they wouldn't know that," Karl replied. "They also wouldn't know that Sturgis is a stone cold killer and strong as a bull. If they did take him, that little move could work out to our advantage. If Sturgis is alive, and gets just one little chance, if somebody gets careless, he'll go wild as a grizzly bear and kill a couple of those old bastards ... especially if he can get his hands on one of them. You all know how he gets. Most of you have seen him go off his rocker before. He goes nuts. It would take a tank to stop him."

"You have a valid point, Karl," Randy agreed. "But Sturgis is also a coward, remember that. I've also seen him fold like a house of cards more than once."

"Yeah, that's true. But he's alone and scared right now. He's like a steam engine building up pressure. He's got to blow, and when he does it'll be a sight to see."

Several of the cons standing around listening nodded their heads. Sturgis had killed several cons during his long years behind bars.

"He's an uncontrollable and unpredictable brute," Sweet Boy stated. "I hate him."

"Oh, shut up, you damned faggot!" Nathan blurted. Sweet Boy and Nathan didn't like one another.

Sweet Boy grinned at Nathan and squeezed his crotch and hunched his hips at the man.

Nathan cursed him.

"Settle down," Karl told them both, stepping between the two men. "We don't need to get on each other's cases. That's the last thing we need."

"Sweet Boy's right about Sturgis," Randy said. "Sturgis is uncontrollable and unpredictable. But then, you're right about him, too, Karl. If those old bastards push him hard enough, he'll blow wide open."

"Yeah? And when he does he'll probably get himself killed," another con said.

Karl looked at the man. "Buddy, who cares, if he takes out one or two of the old dudes?"

Buddy shrugged his shoulders. "Good point, I guess." He walked off to stand with several other men. They had all taken their turn at the women that morning and were, for the moment, sexually sated.

"So what now?" another con asked.

Both Randy and Karl looked at him. "Nothing," Karl said. "We have both ends of the valley guarded, and the old dudes can't get out. But we don't go off and leave camps guarded by only one man from now on, that's for sure. These old dudes will screw up sooner or later, and when they do we'll nail them. It's just a matter of time."

"But for now," Randy added, "we're safer in the wilderness than we would be anywhere else. Just relax."

"Ah . . . Karl?" a con called Dave said, touching Karl's arm.

Karl turned. "Yeah?"

"You mind if I hump Kathy?"

Karl shrugged his shoulders. "If she wants to give you some snatch, go ahead. It'll take some of the strain off me."

Fourteen

Judy Post lay on her sleeping bag on the cave floor and gripped the rock she'd managed to find and conceal from her captors. The rock was just a little bit larger than a baseball, and nearly perfectly round. Judy had plans for that rock, and for the guard's head. She thought the two might go together well. *Just give me one chance to use this rock,* she had prayed over and over.

The fifteen-year-old girl hurt all over. Her breasts were bruised from manhandling, she was bruised from the two beatings she'd received from the cons, and her crotch was so sore she could hardly walk. But she had made up her mind: she was going to escape.

Her brother, Max, was in another cave, with Phil Fisher. Both of them had been raped repeatedly by several of the cons who preferred boys to girls. Judy thought it was all very disgusting. Not nearly as disgusting, though, as when Kathy had taken her sexually earlier that day. Judy endured the sexual attack from the twisted bitch—not that she had any choice in the matter—for several of the cons, including Karl Parsons and Randy O'Donnell, had watched the entire assault, offering suggestions as to what Kathy should do next. And what Judy should do to pleasure the older woman. And Kathy took all the suggestions to heart.

Judy longed for about a gallon of mouthwash.

Judy wasn't sure where her mother was, except that she was being held in another cave. She was aware, however, that her mother, like all the women, was subject to being raped when one, or sometimes two, of the cons felt the urge. Before they had all been moved into the caves she had watched two of the sorry bastards take her mother simultaneously. Her mother had screamed hideously from the pain when one of the cons had bulled his way into her anus. The cons standing around watching thought that was very amusing, offering suggestions.

From that time on, Judy Post, fifteen-years-old, a very beautiful young lady, had very definite plans as to what she was going to do if she ever got the chance. She had been raised in a very liberal-thinking household—politically speaking. No guns in the house, of course. They were evil objects. People who kept guns and believed they had a right to do so were all right-wing whackos. Judy's parents had preached to her from the age of comprehension on that she should feel sorry for criminals, for most of them had been forced into a life of crime by an uncaring society. That didn't matter anymore. Nothing did. Judy had realized quickly that her captors—this particular bunch—were nothing more than savage, rabid animals. And the only thing you could do with savage, rabid animals was destroy them.

And that was exactly what she planned to do, if she got the chance.

Judy moved from her sleeping bag very slowly and very quietly. She held the rock firmly in her right hand. If that guard would just keep his back to her for a couple more minutes, she would bash his fucking head in. And enjoy doing it . . .

"That's it, people," Sturgis said. "That's all I know. Can I have a drink of water? I'm dry from all this yakking."

"The worst criminals in the nation," Dennis said. "A whole huge gang of them, loose in the back country, holding a number of hostages, and sexually assaulting women, girls, and young boys. Jesus H. Christ!"

Bert was silent, sitting on the ground, but his eyes had turned savage. He gripped his old .30-30 rifle with his big, callused hands.

Bert had counted his rounds that morning. He had fifty rounds left for his rifle. He intended to make every one of them count, if at all possible. The story that Sturgis had just told had angered him to the core. The rape of the females was disgusting, and the sexual assaults on the teenage boys was sickening perversion; no other word for it.

Bert cut his eyes to Sturgis, who sat on the ground with a camp cup of water, sipping at it. Dennis and Ted had walked off, muttering and shaking their heads in disgust. Harry was back in the bushes, relieving himself. Jack was sitting close by, staring at the ground and softly cursing. Lindsey was down near the tiny spring they'd found, just sitting and staring at the water as it bubbled out of the ground.

Sturgis suddenly sprang to his feet and charged at Bert, howling curses like a madman. Bert lifted the muzzle of the old .30-30 and pulled the trigger, the slug taking the huge man in the side, turning him on his feet and nearly doubling him over. With a wild scream of defiance, Sturgis jumped for the brush and was gone.

.

* * *

The guard slowly turned his head and said, "I believe when the others get back, I'll have me another taste of that pussy, girl. It's been many a year since I had me all the young pussy I could handle. I—"

Judy brought the baseball-sized rock down on the man's head with all her strength. She could hear the guard's skull crack under the impact. The man slumped to one side. He fell over against the wall of the cave, appearing to be sleeping.

Judy, showing a lot of sense for a young person, swiftly located, pulled on and laced up her boots, then worked quickly to unhook the man's web belt and sling it over one shoulder. She picked u the guard's short-barreled weapon—she didn't know what it was, but she'd seen others like it in action movies and heard them called Uzis. She picked up a heavy rucksack, looked inside, and saw that it was filled with extra clips for the weapon and several grenades. She knew what those were from watching the type of movies her parents didn't approve of. You pulled that little pin out of the thing and threw it real quick and bellied down on the ground. preferably behind something.

She picked up the guard's jacket from the floor and looked around her, spotting a rucksack filled with packets of food, a canteen of water and a bottle of water purification tabs. She walked to the mouth of the cave, hidden by a thick growth of brush, and looked out. She didn't know where her mother and brother were being held. She'd heard the thugs say that there were dozens of small caves all over the place, many of them hidden behind thick stands of brush. Judy knew she'd been held by herself, because several of the convicts were planning to rape her in her butt; she'd heard them talk about doing it and how much they were all looking forward to it. The rotten scum.

Judy looked down at the Uzi. She wondered how you worked the thing?

Well, this is no time to be squatting here worrying about it, she concluded. *I'm free and I intend to stay that way.*

Judy stepped into the brush and vanished.

Several dozen cons heard the rifle shot, but due to the terrain and the low hanging clouds and mist it was difficult to tell which direction it came from. While they were trying to figure it out Jack and the others had quickly broken camp and were moving.

It was slow going, for they all were packing heavy loads. The men had to rest often. Lindsey tried to help, but due to her badly cut and bruised feet, she could do little except hobble along. But she never complained and never was the first one to suggest they stop and rest.

During one of the rest breaks Bert said, "I shot Sturgis low and in the side. My old .thirty-thirty packs a pretty good wallop, but I'm pretty sure it wasn't a killin' shot. But that bastard's definitely hurtin.' "

Andy had said nothing in the hour since leaving their last camp. He sat off to himself during the rest stops.

At the last break, Lindsey had sat down beside Andy. "You don't understand what's happening with the hostages, Mister Dawson. The men holding them are savages."

Andy cut his eyes to the young woman. "They're still human beings, Lindsey."

"They walk upright," she replied.

Andy sighed.

"You ever seen your mother raped and sodomized, and then murdered?"

"No."

"You ever been stripped naked, held down, and fucked up the ass?" Lindsey bluntly asked.

"Good God, no!"

"Well, that's what is happening to some teenage boys being held hostage by that crap and crud."

Andy stared straight ahead, saying nothing.

"I give up," Lindsey said, standing up, and walked back to sit with the older men.

"You're wasting your breath trying to talk to him," Andy's father told the teenager. He did not lower his voice and didn't give a damn if his son heard him or not. For a time, a couple of days back, father and son had been drawn closer than they had been in years. Now the breach between them had widened again; this time it appeared too wide to ever fully close.

"He just doesn't understand what's really going on," the girl said.

"And never will unless the cons get their hands on him," Ted replied. "And I pray that doesn't happen."

"Don't count on Andy in any kind of pinch," Bert said. "I hate to say this, but I don't trust him."

The father nodded his head in silent reluctant agreement.

"Where are we heading, Bert?" Dennis asked.

The packer slowly shook his head. "Hell, I don't know, Boys. I know several good spots where there's springs, but we got to cross that clearing up yonder to get to any of them. We'd be wide open."

"We'll cross it just at dusk," Jack said. He had been studying both sides of the wide meadow through binoculars. "Vision is tricky that time of day. We'll have a much better chance of making it then. We'll stay in the brush and timber as much as possible."

The others nodded in agreement. No one offered any argument against the plan.

"Rest now," Jack said. "Get as much rest as possible.

When we start across, we're not going to stop until we've reached the other side."

Andy broke his silence. "Typical sergeant. Always giving orders."

"What the hell would you know about the military?" the father asked the son.

Andy looked up, hurt in his eyes. "I guess that means you think I'm a coward, right?"

"That's about the size of it," Ted replied.

"It's always good to know where a person stands," Andy said.

The others remained silent, not wanting to get in the middle of a quarrel between father and son, none of them liking the quiet but very heated exchange.

"Let's just drop it, Andy," Ted suggested. "I think that would be best."

"No, Dad, let's settle it here and now. Let's clear the air once and for all."

"Son, we have God only knows how many desperate escaped convicts chasing us, we're in the middle of some of the wildest country in America, and you want to drag up and discuss ancient history?"

"You think I'm a coward, Dad."

Ted paused a few seconds before replying. First he slowly shook his head. "No, Son. I don't think you're a coward. But I do think you're all fucked up politically, and I think you have some very strange ideas about crime and punishment and criminals in general."

"Because I think they're human beings and should be treated with as much dignity as possible, considering their circumstances?" Andy looked at the other men, then at Lindsey. He received nothing but cold stares in return. He nodded his head. "All right. I get the picture. At least now I know for certain where everyone stands."

"Where we stand, boy," Bert said, "is tryin' to get out

of this mess alive. Son, ain't none of us perfect, but all of us here," he waved a work hardened hand, "we're the good guys, for the most part. We all work and pay taxes and try to obey the law. We don't rob and kill and rape and destroy and engage in all kinds of perverted sexual acts—"

"Homosexuality is not a perverted act, Bert. That misguided concept went out about a decade ago. I have some co-workers who are gay, and some very good friends who are gay. I—"

"Shut your fucking mouth, Boy!" Ted flared. "I've had it with you. We're not talking about two people who choose to live a quiet, lawful alternative life-style. We're talking about forcible rape and overt perversion. If you can't understand the difference, then you are one sad, stupid prick!"

Sturgis suddenly burst out of the brush, bloody and shouting like a madman. He headed straight for Andy. Words tumbled out of his mouth, but they were incomprehensible. Lindsey stuck out one foot and tripped the big man. Sturgis fell to his knees and immediately began crawling toward Andy, pain and madness in his eyes.

"Good God, somebody do something!" Andy yelled.

Jack picked up a large stick from the ground and smashed the escaped con over the head. He hit him three times with the club before Sturgis lay still.

"Bastard followed us here," Bert said. "He soaked up that .thirty-thirty round like a wild grizzly, and kept right on comin.' "

"Tie his wrists," Jack ordered. "Do it quick while he's out. We'll leave him. He can work loose after a time. But we'll be long gone."

Dennis quickly tied Sturgis's wrists with a length of rope.

The big man was out cold, but his breathing was even and it wouldn't be long before he started coming around. The stick Jack had hit him with was about half rotten, and on the third whack had disintegrated.

"Let's get out of here," Bert suggested.

Andy was still shaken, his hands trembling. His father glanced at him, not with disgust in his eyes, but with pity. Andy caught the look and misinterpreted it. He flushed but said nothing. Just turned away, picked up his pack, and struggled into the straps.

"Let's go," Jack ordered. "Quickly, before that big bastard comes to."

"You ought to shoot him right now," Dennis said. "Or cut his damn throat."

Andy looked at the man.

"You got something to say, boy?" Dennis asked him, considerable heat in his words.

Andy shook his head and turned away.

The group moved out, Bert taking the lead, Harry taking the drag.

"We'll stay deep in the brush and timber," Bert told them. "It'll take us longer to reach the edge of the meadow, but it'll be a lot safer."

"I don't think I'll ever feel safe again," Lindsey said.

"Yes, you will," Jack told her. "I promise you that, girl. And when this is over you can come live with me and my wife."

"You mean that?"

"I sure do."

The group walked on in silence for a moment. Two men suddenly stepped out of the timber, M-16's in their hands. "Got you!" one said with a very nasty grin. "Now drop them weapons and put your hands in the air. Karl and Randy want to talk to you old boys."

"I want me a taste of that cunt," the other con said, licking his lips and looking at Lindsey. "Everybody said she's got some fine pussy."

"Fuck you!" Jack said, and lifted his weapon and squeezed the trigger.

Fifteen

"Automatic weapons fire," a con told Karl.

"I can hear it," Karl said irritably. "But I can't tell where it's coming from. This damn mist deadens the sound."

"I hate this damn lousy country," a con called Rip said. "Give me the city any time. It just ain't . . . well, civilized out here."

Both Karl and Randy laughed at the man. "How many women did you torture and rape and kill, Rip?" Karl asked.

Rip looked at the man. " 'Bout a dozen or two, I suppose."

"And you speak of civilization?" Randy asked him. "You're a very amusing man, Rip."

"And you're a damn pukey Irishman," Rip came right back. "How many women and kids did your bombs kill?"

"Knock it off!" Karl ordered. "No more bickering between ourselves. That's something we don't need."

The sounds of another burst of gunfire drifted to the cons, then another burst of automatic fire. But the day had turned misty, with low-hanging clouds and occasional cold drizzle.

"Two different types of weapons," Randy remarked. "I'm sure of that."

"Our guys have several different types of weapons," a con spoke, the statement directed at no one in particular.

"And so do the old bastards ... now," Karl said. He kicked at a stick on the ground. "Goddamnit, we're losing people every day to those old farts. Two prisoners have escaped. We've got to put a stop to this crap, and do it quickly."

"And until we do, we don't talk about leaving this area," Randy said.

"Why the hell not?" a con called Billy Boy asked.

"Because the instant those old guys sense we're gone, they'll make a beeline out of here and head straight for the cops. This place will be flooded with law dogs."

"And real dogs, too," another con said. Buster was serving life without benefit of probation, parole, or reduction of sentence—for multiple murder and aggravated rape of several young girls. "I hate dogs. And dogs hate me, too. Every time one comes close to me he bites. I hate dogs."

"We know, Buster," Karl said patiently.

"I kill every dog I see," Buster went on, ignoring Karl. "I like to break their goddamn necks."

Both Karl and Randy sighed, knowing that Buster had to get it all out of his system; he wouldn't shut up until he did.

"I heard a dog last night," Buster said. "Heard him sniffin' around camp. Probably some stray. If I get my hands on him, I'll kill him."

"Yeah, you do that, Buster," Karl told him. "That's fine."

"I will. I hate dogs."

Karl knew, as did most of the cons Buster had served

time with, that one of the young girls he had raped and then killed had a dog that tried to protect his young mistress. The dog, a small mixed breed animal, had bitten Buster several times before Buster had killed it. Buster had then raped and killed the ten-year-old girl. Blood samples taken from the dog's fur had helped convict Buster.

"You sure there was a dog around camp last night, Buster?" a con asked.

"I'm sure. I heard it and smelled its wet fur. I hate all dogs."

Karl and several others walked off, all of them slowly shaking their heads. "If it was a dog, it's just a stray," Karl said. "But I agree with Buster. We can't have a dog hanging around. If any of you see the dog, grab a club and beat it to death."

"I don't like dogs, either," Gunner Monroe said. "As a matter of fact, I hate them."

"Fine," another con said wearily, wishing they would just drop the subject of dogs. "If you see the dog, kill it."

"I will," Gunner said, then walked off.

"Several old men giving us fits, and these guys are worried about a dog," Karl muttered.

"I don't like dogs, either," Randy said.

"Oh, God!" Karl's half sister, Kathy, cried, as Jans Pendley pumped her under the protection of a camouflaged tent at the edge of the camp in the deep timber. "God, that's good!"

Jans had humped every woman taken hostage, several times. The con just couldn't seem to get enough pussy. And now that he was pumping Kathy, she probably would be hanging on the man like a leech, wanting more of the heavy hung bastard. Which suited Karl just fine. He was getting more than a little tired of his half sister and her mouth. Karl grinned at that thought: she did give great head.

* * *

Judy Post awakened from an exhausted nap with a feeling of pure panic. There was a wolf sitting in front of her, looking at her. Frozen in fear, Judy was sure she was about to get attacked and eaten alive.

Then the wolf lifted one paw in greeting and whined softly.

Judy held out a hand and the animal licked it and moved closer to her.

It wasn't a wolf, she concluded. It was one of those hybrids: part wolf, part dog. Husky, or that other type of Alaskan dog—what was it called? Malamute. But it sure looked like a wolf. Judy guessed the animal weighed about a hundred pounds. A big dog, or wolf, or whatever it was.

The animal moved closer and Judy hugged it. The dog licked her face. Judy felt its collar and realized it was much too tight on the animal's neck. She managed to undo the buckle and reattach it in a more comfortable fit. The dog licked her face in gratitude.

Judy looked at the vaccination tag. Last year's tag. But the animal had received its shots and at one time had belonged to somebody. The dog was beautiful.

Judy opened one of the military packets of food and dumped the contents onto the wrapper and laid it on the ground. The dog ate hungrily and then licked the wrapper clean. Finished with its meal, the dog lay down beside Judy, put its big head on her leg, and went to sleep.

"I found a friend," Judy whispered. She again looked at the collar. There was a brass plate on it with the word Max. "Okay, Max. We'll be buddies from now on."

Max opened his eyes, looked at her for a moment, and then went back to sleep.

"And I can sure use one," Judy whispered.

* * *

Sheriff Hawkins looked twice at his calendar, checking it carefully. It was clear. He had no meetings to attend, no functions he had to go to, nothing for several weeks. And he had weeks of vacation time coming.

He called his chief deputy into his office. "I'm taking some time off, Clint. I'm tired. I need to go fishing and lie around and relax."

"Uh huh," Clint said. He didn't believe a word of what he'd just heard. He knew exactly what Hawk was going to do, and it didn't have a damn thing to do with fishing and relaxing.

"Besides, the feds say the threat of these escaped cons is all but over in our part of the country, right?"

"Sure, Hawk. That's what they say. How long you plannin' on takin' off?"

"Couple of weeks, Clint. At least that long."

"You gonna take a walkie-talkie?"

Hawk looked at his chief deputy. "I was planning on it, yeah."

"Good." The chief deputy moved to a huge wall map. "Now tell me exactly where you'll be in the back country."

"I don't know yet, Clint. I really don't. I'm gonna gear up and pull out tomorrow. I'll let you know before I go."

"You be careful in there, Hawk. You and me, we both know there are some cons in the back country."

"That's why I'm going in."

"You ought to take some volunteers."

Sheriff Hawkins shook his head. "I think one man is better. Viv agrees with me on that. She agreed after we had a brief but very heated argument about me even going," he added drily and with a grimace.

Clint smiled. "I bet that was some argument."

"We'll make up tonight."

"That'll be fun." Clint walked to the gun rack, studied the rifles for a moment, then opened the glass front and took down a bolt action 7mm magnum with scope. He turned back to the sheriff, questions in his eyes.

"Yeah. That'll be a good one, Clint. Nice choice."

"What kind of sidearm? Your nine?"

Hawk shook his head. "My .forty-four mag."

The chief deputy nodded his head. "I like it. Less chance of it jammin' up in there. Several boxes of rounds for each of them?"

"Yeah."

"I'll get them and put them in your car."

" 'Preciate it, Clint. And keep quiet about this, will you?"

"You know it, Hawk. Anybody asks, and they will, I'll tell them you went in another direction."

"Good deal. This may turn out to be a big zero. But I just got a hunch. You know what I mean?"

"Oh, yeah. I sure do."

Hawk stood up. "Then I'm out of here, Clint."

"You be careful in there, old buddy."

"You know it, man."

"You're headin' smack for the center of the back country, aren't you?"

"Yeah."

"Rough country. I've seen grown men break down in tears in there."

"I won't." Hawk was thinking of a valley he'd been in several times, years back. It was a long valley, twenty miles or so. One way in from the south, one way in from the north. High towering mountains on both sides. Dozens of caves, many of them concealed by brush and timber. Some of the caves, probably a lot of them, unexplored. It would be an ideal place for the cons to hide . . . providing one of them knew about it. And Hawk knew a couple of them did. Packers seldom took tourists into that valley. Too

much danger of getting trapped in there by a sudden
snowstorm. It was mean, rough country. No place for tourists.

"You packed up, Hawk?"

"Some of the gear, yes. Won't take me long to get the
rest of it together."

"Where you gonna leave your car?"

"MacMickles' place."

Clint nodded his head. "I'll case this rifle and get it out
to your unit."

"Thanks."

Clint took the rifle and left the office. Hawk turned and
looked out the window. He wondered if he was on a fool's
errand.

"I'll soon know," he muttered. He picked up his hat
and turned out the lights in his office, then stood for a
moment by the hall door. Then he walked out of his office
and outside the building.

He had a lot of packing left to do. He wanted to be out
at MacMickles' place that day, and several miles into the
back country by dark.

Tell the truth, he was looking forward to the hunt.

Sixteen

The sun was hidden by fog and mist and Judy couldn't tell one direction from the other. But she thought she was slowly making her way west.

"How do we get out of here, Max?" she asked the dog.

Max looked at her, the expression in his eyes seeming to say "You're asking *me?*"

Judy managed a smile and patted the big dog. "We'll make it. I just know we will."

The two trudged on.

Judy longed for a hot bath and a change of clothing. She also wished for a hot cup of coffee. She had begun drinking coffee before she reached her teen years. Black, with one sugar. She did her best to stop thinking about a bath, a change of clothing, and the cup of coffee.

She'd been afraid that when she woke from her night's sleep Max would be gone. But the big dog was right beside her when she awakened, and had not strayed far from her side since they started out. It was Max who had found the tiny spring where Judy filled her canteen with cold water.

She also tried not to think what might be happening to her mother and brother. She knew they were having a really bad time of it—if they were still alive.

Then she saw movement in the distance and immediately stopped, kneeling down and pulling Max close to her. Both shoulders ached from the straps on the rucksacks and the gun. She wished she had a couple of aspirin.

"Might as well wish for Tom Cruise," she muttered.

Max gave her a big lick on the side of her face and the teenager smiled.

"Thank you, Max," she whispered.

She saw the movement again, and this time she was able to pick out the shape of people. Whoever they were, they were staying in the timber, out of the small clearing to their left. The smaller of the group was walking slowly and sort of oddly. The line of people—Judy counted half a dozen or so—disappeared for a couple of minutes, then again came into view. They seemed to be hesitating, unsure of what to do next. Judy moved closer, walking a few hundred feet toward the clearing, but staying with cover.

Then she stood up from her crouch, suddenly filled with a sense of giddy relief. It must be the older men she'd heard the convicts cussing and discussing. The smaller figure had to be the girl who'd escaped, Lindsey something or another. She'd heard the convicts talking about her.

Judy stepped out from cover and into the clearing. She waved a hand and yelled. The line of people stopped, turned, and looked at her. Judy began slowly limping across the clearing, Max padding along beside her, staying close. Judy could tell the big dog wasn't happy about approaching the group of people. His ears were laid back flat against his head.

"It's all right, Max," she assured him. "It's all right. They're friends."

As she approached the group, she called, "I'm Judy Post. This is Max. He found me yesterday. God, I can't tell you how glad I am to see you people."

Jack smiled at her. "You're carrying a heavy load there, Judy. Let's all get back into the brush and take a rest. You can tell us how you got away."

"You have any coffee?" Judy asked.

Bert grinned. "Now there's a girl after my own heart."

"We have some," Ted said. "But lighting a fire would be dangerous."

Judy let her rucksack slip to the ground with a sigh of relief. "I don't think the convicts are anywhere close to here. They don't have to be. They've got both ends of this long valley sealed tight. We can't get out." Then she started to cry. "Shit! I promised myself I wouldn't do that."

Jack stepped close and put his arms around the girl, holding her to him. "It's all right, Judy. You cry if you want to. I've felt like it myself a time or two."

Judy, between sobs, told about her escape and about Max finding her.

"Well, to hell with it," Bert said, easing his pack to the ground. "I'm going to gather up some dry sticks and build a small fire. Let's have some coffee, gang. By God, we've all damn well earned it."

Max yawned, exposing a mouthful of very healthy teeth.

"That's a heck of a dog there, girl," Harry said.

"He's my friend," Judy told them, wiping her eyes on the sleeve of her shirt.

"I'd sure hate to have him for an enemy," Jack said, as he and Max eyeballed each other.

* * *

Sheriff Hawkins checked his compass and swung back into the saddle, lifting the reins. It had been a long time since he'd been in this part of the back country, and he wanted to be sure of his bearings. His plan was to ride to the west side of the valley, throw together a makeshift corral out of brush (one the horses could easily bust out of and make their way back to home range if Hawk didn't return) and then slip into the valley through the south pass.

And Hawk was fully aware that he might not return.

His Ruger Redhawk .44 mag, five and a half inch barrel, was in leather at his side, his cartridge belt filled with rounds. His 7mm magnum rifle was in a saddle scabbard.

He rode on. All vestiges of civilization were miles behind him now. There were no honking horns, no squealing tires and stink of exhaust, no houses, no TV antennas, no huge satellite systems capable of pulling in several hundred channels of mostly mindless TV crap. In the back country one could really experience the sensation of being alone. And the deeper one rode, the better the chances were of getting lost if you weren't careful and didn't have some knowledge of the country.

Hawk had snuggled into his warm sleeping bag about an hour after dark, and had slept a good ten hours. He awakened refreshed and rarin' to begin the hunt. He was glad to be in the back country alone: this was his country. He was Montana born and reared, and had been prowling this neck of the woods since he was old enough to sit a saddle. He might not know the country as well as some of the longtime guides, but he wasn't going to get lost, either. Besides, he thought with a smile, he knew how to read a compass.

He figured two more days of hard riding would put him near the valley; maybe two and a half day's ride, for this was rough country. And the deeper he went, the rougher it got.

Not very many packers brought their charges into the back country by the route Hawk was taking, for this was not the fastest or safest way, and inexperienced riders could easily get hurt.

Hawk slowly looked all around him. There were no thin trails of smoke from campfires lining upward. He was alone in some of the wildest and most beautiful country in all of America. Alone, he thought, except for about thirty or so of the nation's most dangerous criminals.

And, he silently added, about a dozen or so very frightened tourists being held hostage and sexually abused . . . male and female, probably. Hawk's expression changed, turning grimmer as those thoughts drifted through his head.

"Hang on, folks," he whispered to the winds that sighed down off the mountains that loomed all around the solitary rider. "Hang on."

Bert built a small fire using dry twigs and sticks, the fire under low hanging branches that would break up the tiny amount of smoke that drifted upward. The tired group ate their first hot meal in several days and then leaned back on their blankets, each with a cup of coffee. Max enjoyed an MRE meal and then stretched out and went to sleep by Judy's side. The big mixed breed never strayed far from her.

"So you really don't know how many people are being held hostage by the cons?" Jack asked Judy.

She shook her head. "No, I don't. Not really. But from the way the convicts talked it's over a dozen. Maybe twice that number."

"But they're all being held in the caves, right here in this valley?"

"Yes. All of them on the east side of the valley."

"The roughest side," Bert said. "Some of the cons surely know this country."

"You bet they do. Karl Parsons and a man called Nathan," Judy told the group, after taking another sip of the hot coffee. She looked down at the ground. "And Karl's sister, Kathy. That twisted bitch."

None of the men opted to pursue that last bit.

"And you're sure both ends of the valley are guarded?" Ted asked.

"Oh, yes. I know that for a fact. I heard Kathy tell some of the convicts that guides seldom brought people into the valley, that it's too rough getting in and out, and there's always the danger of getting trapped in here."

Bert nodded his head. "She knows what she's talkin' about, for a fact."

"She seems like a very experienced guide," Judy said.

"She is. One of the best. And she was well-liked, too. I guess that proves you don't never really know a person, and you don't never really know what's goin' on in someone's mind."

"I don't understand why the police aren't in here searching for us," Judy said.

"The cons laid a false trail," Harry told her. "The police think the two ringleaders are dead and nearly all the escapees headed away from the wilderness. We were told that by one of the cons we captured."

"Where is he?" the girl asked.

"He broke loose," Jack told her. "Bert shot him, but he still managed to get away. But before he did, he told us the whole sorry story."

"They're going to kill all the hostages," Judy said softly. "I heard them talking one time when they thought I was asleep. They're going to put them all in one of the caves and use grenades to blow the entrance closed, trapping those inside. They'll either starve to death or die from lack of oxygen.''

"What a bunch of lousy bastards," Ted muttered, a look of pure disgust on his face.

Judy looked at him. "Yes, sir. They sure are. Every one of them. They sure changed my opinion of convicts. I used to feel sorry for them. Well, you can hang that up.''

"Many convicts are decent people who simply made one tragic mistake. Then they're thrown into prison with a few dregs of society," Andy said. "It's the process of brutalization while behind bars that turns them somewhat savage. One of my professors in school told us that prison is simply not the answer, that a more humane form of punishment should be explored. He said—"

"Shut your goddamn stupid mouth, boy!" Andy's father lashed out, his words hard and bitter. "My God, I've never heard such bullshit from one person . . ."

Bert smiled sadly and placed a couple more sticks of dry wood on the small fire and poured some more water into the battered coffee pot. One cup of coffee apiece was just not going to be enough. During this verbal go-round he planned on staying out of the quarrel and the ever widening rift between father and son.

"What kind of people are teaching at the colleges now?" Ted asked.

"It's not just in the colleges," Lindsey told him. "It's in high school, too."

"Sure is," Judy said. She stared at the coffeepot, wishing the water would hurry up and boil.

"In high schools?" Dennis asked.

"Oh, yes, sir," the girl replied. "It's not so much what they teach, but what they *don't* teach."

"And how they teach it," Lindsey nodded. "And what they can't do anymore."

"They certainly can't beat children on the behind until

they're raw and bruised," Andy piped up. "Not anymore. And that is something those of us who fought against corporal punishment are proud of."

Ted sighed in exasperation, and Dennis rose to his feet and wandered off into the brush to relieve himself. Bert shook his head and reached for the container that held the coffee. Harry stared at Andy as if seeing him for the first time and he thought, *Maybe I am.* Jack leaned back on his ground sheet, waiting for Andy to babble some more. Jack had known Ted since they were just kids in the Korean War, and he could sense that Ted was not going to interrupt his son again. He was going to let him verbally dig his own deep hole.

Jack turned his head for a moment. He thought he had heard something out of place in the brush and timber. He listened intently for a few seconds, but all was silent. A falling branch, he decided.

When his father made no effort to cut him down, Andy said, "It's been proven time after time that corporal punishment really is detrimental. It accomplishes nothing constructive."

Bert hid his smile. He was remembering the time he got the crap whaled out of him by a junior high teacher. He couldn't recall exactly what he'd done to warrant the butt-whipping, but he knew damn well that whatever it was, he sure never did it again after that.

And when Bert got home his father had already been informed about the incident by the school principal. His dad made him drop his jeans, bent him over a chair, and laid the belt to his butt.

Bert heard the same noise Jack had heard and paused for a few seconds. When the noise was not repeated he directed his attention toward making a fresh pot of coffee: Bert was known for making the best camp coffee of all the back country guides.

Andy said, "Personally, I think the public schools are doing a wonderful job with the students of today . . ."

Judy and Lindsey exchanged glances at this, both of them wondering where this guy was coming from, or more importantly, where had he been? There were armed guards all over the place in public schools, metal detectors were used in an attempt to keep guns and knives out of the classrooms, there was some sort of racial incident nearly every week, teachers were being physically assaulted, the tires on their cars slashed . . . and this guy was talking about how wonderful the nation's public schools were.

Both Judy and Lindsey were straight A students, and both of them had already picked out the college they were planning to attend after high school graduation. Neither girl was known as a party girl by her peers. Neither had had any experience with sex until being seized by the escaped cons.

"I personally think you're full of crap, Andy," Harry said. "Everything I read about the nation's public schools shows they're in deep trouble. For one thing—"

A hard blast of gunfire put an abrupt halt to the conversation and sent the men and two teenagers scrambling for their weapons and for some sort of cover.

"Heads up!" Dennis shouted from the brush. "Four guys coming in from the north . . ."

More gunfire cut off the rest of Dennis's warning.

Jack had been sitting next to Judy. He reached down and picked up the Uzi she'd taken from the guard in the cave. He'd been looking at the weapon and knew its operation. The selector switch was set on full auto. He turned to face the north, gripping the weapon.

"There's one!" Lindsey shouted, pointing.

Bert had been sitting close to Lindsey and at her shout he leveled his .30-30, locating the wild-eyed stranger bursting through the brush, a shotgun in his hands, and pulled the trigger. The round took the man in the center of the chest and sat him down abruptly, a strange expression on his face.

Jack cut loose with the Uzi and stitched a man in the belly just as the stranger made the tiny clearing, a pistol in his right hand. The automatic fire from the Uzi knocked the man spinning and threw him against the trunk of a tree. He dropped the pistol and slumped to the ground.

"Don't kill them girls!" a man shouted. "I want some pussy!"

"These guys have a one-track mind," Judy muttered.

Jack heard the comment and smiled at the gutsy teenager.

Then the camp erupted in gunfire as several men burst into the camp, weapons leveled.

Seventeen

"Stay down!" Jack called, and again squeezed the trigger of the Uzi.

He would have missed with every round except that one of the charging men made the mistake of stepping directly into the line of fire. The 9mm slugs stitched the man from left to right, hip to shoulder, and knocked him sprawling to the ground, dead before he stretched out.

A pistol banged in the timber and brush and a few seconds later, Dennis stepped out. "One ran off," Dennis said. "But he's hard hit. His buddy sure as hell isn't going anywhere . . . ever again," he added with a definite note of satisfaction.

"This one's still alive," Bert called, kneeling down beside the man he'd shot. "But he ain't gonna last long, I can tell you that."

The group gathered around the man. He looked up at them, pure hate in his fading eyes. "Won't none of you get out of here alive. You're hard trapped in this valley."

"I never saw you before," Judy said. "Where did you come from?"

"Me and my buddies joined up a couple of days ago, bitch. I was lookin' forward to screwin' you."

Judy sighed. Lindsey was a bit more graphic: she gave the man the middle finger.

"God, you're a sorry bastard!" Ted told the man.

"Hell with you," the dying man said.

"I think it's you that better be worried about hell," Bert told him.

"I don't believe in that shit," the man gasped. "When you're dead, you're dead, and that's it."

"You people start packing up," Jack told the group. "We've got to get out of here."

"Run all you want to, sucker," the wounded man said, blood leaking out of one side of his mouth. "My buddies will get you, sooner or later." He cut his eyes to Lindsey. "And when Jans runs that root of his up your snatch, you gonna scream until you're hoarse."

Lindsey got up and walked off to help with the packing.

Bert jacked the hammer back on his lever action rifle. Andy stepped in front of the man. "What do you think you're going to do?"

"I'm fixin' to send this rotten bastard to hell," the guide told him.

"Are you crazy!" the younger man almost shouted the question. "That would be murder."

When the gunfire started, Max had beaten a very hasty exit behind the nearest tree, headed for a safe spot; he was no dummy. He was now peering out around the trunk.

For a moment it looked as though Bert just might pop Andy with the butt of the rifle. Andy suddenly realized he was in a lot of danger and backed up a few feet.

"Bert, you can't just shoot the man," Andy pleaded. "He's dying, anyway."

Bert stared at Andy for a moment, then turned and walked off. Andy's face regained some of its color and his breathing began to even out.

"You one stupid asshole," the dying convict gasped the words. "That ole' boy is mean as a snake. You 'bout got your ass killed for nothin.' "

Andy turned and looked down at the man. Blood now covered the front of his shirt and light jacket and every time he exhaled or coughed, blood sprayed from his mouth. "You wouldn't understand," Andy told the man, his words spoken low.

"You'd be surprised what I do and don't understand," the convict replied. "And I don't have the time to explain it all. Besides, it would just mess up your stupid head if I did try."

"You have any relatives?" Andy asked.

The convict laughed at him, the laughter grotesque through his bloody mouth. "God, you are a dumb man. Sure, I got relatives. Who don't? But they don't want anything to do with the kid here. Didn't take them long to get smart 'bout me."

"I don't know what you mean."

The convict chuckled. "My father is a retired banker, and my mother was an educator. I got one brother who's a lawyer and a sister who's a doctor. We grew up in a house built on two acres of land with a swimming pool in the backyard and a four car garage filled up. That tell you anything, twinkie?" He coughed and spat out blood.

Andy didn't really grasp what the con was talking about, but he knew what a twinkie was, and he flushed beet red. "I'm not homosexual."

"Wouldn't take you long to become one in the joint, punk. You'd be suckin' me hard and I'd be fuckin' your prissy ass first night in general population."

"I doubt that!"

"I don't."

The others had gathered around, listening, all except the girls. They had doused the fire and were busy packing up.

"What did you mean, telling me about your family?"

"He means," Jack said, "that he grew up in a good family, with plenty of money, plenty of love, plenty of opportunities. It means he was born bad, Andy."

"I don't believe in that theory," Andy came right back.

"Then that really does make you a fool," the dying con said. He coughed up more blood, and for a moment those gathered around thought he was finished.

Everyone had taken note that the man's vocabulary had dramatically improved. They looked at each other and shrugged their shoulders.

"What were you in prison for?" Ted asked.

"I like pussy." The dying con laughed sarcastically: a bitter bark of dark humor.

"You're a rapist," Jack said. It was a statement, not a question.

The con began coughing up gobs of blood. When he finally caught his breath, he said, "I got a little rough with a bitch one night, while I was in college. My sophomore year. Broke her neck. All of a sudden she just went limp. She was dead. I liked it."

"You liked to kill women?" Ted asked, a note of incredulity in his voice.

"You obviously need some psychiatric help," Andy said.

"All of you get the hell away from me and leave me alone," the con said. "Let me die in peace."

"With pleasure," Jack said. He looked at Dennis. "Watch him."

"You bet I will, from a safe distance."

The con arched his back as sudden pain ripped through

him. He cussed savagely, then relaxed, his eyes wide open and staring, but seeing nothing.

He was dead.

"Good riddance," Bert said, walking up.

"My sentiments exactly," Ted said.

Andy looked at his father, opened his mouth to speak, then thought better of it. He shook his head.

"Pack it up," Jack ordered. "We're getting the hell out of here."

"What about the bodies?" Andy asked. "Are we going to bury them properly?"

Jack laughed and the others laughed with him.

Andy got the message.

Eighteen

Sturgis was tracking the group.

Through the pain in his head and the bullet wound, which was now badly infected, he was like a bloodhound, staying on their trail, always a few miles behind them, never quite closing the distance. He staggered along, occasionally falling down, sometimes crashing into trees, sometimes losing the trail for hours. But he always managed to find their trail and stumble along. The big man had but one thought in his fevered brain: Kill those who had caused this terrible pain in his body.

Sheriff Hawkins was a day and a half's ride from the valley. He was riding more cautiously now, stopping often to scan his surroundings. He stayed in the timber and brush when that was possible. He had seen no campers as he put the miles behind him, and he hoped he would not; hoped their guides had taken their charges either north or south of this section of the back country. But deep down in his guts he could bet there were a few campers in the area, with more coming in. It was only a matter of time before the escaped cons would find them.

Hawk shoved those thoughts out of his mind. He didn't like to think about that.

Randy and Karl sat in one of the smaller caves and drank coffee and looked at each other, neither one speaking. They were enjoying hot coffee now, for small fires could be built in the caves with no danger of the smoke being seen: the smoke drifted out through cracks in the rock; the ceilings of many of the caves were blackened from fires of centuries past.

Randy broke the silence. "These old farts have been eluding us for days now. And that just doesn't make any sense to me. We're six or seven times their number and half their age, in most cases. Still, they're killing us off and then disappearing into the brush and timber. It just isn't logical."

"Logical or not, they're doing it," Karl replied. "I got me a hunch these guys are all ex-combat vets, maybe even Special Forces. They sure as hell are falling back on some hardass training or experience . . . probably the latter, I'd guess."

"But they're *old!*" Randy flared in sudden anger. "Goddamn old men!"

"Early sixties, from what those who came out alive from tangling with them have said. But we're reasonably safe in this valley. Kathy says no guide brings campers in here—"

"There's always a first time for that," Randy interrupted sourly.

Karl ignored that. "We know from listening to shortwave the cops aren't looking for us in this area. Hell, they think you and me are dead—"

"For a couple more weeks, max," Randy said. "Soon as the autopsies are done they'll know the bodies in that burned up car weren't us, and we're still alive. Then there'll be cops all over this area, swarming all over the place. And you know it, Karl. Whatever we come up with on how to deal with those old bastards, we'd better get it done, get it done quickly, and get the hell out of here."

Karl didn't argue that. He knew the international terrorist was right. But Karl was no soldier; he had no training in tactics. Few of the escaped cons did.

Karl Parsons and Randy O'Donnell sat in the cave and looked at each other.

"You left a piece of shirt on the ground," Andy pointed out to Jack.

Jack smiled. "Yes, I did, Andy."

"Deliberately?"

"Yes."

"You want those men chasing us to find it?"

"Yes."

"Come on, Son," Ted told him after a long, very patient sigh. "Fall in behind me and let's go."

"But I would like to know why Jack wants to leave our trail so clearly marked."

"I left a surprise for them, Andy," Jack told the younger man. "I want them to find it."

Andy blinked. He did not have the foggiest idea what Jack was talking about. He did not read books that featured action and adventure, watch TV shows or go to movies that had much violence in them, and no one else in his family did, either. Those types of shows were forbidden. None of his children had ever been allowed to play with toy guns, toy tanks, or toy fighter planes. He knew nothing about the military (except that he didn't like it and felt it should be drastically downsized and used only for peacekeeping operations). He knew nothing about survival.

"Move out," Jack ordered. "Now!" Jack took the drag and Bert took the point. When the others were moving, Jack paused and looked back at the rest area they'd just vacated. He smiled.

"Come on, you bastards," he whispered. "Find this campsite and investigate." He laughed, but the laughter was totally devoid of humor.

Jack turned and closed the distance with the group.

Sheriff Hawkins found a tiny spring that spewed forth ample water for the horses and built a corral out of brush, temporarily closing the only entrance to the small box canyon several miles from the south pass that led into the valley. The horses would have plenty of graze and could break out easily enough if Hawk didn't return.

Hawk struggled into his heavy pack, picked up his rifle, and started walking. He would make the south entrance to the valley at dusk, and that was how he planned it: he was right on schedule, and that pleased him.

Call it a hunch, a guess, but Hawk just felt in his guts that a group of escaped cons were in the valley. Probably hiding in the caves along the high ridges just before the mountains loomed up on both sides of the long valley.

He had made a few quiet inquiries since the back country had opened up after the prison break, and could find no one in his area who was guiding tourists into the valley. However, there were any number of guides located all around the wilderness; Hawk sure as hell didn't know them all. None of the guides he knew ever led people into the valley, and didn't know anyone who did, but there was always a first time.

Hawk walked on.

* * *

Bert had left the group resting and scouted ahead for a couple of miles. He returned and sat down wearily. Bert was a pure western man—he could sit a saddle all day—but when it came to walking he was not thrilled. He took off his boots and rubbed his aching feet.

"The south end of the pass is blocked, and blocked good," Bert said. "We can forget about getting out that way. And you can bet the north end is blocked just as well."

"Well, what are we going to do?" Andy asked, just a touch of panic in his voice.

No one spoke for a moment. Jack finally said, "We fight."

Andy turned and looked at the man. "What did you say, Jack?"

"I said we fight. We find our balls—excuse me, girls—and stand up on our hind legs and fight."

Dennis slowly nodded in agreement. "Yeah. That sounds good to me. I've been thinking about that for the past couple of days."

"You guys are crazy!" Andy blurted.

Harry ignored him. "I've had my ass whipped more than once in my life. But this is the first time I ever ran from a fight. I don't like the feeling."

Ted met the eyes of his friends and smiled. "I'm for it, boys. Let's take the fight to the crud."

Bert pulled his boots back on and laced them up. "I'm with you guys, and standin' up and makin' a fight of it sounds damn good to me. Let's do it."

"People," Andy pleaded with the men, "none of you will ever see sixty again. We should continue to march and hide out and leave the fighting to the professionals."

The group of older men ignored him. Jack said, "We've

got plenty of ammo and weapons. Hell, we're overloaded with weapons. We've got several rucksacks filled with grenades, and we all know how to use them. Maybe we can't toss a pineapple as far as we could thirty odd years ago . . ." He grinned. "Actually, it's forty years ago. But we can still chunk one a respectable distance. It's time we took the fight to them."

Andy looked at the teenage girls. "You two try to talk some sense into these guys, will you?"

Lindsey and Judy exchanged glances. "What they're saying makes plenty of sense to us," Lindsey said. "We'll do what we can to help."

"That's the spirit, girls," Jack said.

"You have a plan, Jack?" Ted asked.

"Not yet. I think we should talk about it, exchange ideas."

"Sounds good to me," Harry said.

"Ridiculous!" Andy snorted. "The testosterone is really flowing today."

"You really are chickenshit, aren't you?" Lindsey asked him.

"I don't have to put up with insults," Andy whirled around to face her.

"What are you going to do about it?" the teenager challenged him. "Talk me to death?"

Andy stared at the girl for a moment; there was open defiance in her eyes, all of it directed at him. He turned and walked off a few yards to stand by himself.

"Okay, boys," Jack said. "See what you think about this plan. . . ."

"We're on the right track!" a con yelled to the group behind him. "Look here what I found."

The others began to gather around, all looking at the torn piece of shirt Jack had left behind.

One stepped off to his left, and his foot hit a piece of rope that Jack had camouflaged by rubbing fresh leaves on the fiber until the color melted in with the surroundings. A thick limb, bent down taut, sprang forward. There were three sharpened stakes secured to the limb. The sharpened points slammed into the chest of the convict, piercing heart and lungs. The man died without making a sound.

"Jesus Christ!" another one shouted, eyes bulging at the horrible sight in front of him. "It's a damn trap!" he shouted. He stepped back and his foot dropped eighteen inches into a hole Jack had dug. Sharpened stakes, the points arched upward, were secured in the bottom of the hole. Several of the stakes penetrated the man's foot and calf. The con began screaming in pain.

"Shit!" a third con yelled. "Back up slow, boys. Look all around you careful before you touch anything or take a step."

"Those damned old bastards!" another con hissed, looking all around him, his eyes suddenly full of fear. "I hate old men. You can't trust none of them."

"Help me, damnit!" the con with the stakes in his foot and leg called.

The remaining cons gathered around, carefully looking all around them, up and down, and stared at the punctured foot and calf.

"Pull them damn stakes out!" the con screamed.

"It's gonna hurt."

"Shit, I know that! It's killin' me now. Get me off these stakes."

The con passed out, screaming his hatred for the 'old men' as he was being pulled from the hole and the stakes pulled from his foot and leg.

"Pour some water on him," a con said once the injured

man was stretched out on the ground. "He's gonna have to hobble along, leanin' on us. We'll take turns."

"What about Larson?" a con asked, cutting his eyes to the dead man.

"We'll get him down and lay him out. We ain't got nothin' to dig no holes with. It's the best we can do."

"Aw, come on, now. That ain't right. The animals will eat him, Hobby."

"You think he's gonna feel that?"

"No. But it's disgusting."

"Oh, shit, Bruce! So what? He was totally disgustin' when he was alive. Come on. Hold the limb while me and Don pull him loose."

The smell was terrible, for the dead con's bowels and bladder had relaxed upon death. He was finally pulled loose and stretched out on the ground.

"Let's get Sam awake and up," Hobby said. Hobby had been serving life without parole for multiple murders and rape and a half dozen lesser charges. "We got to get the hell out of here."

"I hate those old men," Don said. "They're mean old bastards. They'll pay for doin' this, won't they, Hobby?"

"They'll pay, all right. You can make book on that."

"I want to hear them scream. I like it when they scream. The louder they scream, the better I like it. That's why I like this wild ass country. No . . . I *love* this country. I really, really do. Can't nobody hear 'em when they scream. A woman's screamin' turns me on." Don was perverted to his very core—just about as worthless a human being as could be found—and he had been that way since childhood. He had begun his long career by torturing animals. Someday some judges might get their heads out of their asses and realize that young people who torture animals have already taken several long steps toward a life of crime and perversion.

"Yeah, Don, We know all about that," said Bruce, another murderer and rapist who was serving life without benefit of probation, parole, or reduction of sentence.

"Karl and Randy ain't gonna like this," Bruce opined, pouring water on Sam's face. Sam remained unconscious. "They ain't gonna like it at all."

"Well, let them come up with a way to fix the problem, then," Hobby said. "I'm fresh out of ideas."

"We're runnin' out of water, Hobby," Don said. "What do we do if we run out of water?"

"We stand around and piss on him," Hobby said. "Good God, man, I don't know."

"Let's leave him," Bruce suggested. "I never did like the son of a bitch no way."

Hobby looked at Don. "You got anything you want to say about that?"

"I guess I ain't got nothin' to say about nothin,' " the con replied.

"As usual," Bruce said.

"Fuck you," Don told him.

"You'll never go back to girls if you do," Bruce said with a very exaggerated simper and lisp.

"Knock it off," Hobby told them. He looked down at the unconscious con. "Hell with him. Let's get out of here."

Don looked down at Sam. "Bye, Sam."

"How touchin,' " Bruce said.

"Yeah," Hobby said. "Makes me feel all gooey inside."

"You guys ain't normal," Don said.

It took Hawk hours to claw and climb his way into the valley. Several times he actually felt he wasn't going to make it. Sometimes he doubted his own sanity at even attempting the rugged climb in. It had been many years since he'd taken this route, and he'd been a much younger man then . . . about twenty years younger, he recalled with a rueful grin. And the years did take a toll. He sighed and got to his feet, starting out once more.

Finally he made it into the beautiful and isolated valley, and he sat down wearily for a long rest. He pulled his boots off and rubbed his tired feet. He hadn't spotted anyone, and that had caused him more than once to question the entire trip in.

"The bastards are in here," he muttered. "I know they are. I just know they are. And I'm going to find them."

A cold voice came out of the shadows. "You don't have to worry about that, sucker, 'Cause we done found you!"

Nineteen

Hawk threw himself to one side, the move totally unexpected by the men standing in the shadows off to his right. He rolled to a stop, clawing for his pistol.

"Shoot the son of a bitch!" someone shouted.

But Hawk triggered off the first shot. The .44 mag roared and the big hollow-point slug took a con in the belly, doubling him over, knocking him backward, and sitting him down hard on the ground. He began bellowing in pain.

There was no way Hawk was going to leave his pack and his rifle. This was going to be a fight until one side either ran or was the clear victor, with no survivors.

"How the hell did he get in here?" someone shouted.

"I told you all I seen someone climbing up them rocks, didn't I?" was the reply.

"I knew you were in here," Hawk muttered, crawling behind better cover. Hawk knew in his guts this was no bunch of poachers or dopers: he had found the escaped convicts.

It had taken Hawk much longer to get into the valley than he anticipated. It would be full light soon. The stars had faded and the approaching day was going to be clear and bright.

"I can't see the son of a bitch," a voice called. "Where is he?"

"Can't tell." The second voice came from his left. The con Hawk had shot was moaning and crying as the pain in his belly intensified.

"Who the hell is he?" a third voice called.

"How do I know?" the first voice replied. "All I know is, we'd better get him."

"He can't get out of the valley. We got the trail he took blocked. Jimmy sealed it tight with boulders."

Hawk had faintly heard the noise hours back. The cons had started a rock slide. That pass was closed forever.

"It's just a matter of time before we nail him."

Don't count on that, Hawk thought. He was about twenty feet from his pack and rifle, and if he was going to make a move to retrieve them, he was going to have to do it right now, and then get the hell gone into the timber and brush. It would be light in a very few minutes, and if he waited any longer he would be hard trapped and eventually dead.

Hawk began inching toward his supplies, moving as silently as a snake. His hand closed around a baseball sized rock, and he hefted it, thinking hard. Maybe it would work; maybe it would buy him five or ten seconds. He was sure that was all the time he needed.

He hurled the rock up high, in a slight arc. It landed about twenty or so feet behind where he felt the cons were. The noise was startlingly loud. The silver darkness before dawn erupted in gunfire. Hawk scrambled for his supplies and retrieved pack and rifle, then faded back into the brush. He was breathing hard and tried to keep the hard breathing in and out of his mouth, to cut down on the noise.

"Did we get him?"

"Can't tell. But I don't think so. I don't think that was him. I think he tricked us."

"Why?"

"How the hell do I know?"

The badly wounded con began screaming in pain and Hawk took that time to move back, deeper and deeper into the brush, the loud squalling covering any noise he made. He had no idea how much cover he had in this direction, but he knew he had to get the hell out of this bind. He silently slipped into his heavy pack, holstered his pistol, carefully securing the strap over the hammer, and found another rock about the same size as the one he'd just thrown. It might work again, and if it did that would buy him the time he needed to get clear.

He hurled the rock. It was one of those one in a million tosses: it struck a con. Hawk didn't know where it hit the man, but it wasn't in the head, for the con let out a scream of shock and pain.

"I been shot!" he yelled. "The guy's usin' a silencer. He shot me in the leg."

"What!"

"I been shot, I tell you. My whole leg's numb. I'm hard hit."

Hawk was slipping backward, deeper into the timber. He could not keep the wide smile from creasing his lips at what had just occurred.

"Shot?" The third con's voice called the question. "You bleedin' bad?"

"Somebody help me!" the con who'd been shot screamed his anguish. "Help me!"

He was ignored.

"I ain't bleedin' at all," the con injured by the rock called after a few seconds.

"Well, how the hell can you be shot if you ain't bleedin?' That's stupid."

Hawk was deep in the timber now, working his way silently back and slightly to his left, toward the long valley.

"I was shot, damnit! Hell, I been shot before. I know what gettin' shot feels like."

Hawk figured he was now a good fifty or sixty yards from the shoot-out site. He could no longer make out the words being exchanged. He kept moving, more to the east now, deeper into the valley.

"Shit!" Hawk heard the very faint shout. "You was hit by a rock, you idiot."

"A rock?"

"The bastard threw a rock at you. Here it is right by your leg. It's the only rock of any size anywheres near you. Now he's gettin' away. Come on, damnit!"

"He hit me with a rock?"

Hawk could no longer hear the voices. He was moving very swiftly down the slope, behind the cons. He was almost to the valley floor. He stopped to rest for just a moment, until his breathing settled down. He continued walking, staying right on the edge of the timber, the valley floor to his right.

He was clear of the ambush. And with any kind of luck, Hawk intended to stay clear. Then the full realization of what he had heard the cons say touched him: He was trapped. The cons had him boxed in at this end of the valley, and he knew the north end of the valley, some twenty odd miles away, maybe closer to thirty miles, was pure hell getting through.

"All right, boys," Hawk muttered as the sky began turning from silver to red and gold. "You want a fight? Okay. I'll damn sure give you a fight."

A rifle shot roared through the morning quiet and knocked an escaped convict spinning. The man dropped to the ground in front of the brush that hid the opening to a cave and lay still. Another con ran out of the thick growth, hesitated for just a couple of seconds at the sight before him, then hit the ground and crawled back into the brush.

A mile down the rocky ridge Karl Parsons looked up at the sound of the shot and listened for a couple of heartbeats, then picked up his M-16 and stepped out of the brush. He was sure that had been a shot. Trouble was, in these mountains it was difficult to tell which direction it came from. He stood for a full minute, listening, but no other shot—if it *was* a shot—was heard. Karl shrugged his shoulders and made his way back through the brush and into the cave.

"What's the matter, Baby?" his sister, Kathy, asked. She was lying on a bed of blankets, her shirt unbuttoned and her breasts exposed.

Her bare breasts did nothing for Karl. For the moment, he was sexually sated. "Nothing, I guess. But I thought I heard a shot a couple of minutes ago."

"I didn't hear a thing." She grinned. Her teeth were perfect and very white. "Of course, I was still half asleep." Jans Pendley had just finished humping her not long before Karl thought he heard the shot. After the coupling, she had slept for half a hour, thoroughly satisfied, for the moment.

"Don't get hung up on Jans, Kathy," Karl warned her. "The man's crazy."

"But he fucks good," she said. "I never had a cock like that before. I can't get enough of it."

Karl chose not to respond to that. He squatted down and poured a cup of coffee from a pot hanging over the small fire. The smoke drifted upward and disappeared into a large crack in the rock ceiling.

Back in the cave, lying on his side, his hands and feet bound securely, Kathy's husband, Dave, gritted his teeth at his wife's words. Dick Jamison, only a few feet away from Dave, whispered, "She isn't worth getting all worked up over, Dave. She really isn't."

"I know it," the guide returned the whisper. "But God, what a filthy perverted bitch she turned out to be." He sighed. "How's your wife, Dick?"

"They hurt her when they raped her . . . from behind. I can't get the sound of her screaming out of my head. But she told me about an hour ago to stay tough. She's a strong woman."

Henry Matthews wormed his way a little closer to the two men. "Have any of you seen my wife or either of my kids?"

"Several men took Christine and Patti away a couple of hours ago," Dave told him. "I don't know where Paul is. I haven't seen him in a couple of days."

Paul was getting gang-shagged by a couple of the more perverted types who busted of the federal lock-up. Phil Fisher and Max Post were with him, the three of them being forced to sexually entertain several of the cons.

A woman's screaming drifted to the men tied up on the cave floor. Dave grimaced. "That's the woman from that other group that linked up with us the other day. Abby something or another. They've got her in the cave right next to us. Kathy told me—bragged actually—that two of the cons were going to double-team the woman. I think we all know what that means."

"Dirty, miserable, lousy no-good scum!" Dick said, considerable heat in his voice. "Where the hell are the cops when you need them?"

"Not in this part of the back country," Dave told him. "No one brings inexperienced people into this area. Too much danger of getting cut off and trapped. Some of these caves along the ridges have never been fully explored. I'm sure there are some that have never even been *found*."

"Oh, God!" Abby wailed. "Please stop. For the love of God, stop!"

Rough laughter followed the wailing and pleading.

"Goddamn those people," Dick said.

"Knock it off back there!" Karl said. "Shut up or I'll put a rifle butt against your heads."

The men fell silent. They could do nothing except listen grimly to the sounds of Abby Hayes screaming as she was sodomized over and over.

It was going to be a long day for the women being held hostage . . . and for several of the boys.

Twenty

"One down and dead," Jack said, a grim note of satisfaction in his words.

"You're sure he's hard hit?" Ted asked.

"I'm sure." Jack patted the bolt action rifle taken from a dead con. "This is a good rifle. Shoots true, and the scope is right on the money."

"Let's get out of here."

The two men faded back into thick cover.

Word was sent to Karl and Randy that the cons had lost another man. They received it just about the time another con reported having heard gunfire at the south end of the valley just about dawn.

"That's where Hobby and his boys were standing guard last night," Karl said.

"Have you been able to make contact with any of them?" Randy asked.

"No. So it must not have been anything of importance."

"The way things are going," Randy said acidly, "I wouldn't count on that."

Karl said nothing for a moment, but in his guts he agreed with the terrorist. The problem was, while the cons did have the old men trapped in the valley, they had also managed to pretty much trap themselves, too.

"Goddamn Mexican standoff," Karl muttered.

"You just now reached that conclusion?" Randy asked. "Hell, Man, we've got ourselves trapped in this godforsaken place, too . . . in more ways than one."

Karl exhaled audibly and nodded in agreement. "Yeah, Randy, I know."

"Well, from now on I run the operation against the old men, Karl. Me. Any objections to that?"

Karl immediately shook his head. "No, Randy. You can handle it, I don't give a damn. Just as long as those old bastards are put out of the way. You want to tell me just exactly what you have in mind?"

"We begin a sweep of the valley. We've got enough people to do a search and destroy mission."

Karl was a war movie buff; he knew what that meant. "All right. That's fine with me."

"Just how wide is this valley, at its widest point?"

"Five miles. It narrows down in several places to about a mile."

"Why?"

Karl shrugged his shoulders. "Marshes, ravines, so forth. They're impassable."

"Do you recall exactly where those places are?"

"Kathy would. My memory's a little hazy after all these years of being gone."

"All right. I'll get with her in a few minutes."

"Better make it an hour."

"Why?"

"She's screwin' one of the guys."

Randy shook his head and sighed. "Does your sister keep her brains between her legs."

"To some degree, yes. She's waiting on Jans to get another hard on."

"I don't like that, Karl. You told her the man is about half crazy, did you not?"

"Yes. But I don't think she believed me. She's in love with his dick."

Abby's moaning and sobbing drifted to the men as they sat in the sunlight in front of the cave. They were concealed from prying eyes by a thick stand of brush. The woman was begging her captors to stop.

The men sexually abusing the woman were laughing at her, and making some wild suggestions as to what they should do next.

In another cave, the three teenage boys were receiving the dubious favors of several other cons. The cons had been in lockup for so long, getting sucked off by and butt-banging queens, they had difficulty making it with a woman.

"I will be eternally grateful to get away from those miserable people," Randy said.

"We sure agree on that," Karl said. "When do we start the sweep for the old men?"

"In the morning."

Sturgis staggered up to the camp, a club in each hand, a wild expression on his face. Lindsey spotted him and yelled. Judy chunked a fist-sized rock that caught the big man on the forehead and sat him down hard on the ground, blood pouring from a cut and swelling lump in the center of his forehead.

"I actually hit him," Judy said, wonderment in her voice.

Jack and the others were all over the stunned man, lashing his hands behind his back and tying his ankles tightly.

"I'm really gettin' tired of foolin' with this ole' boy," Bert said. "I've 'bout reached the limits of my patience with him."

"Well, you can't shoot him!" Andy said.

Bert fixed the younger man with a hard look. "Boy, I've just about had it with you, too."

"Be quiet, Andy," Ted told his son. "Before your ass overloads your mouth."

Andy stared at his father for a moment, started to speak, then turned and stalked off a few yards.

"Hell, I wasn't goin' to shoot the bastard," Bert said. He looked at Ted and blinked a couple of times. "I'm talkin' 'bout the convict, Ted, not your son."

Ted laughed and lightly punched the guide on the shoulder. "I know that, Bert!"

Sturgis groaned and tried to sit up. "Kill you all," he growled. "All of you."

"What the hell are we going to do with the guy?" Harry questioned.

"Leave him," Jack said. "He'll work his way loose in a few hours and by that time, we'll be long gone."

"You don't know that for sure," Andy said. "He might well die right here. And his wounds need attention."

"Andy, please be quiet," Ted told him.

"No, I won't be quiet! The man may be a criminal, but he's a human being. He probably has a concussion from that blow to the head and he needs medical attention."

"Well, boy," Bert said, losing his grip on his temper. "I

have an idea, then. Why don't you stay here with him and see to his medical needs? We'll just head on out and maybe we'll see you again. Does that suit you?''

"You'd leave me here alone?" Andy asked.

"Don't force us to make that decision, Son," his father said.

"It wouldn't be a hard decision for me," Jack said. " 'Cause I'm damn tired of his whining.''

"Get into your pack, Son," Ted told his son. "We're moving out. Just do it.''

"The sad thing is, I bet you people call yourselves good Christians," Andy replied.

Bert picked up his pack and slipped it on. "Andy, I heard this preacher say that after his second arrest Jesus told his followers, 'Those of you who do not have a sword, get one.' Personally, I've never seen that particular bit of scripture, but I don't doubt it. Sounds pretty good to me. I think when you come right down to it, Jesus was a realist. I think what he was sayin' to his people is there's a time to be forgivin' toward your enemies, and a time to fight.' And right now, boy, we just don't have the luxury of bein' very forgivin.' ''

Andy stared at Bert for a moment. "Not that it makes any difference to me, Bert, but did Jesus really say that?''

Bert shrugged his shoulders. "You couldn't prove by me. I'm just repeatin' what the preacher said. I'm no student of the Bible. And yeah, Andy, I think I'm a Christian. I'm not the best Christian. I don't get to church as often as I should. I just try to live a decent life, that's all.''

"Fuck Jesus, and fuck you all," Sturgis mumbled.

Andy looked at the convict for a moment, then picked up his pack. "All right. Obviously, I'm not going to stay here alone. I'm ready to move out when you are.''

"Let's get away from here," Jack said.

"I'll kill you all," Sturgis said.

"Nice fellow," Dennis muttered.

Hawk made a cold camp in a thicket of brush, several miles from the site of the shoot-out. He ate one of his Hi-Energy bars, washing it down with water, then took a nap, sleeping for about an hour. He awakened feeling refreshed.

Hawk inspected the contents of his pack, turning on his radio. It was dead as a rock. He had checked it carefully before pulling out and it had been working just fine, so whatever had happened to it had happened on the way into the back country.

"Shit!" Hawk muttered. He was trapped in the valley.

He inspected his binoculars. They were still in good shape and had not been knocked out of focus. He lifted the small but very powerful binoculars to his eyes and scanned the terrain all around him. Far in the distance, he could see carrion birds slowly circling, edging ever so gradually downward toward a meal. Might be a dead animal, but if Hawk had to make a bet on it he'd bet it wasn't.

Hawk struggled into his heavy pack, picked up his rifle, and moved out, staying in the timber near the foot of the slopes. He moved slowly and carefully, stopping often to scan the terrain, but still managing to cover a lot of ground.

He spotted no human life, no smoke from campfires, nothing to indicate there was anyone in the valley.

But he knew there most certainly was human life in the valley. Probably a dozen or so of the escaped cons. Maybe more than that. Probably more than that. Twice, while resting, he had gotten an unmistakable whiff of wood smoke drifting to him. Just a tiny whiff, but he knew what it was.

"They're in the caves on the other side," he whispered to the breeze that floated down from the mountains. "Hiding out in the caves. A damn smart move on their part. Somebody knows this country.''

Hawk also knew there were dozens and dozens of caves spread out along the twenty or thirty miles of the long valley. It would take a battalion of troops to effectively search all the caves . . . and it would take them days, maybe even weeks.

He walked on.

Max stepped in front of Judy and refused to get out of the girl's way. The others noticed and the short column paused.

"Quiet, now," Jack whispered. "Pass the word. That dog senses something up ahead he doesn't like. Stand easy and quiet. I'll check it out."

It was Sam, the convict who had stepped into the punji pit. He was crawling along, mumbling and cussing and dragging his grotesquely swollen leg and foot. His hands were cut and bleeding, and he had worn out the knees of his trousers. He must have crawled four or five miles. Jack knew at first glance what had happened to the man. His lips creased in a savage smile. One less worthless bastard in this world. And Jack knew the man was going to die. He knew what he'd put on those stakes.

Jack waved the others up to him. Andy took one look and said, "Oh, my God. The man must be in terrible agony."

"I hope so," Judy said. "I really do."

"You don't mean that!" Andy said.

"You wanna bet?" the girl came right back at him. "That's one of the men who raped me. He tried to get his dick up my ass but it wouldn't fit. But that sure didn't stop him from trying several times. Now you want me to feel some sort of compassion for him? You're crazy!"

Sam had turned like a huge ugly bug to face the group gathered behind him. He cussed them. Then his eyes fell on Judy and he cussed her. He stopped cussing when Judy had to hold Max back by the rope they'd attached to his collar. The malamute's teeth were bared in a hideous snarl.

"You keep that goddamn dog away from me." Sam panted the words. "I'll kill that son of a bitch."

"You're all through killing—and raping," Jack told the man. "Those stakes were smeared with shit I found in the timber. Deer or bear or wolf or coyote . . . some kind of animal. I don't know what produced it. But it was shit. Fresh shit. You've got blood poisoning in that leg by now."

Sam cussed Jack. He called him every filthy name he could think of. Jack stood smiling at him.

"I seen what you done to Larsen," he gasped the words. "I seen them awful stakes you rigged up in that spring trap go into him. No normal human bein' would do something like 'at. You a mean, cruel son of a bitch, you are."

"Stakes? Spring trap?" Andy asked. "What stakes? What spring trap? What kind of shit did he smear on the stakes . . . what about these stakes? What kind of stakes went into Larsen? Who is Larsen?"

No one chose to reply to his questions.

"Let's get out of here," Jack said. "Turn around and move out."

"You can't just leave that man here!" Andy protested. "That would be inhuman. He needs medical care."

"Well, then, Andy," Jack replied. "Why don't you stay here with him? You can kiss him and hug him and whisper sweet nothin's in his ear. I'm sure that would make him feel better. How about that, Andy?"

"Don't be ridiculous, Jack. That's absurd!"

A gunshot roared and startled all the men. They spun around. Max was tied to a tree and Judy was standing over the body of Sam, a pistol in her hand. She had shot Sam through the head.

Judy said, "You'll never rape another woman, you son of a bitch!"

Then she lowered the pistol and began crying.

Twenty-One

A man said to the universe: "Sir, I exist!"
"However," replied the universe, "the fact has not
created in me a sense of obligation."

Stephen Crane

Andy did not speak to Judy the rest of that day. He was shocked and sickened by what she had done to Sam.

Once Judy got all her crying finished, she said nothing about the incident.

The group had left Sam where he died and moved on. They made camp that afternoon not a mile from where Sheriff Hawkins was making a cold camp.

Randy and Karl had sat in front of the caves all that afternoon, just inside the thickets of brush, and scanned the valley below through powerful binoculars. They could spot no human movement.

"They're either damn lucky or know what they're doing," Karl said, lowering the binoculars and rubbing his tired eyes.

"I think it's probably a combination of both," Randy replied. "These guys are no bunch of sweethearts. They may be old, but there is no back-up in any of them. They've had some experience at warfare."

"Pretty good shots, too. At least one of them is. And speaking of that, how's Ray?"

"Dead as a hammer. A clean shot right through the heart. Some of the boys tossed him in one of the small caves; 'way in the rear, so the stink won't be so bad. Probably won't even be able to smell him."

"You doubled the guards at both ends of the valley?"

"I did for a fact. The old men, and that new person—whoever the hell he is—are trapped. They can't get out."

"And it's a pretty good bet that new person doesn't have any means of communicating with the outside. If he did, this place would be swarming with cops by now."

"Very true."

"So we've bought ourselves another few days, or week, or two weeks."

"I would say so. Two weeks, max. Certainly no more than that."

"Why?" Karl knew the answer; he just wanted to see if Randy was as sharp as he thought himself to be.

He was.

"Those old men must have families, and if they don't return on some given day their families will report them missing. That's when we've really got troubles, because we'll have search teams all over the back country."

Karl was silent for a moment, chewing on his lip. "Well, Kathy has agreed to lead one search team. I'll take another.

You said you wanted to lead another one. That will give us enough men to effectively sweep the valley. We start moving into place in the morning?"

"Correct."

"From the south end?"

"That's right. We fan out across the valley floor and start moving very slowly and very carefully north. If it takes us a week, that's fine. But we're going to do it right. Measure twice, cut once."

"What?"

"Old carpenter's motto. Measure twice, cut once. It means do it right the first time," he added drily.

Karl gave him a long dirty look. The two were not friends, didn't even really like one another . . . neither one possessed many likeable qualities. They were cohorts in this by necessity. "Yeah, Randy, I know what it means."

"How wonderful for you." Randy was thinking: *Give me half a chance, you big buffoon, and I'll kill you when this is over.*

Karl was thinking: *I'm going to kill you when this is over, you goofy Irishman.*

Sheriff Hawkins came face to face with Jack's group about an hour after dawn the next day. Jack and the sheriff looked at each other in surprise, then both jerked up their rifles, and for a few heartbeats there was a silent staring standoff.

"I never saw that one before," Judy said. "I don't think he's one of them."

"Who the hell are you people?" Hawk asked.

"Well, just who the hell are you?" Jack came right back. "And you'd better give the right answer or I'll put some lead in you."

"I'm Sheriff Hawkins. Who the hell are you?"

"Sheriff!" several in the group blurted.

"Yes. Of the county just west of here. You folks look like you've had a bad time of it."

"You could say that," Jack said, lowering his M-16. The bolt action scoped rifle was slung over one shoulder. "Where are your men?"

Hawk laughed bitterly. "What men? I came in here alone."

"You're kidding, I hope," Dennis said.

"I wish I was. I've already tangled with some of the escaped cons. You people look like you've tangled with them several times."

"We have," Jack said.

Bert stepped up from his position at the drag and smiled at the sheriff. "Hello, Hawk."

"Well, I'll be damned!" Hawk said with a smile. "Bert! You old goat. Jesus, man, I'm glad to see you alive."

"I'm kinda proud of that myself, Hawk. Did you really come in this country alone?"

"I really did. I didn't know whether any of the cons were in here or not. But I had me a good hunch. Looks like it proved out, too."

"For a fact. These young ladies have had a real rough time of it, Hawk. Tell you what, let's make some coffee and we'll sit and jaw for a time."

"Sounds good to me. I haven't had a cup of coffee in days."

Bert laughed. "Well, neither have we. But we've got another gun now, and I know the man behind it won't hesitate to use it. We'll take a chance and build a small fire."

"Let's do it," Jack said.

"I want you young ladies to tell me what happened," Hawk said, slipped out of his pack with an sigh.

"Long story," Lindsey said. "Did you people find my mother? The body of my mother."

"Your name Lindsey?"

"Yes, sir."

Hawk slowly nodded his head. "Yes. She was found."

"I know she's dead," Lindsey said. "I was there when they killed her. I've accepted it."

"Jesus," Hawk whispered.

"These are some pretty tough young ladies, Hawk," Bert said.

"I believe it."

Max growled gently—not an unfriendly growl, more a sound of greeting.

"And this is Max," Judy said. "He found me and we're friends."

Hawk and the big malamute exchanged glances. "I would say you found a good friend, girl."

"I think so."

"Two people stand guard at all times," Jack ordered. "Right now."

"I believe since we now have some duly authorized law enforcement among us," Andy said, "we should take orders from him."

Hawk stared at the younger man. Andy bore a striking resemblance to the original Sad Sack. Hawk formed an opinion very quickly, and that opinion was not good. "As far as I'm concerned whoever's been giving the orders can continue to give them. Obviously, he's kept you alive for several days. He must be doing something right."

"But you're the sheriff!" Andy protested.

"Not in here," Hawk corrected. "My county is west of here. In here I'm just a citizen."

"You have no power?"

"No more than you do."

"You do at least have a radio with you?" Andy persisted.
"I hope."

"I had one. It's busted."

"Oh, my God!" Andy said. "We're all going to be killed in here."

Hawk looked at the man and sighed. Here was a fellow he damn sure would never count on in a bind. Probably hated guns and thought everyone who supports the right to own one was a right-wing whacko.

"You know this valley, Bert?" Hawk asked.

"Years back, I did. I don't ever bring campers in here. But Kathy knows it."

"Kathy?"

"Dave's Kathy."

"The guide team?"

"Yes."

"She's with you?"

"She's with them. Karl Parsons is her half brother."

"Karl Parsons is really here? Not dead?" Hawk sat down on the ground. Karl being here would explain a lot of things.

"Yes, sir," Judy said. "And about forty of the worst criminals in the nation. Including some guy from Ireland that the IRA threw out of their organization 'cause he was too bloodthirsty. Name is Randy O'Donnell."

"Are you sure, Honey?"

"I'm positive."

"Is Dave alive?"

"He was when I escaped."

"And Kathy is helping her brother?"

Judy laughed, but there was no humor in it. "Yes, sir. You could say that. She's having sex with him."

"Dear God," Hawk whispered.

"I have an idea," Andy said. "I think it's a good one."
The others looked at him.

"Let's start a fire."

"I'm starting one for the coffee, Andy," Bert told him. "See the flames?"

"No. I mean yes, I see the flames. But I mean a really big fire. A forest fire. The smoke would bring help in here quickly, right?"

"Son," Bert said, as he unscrewed the cap on the coffee can. "We're in a valley. Trapped. We can't get out. Where would we be safe from a raging fire?"

"Oh," Andy said. "Yes. You're right. I hadn't thought of that." He looked at Hawk. "How did you get into the valley without being seen?"

"I knew another way in. But it's been closed up tight by the cons."

"Over the rocks, Hawk?" Bert asked.

"Yes."

Bert shook his head. "That's a mean way in. Took you a while, didn't it?"

"Hours. Several times I didn't think I would make it. Tell you the truth, even if it wasn't blocked I wouldn't want to try that route again."

"I know damn well I wouldn't," Bert replied.

"So we have another gun, but we're still trapped," Andy said.

"That's about the size of it, Son," his father replied. "But thanks for your idea, and I mean that."

Father and son looked at one another for a few seconds. Andy nodded his head. "Thank you, Dad."

Hawk gave the group a furtive once-over. They were all damn rough looking. They had all been in the same clothing for several days, and were filthy, the men unshaven. Hawk knew the girls especially would enjoy a long hot bath and a change of clothing. But they both were gutsy young ladies . . . they were holding up better than most, considering what they'd both been through at the hands of the cons.

"Coffee will be ready in a few minutes," Bert announced. "Let's break out some of those miserable army rations. We might as well have something to eat, too."

"We're going to be on short rations pretty quick," Jack said. "Unless we can steal some more."

"We might have to think about shooting some game," Hawk said. "But a shot could bring the cons running straight to us."

"We have enough food for two more days of full rations," Jack said. "Then we're gonna have to think of something." He met Hawk's eyes. "How long did you tell your office you'd be gone?"

"Couple of weeks. We're not going to get any help there. Not any time soon." Hawk looked up at the sky. Clouds were moving in with another front. This part of the back country was going to be socked in tight.

"Yeah, I noticed the sky too," Jack said, following the sheriff's eyes. "Even if planes were searching this area, they wouldn't be able to spot us."

Hawk nodded in agreement. Looked at Judy. "You said there were about forty of the cons?"

"At least that many," the girl replied. "They have automatic weapons, cases of bullets and stuff, and lots of grenades and food and water."

"Somebody planned the breakout very carefully," Hawk mused.

"Randy's friends," Judy said. "I heard him boasting about it. That man is crazy."

"He's an international terrorist," Hawk told her. "In prison for multiple bombing of buildings. Killed several people. Including some kids. Why he wasn't given the death sentence is beyond me."

"We all know the answer to that," Jack said, disgust in his words.

Andy suddenly got a very pained expression on his face, but he wisely kept his mouth shut.

"Yeah," Hawk said. "We sure do."

"All right," Jack said. "Nothing has happened to change our plans. We still take the fight to the cons. Everybody still in agreement on that?"

"I'm for it," Dennis said.

"Sure," Ted said.

Harry nodded his head. Looked at Hawk. "How about you, Sheriff?"

Hawk smiled. "You boys were born with the bark on, weren't you?"

"Two wars will do that, Hawk," Jack said.

"What does that mean?" Andy asked. "Born with the bark on?"

"It's an old western expression, Andy," Bert told him. "Means rough and ready for anything."

"How quaint," Andy muttered.

"Don't you ever read western novels, Andy?" Hawk asked.

"I never read pulp fiction. I only read serious work. Quality fiction."

Hawk looked heavenward and rolled his eyes as the others laughed. "Sure, I'm ready for a fight," Hawk said. "Running has never much appealed to me."

"Oh, Lord," Andy said.

"Cheer up, Andy," his dad told him. "We've cut the odds down to only about eight to one."

"And we're almost out of food. We'll probably all contract some horrible intestinal disease from drinking untreated water. Our blankets smell bad. We smell bad. We all need long, hot, soapy baths."

"But we're alive," Dennis pointed out. "And doing

pretty well, I think. And each day we stay alive increases our chances of making it out in one piece."

"Besides, Andy," Ted said, "we're in the valley and the cons have the high ground. We can't hide out in one spot for more than a day or a night. We have to keep moving. And as long as we have to do that . . . well, let's fight the bastards."

Andy shrugged his shoulders in resigned acceptance. He had no choice in the matter, and knew it.

"Is that okay with you young ladies?" Hawk asked.

"Sure," Judy and Lindsey said together without hesitation. Judy added, "Maybe if we get close enough to the caves we can rescue my mother and brother. I mean, that is, if they're still . . ." She looked down at the ground and trailed that off into silence.

"They'll be alive, Baby," Ted told the young woman. "The cons will keep them alive."

Judy nodded her head. "Raping them both," she said softly. "Neither one will ever be the same after this." She looked at the sheriff. "Tell me this—those scum who are torturing and raping my mother and brother and the other people, if the police take them alive will they be put to death?"

Hawk shook his head. "No. Not unless they're responsible for some deaths, and even then that's iffy."

"Then where is the justice in this country? What happened to it?"

"I don't know, girl," Hawk replied. "Oh . . . that's a lie. I know. Every cop knows."

"It sucks," Lindsey said.

The sheriff nodded his head in agreement. "That's a good way of putting it."

"In this valley," Jack said, "maybe true justice will be served."

"What do you mean, Jack?" Harry asked.

"We're here, aren't we?" Jack smiled at the group. "It's all in our hands."

"Yeah," Lindsey said, remembering vividly the rape she had to endure and her mother's brutal death. She patted her M-16. "It damn sure is."

Twenty-Two

A big con stepped out of the cave and stretched. He zipped up his pants and then contentedly scratched his crotch for a moment. The old broad might be in her fifties, but she still had some fine nookie. After Doris Fisher was beaten two times, she had started to obey and move her ass and get in the spirit of the game while she was getting the meat put to her. Doris had some great-looking tits too. Kinda saggy, but a good handful still. And she could give some great head, too.

The con yawned just as a rifle barked from several hundred yards out, the bullet taking him in the belly and knocking him backward. Feeling as if a giant fist had struck him, he sat down hard on the ground as the first wave of pain hit him hard. He screamed in agony and beat his fists on the ground.

Another con ran out and another rifle barked, the bullet striking him in the hip and spinning him like a top. He yelled in pain as he fell to the ground, crawling like a crab back behind the bushes.

Only two cons were left inside each cave where the prisoners were held, there solely to guard the hostages. The rest were down at the south end of the valley, getting ready to slowly work north, starting their sweep.

"Two down," Jack said to Harry. The two men were several hundred yards out from the caves, Jack using his scope-mounted rifle.

The old friends had no idea how many cons had been left behind in the caves. Perhaps that was a good thing, for had they known there were so few they might have tried a rescue and gotten killed in the process. Those in the caves held the high ground, and taking the high ground is always very costly.

The two men heard the very faint boom of Sheriff Hawkins 7mm mag a couple of miles south of their position, followed by the crash of Bert's .30-30. Jack and Harry smiled at each other. One of the teams of escaped cons they'd seen forming early that morning had walked right into an ambush.

"Let's get out of here," Jack said, and the two men began crawling away from the ridges.

A couple of miles away, Hawk and Bert were doing the same, having inflicted as much damage as they dared for that ambush.

"Two down," Karl was notified by walkie-talkie. The little walkie-talkies did not have much range, and the chances of the signal getting out of the mountains that surrounded the valley were slight.

"All right," Karl radioed. "Stay put. Don't move out until you get my signal."

Karl cussed, then lifted the radio and informed Randy what had happened.

The Irishman cursed for a moment, then savagely clicked off the walkie-talkie. He was getting a gut full of those damned old men.

Karl was busy trying to raise somebody back at the caves. He finally made contact and was told, "We've got two down here. One of 'em's dyin.' He's hard hit. Cal's shot in the hip. He's in bad shape. Can't walk."

Again, Karl cussed. He was just about at the end of his rope. Those old bastards were out-slicking him at every turn.

"Shit!" Karl said.

"They might decide to give it up and make a break for it," Jack told the others over a hot cup of coffee. The front had moved in and the clouds were hanging low. Visibility was down to about half a mile, or less.

"What happens to the prisoners if they do that?" Lindsey asked.

"They'll probably kill them," Hawk told her. "I hate to be so damned blunt, but you've got a right to know."

Lindsey slowly nodded her head. "I understand. I guess I knew that before I asked." She looked over at Judy, who was standing at the edge of the tiny clearing. "Tough on her, though."

"Yeah," Hawk said, a hard grimness behind his words. "I know it is."

Abby Hayes saw a small window of opportunity and decided to take it. She had found a baseball-sized rock and for hours had concealed it under the stinking blankets where she lay. She was filthy, her hair matted and sticky. She had been raped and sodomized so many times she had lost count of the number. She had reached the end of her endurance, and was at the point where she just didn't care any more.

When a convict called Chambers turned his back on her for a few seconds, she jumped up and smashed him on the back of the head with all her strength. He went down without making a sound, a dent in the back of his head and blood leaking from his mouth and nose. She swiftly pulled on her clothes and picked up two rucksacks from the cave floor. She did not know what was in them. She just wanted out, and away. She did not know where the others were being held. For the past day and night she had been held alone in a small cave and abused hideously. She did not know if her husband was alive or dead.

The unconscious guard was wearing a web belt with a lot of things hooked onto it, including a canteen. She ripped that from him and slung it over one shoulder. She quickly rolled up her blankets and moved to the mouth of the cave, looking out into the mist. She could see no one and could not hear any sounds of life. She stepped out and quickly disappeared into the brush. She did not know where she was, but she was free, and she intended to remain that way. They might kill her, but the cons would never rape her again.

Never.

Paul Matthews had found a jagged and rusted piece of metal half buried in the dirt. He had been sharpening it whenever he got the chance, quietly working one side of the metal against a large rock in the cave until the rust was gone and the metal gleamed with sharpness. He was a slightly built teenager, neither strong nor athletic. He had been raped a dozen or more times and forced to perform oral sex on the convicts. He had been degraded and humiliated. He had been laughed at and forced to endure the most unspeakable acts a male could tolerate. He could not take the pain and humiliation any longer, would not. He had made up his mind.

Paul leaped at the guard and cut the man's face from just below the eye to the point of his chin. The guard screamed in pain and anger and fell backward against the wall of the cave. Paul raced for the mouth of the cave. The last thing he would remember on this earth was the roaring of a pistol and three hammer blows in his back. He sprawled dying and naked at the mouth of the cave. The teenager's days and nights of torture and humiliation were over. His body was tossed into a cave to rot alongside the body the convict called Ray.

A few hours before dusk, Randy O'Donnell sat just inside the mouth of a cave, occasionally tossing pebbles into the brush. He was outwardly calm; inside he was seething. The sweep of the valley had been canceled for a time after four men had been put out of action: two dead, two wounded. Another man had been severely injured by that cunt, Abby Hayes, and another savagely cut by the punk kid, Paul.

Everything was unraveling. All the carefully laid plans were coming unglued. All the meticulously thought-out strategy was to be for naught. All the efforts of his friends on the outside were to be for nothing. No more than a few days of freedom, and then back behind bars . . . for if they stayed here in this miserable valley, they would all be either captured or killed. Randy was certain of that.

Randy stood up and looked carefully all around him. No one was close to him or watching his actions. He stepped back into the cave and buckled on his web belt, then picked up a pack.

Randy again stepped outside and looked all around. Nobody to be seen. He quickly walked into the brush and disappeared. He was through with this bunch. Hell with them.

"What will you do if the convicts threaten to kill the hostages if we don't give up?" Judy asked.

"What would you have us do?" Jack asked the young woman.

"Don't give up," she answered quickly. "They won't keep their word."

"You don't know that for certain," Andy said.

He was ignored.

"They have nothing to live for," Judy said. "Some of them are facing murder charges—new charges. The rest will spend their lives in prison." She looked at Andy. "Yes, Andy. I know that for sure. I listened to them talk. I heard what they all had to say about it. When they weren't taking turns raping me," she added very acidly. "They're not going to surrender. They're not going back to prison. They'll die first."

Andy looked down at his cup of coffee for a few seconds. "I guess everyone wishes I would shut my mouth and keep it shut, right?"

"It's gone past that point, Son," his father told him.

Hawk listened to the exchange and wondered if maybe the babies hadn't got mixed up at the hospital shortly after Andy's birth. Ted was tough as a boot; Andy was a marshmallow all the way through.

"Well, that does it, then," Andy said, his voice shaking with anger.

"Does what?" Ted asked.

"I think," Andy said, pointing a finger at his father,

"that when, or if, we get out of this mess, I would prefer it if you never contacted me again."

Harry sighed and Dennis shook his head in disbelief.

"If that's what you want, boy," Ted said. There was no emotion at all in his voice. It sounded to the others as though Ted had already made up his mind to do what his son had just gotten around to suggesting. "I thought when this trouble started, you might shape up and started acting like a man. I was wrong."

"I think I *am* behaving as a man should," Andy came right back.

For a moment the group thought Ted was going to punch his son. But instead he walked off, calling over his shoulder, "I'll stand guard for an hour. Relieve me then, Jack."

"Will do, Ted."

"Sheriff, you got into a hell of a group when you linked up with us," Harry said.

"Why, Harry?" Andy asked, before Hawk could speak. "Because I don't want to kill every escaped convict I see?"

"Andy," Harry said, almost a pleading tone to his voice. "They're trying to kill us. We're trying to get them before they get us. Why can't you understand that?"

"*Some* of them are trying to kill us," Andy replied. "I imagine that some of the others are fairly decent people who just got a bad break in life."

"Shit!" Judy said. "Andy, I may be just a kid, but mister, you don't know what in the hell you're talking about." She got up and walked off to be with Ted on the ridge overlooking the encampment.

"Yeah," Lindsey said. "I agree with Judy." She rose to her feet and walked off to the ridge.

Andy started to retort, and Max got to his feet and walked off, joining Ted and Lindsey and Judy.

"Not even the dog wants to hear what you have to say, Andy," Dennis told him.

"I don't find that amusing," Andy replied.

"It wasn't meant to be," Dennis said.

"I guess I know where I stand now."

"You don't stand very tall, boy," Bert told him. "Not in my book, anyway."

Andy stared at the men, giving each of them a long look. Then he nodded in acceptance. "I can live with my decision."

"Well, *I* sure as hell couldn't," Hawk broke his silence. He sat his empty coffee cup on the ground and got up and started to walk away.

"You wait just a minute!" Andy raised his voice.

Hawk turned around.

"I don't believe you have any idea what it's like to live with a father who was a war hero. My father doesn't have any close friends who didn't serve in some branch of the military. All these guys served." He waved a hand. "Once a month it's the VFW meeting. Then it's the Korean War Vets meeting. Then it's the Vietnam something-or-another. Then it's something else, and something else after that. I got sick of it very early—as soon as I made friends with boys whose fathers didn't serve. They lived in normal households—"

Harry flared at him. "Oh, that's bullshit, Andy. Your dad never talked up the service to you. I know that for a fact. He never pushed you toward any branch of the military. His medals are in a trunk stored away in the attic. I know that for a fact, too. Your dad was a good father. You're talking out your ass, boy—"

"Somebody's coming up from the east," Ted called from the ridge. "It looks like a woman. I think somebody else escaped from those bastards."

"We'll hear her story," Dennis said, and Andy knew immediately it was all directed at him. "I'm sure she can tell us all about the various acts of compassion shown the hostages by the convicts."

Twenty-Three

"Gone," Karl told his sister. "He pulled out."

"But why?" she asked.

"He gave up on us, Kathy. He thinks the old men are going to beat us. I should have seen it coming and talked to him about it."

"Are they, Karl?"

Brother met sister's steady gaze and held it for a moment. "As incredible as it seems, Sis, they just might if we don't come up with a plan damn quick."

"You got anything in mind?"

"Not really. We could threaten to kill the hostages if they didn't back off or surrender, but I think they'd just tell us to go ahead. These old boys are tough. And smart. They know we can't, won't, pull out and leave them alive. And they probably know, or sense, that going back to the bucket is not in our plans."

"You and me, Karl . . . we're not going to be separated

ever again. That's the deal we made when I agreed to my part in this thing.''

Karl never had any intention of sticking with that agreement . . . not from the beginning. He was free from prison and he intended to remain free . . . either that, or dead. Kathy did not figure in his plans once outside of this valley. He didn't give a damn what happened to her. If it came right down to it, he'd shoot her himself and have done with it.

He slowly nodded his head. "Sure, kid. That's right. It's you and me all the way."

"Forever, Karl?"

"Forever, Baby. That's the deal we made. You know me. I don't go back on my word."

But Karl was already thinking of how to leave the whole damn crew behind and cut out on his own. Randy had the right idea. Karl just wished he'd thought of it first.

"We'll come up with something, Karl."

"Sure, Baby. We will. You can bet on that." *But we'd better do it damn quick,* Karl mused, *or my ass is out of here.*

"Abby Hayes," the woman told the men. She gave the group a quick once-over. "You guys aren't old," she said. "The cons keep referring to you as old men."

"We ain't young," Bert said with a smile. "But thanks for the compliment, Miss Hayes."

"Abby. Call me Abby. Miss Hayes is going to get old pretty quickly," She accepted a tin cup of coffee and sipped it, a smile on her lips. "You don't know how good that tastes."

"If you want to take the chance of freezing to death," Judy told her, "there's a little creek just over the ridge. Lindsey and me took a quick bath over there."

"Real quick," Lindsey added.

Judy had asked about her mother, and had been told she was still alive. The girl had closed her eyes for a few seconds, breathing a silent prayer of thanks.

"A bath sounds great," Abby said. "But after I finish this coffee . . . and maybe another cup. If you folks can stand me for that long."

"None of us smell real great," Jack told her. "Or look any better." He smiled. "Bring us up to date on the cons, if you feel like it. If you don't want to talk about it, we'll understand."

"I don't know everything that's been going on," the woman said. "But you guys are taking a toll on them. However, there are still a number of them looking for you. And I think they're getting desperate. Pretty soon they're going to start pulling out all the stops."

Everyone in the group smiled at that.

Abby picked up on the smiles and flashed one of her own. "For a fact, you guys are making them nervous." She told them about the planned sweep of the valley . . . and that it had been called off after the ambush.

"But you don't have any idea what they're planning next?" Dennis asked.

"They don't know what they're going to do next," Abby told him. "Everything they've come up with, you guys have blocked."

"But they haven't started killing the hostages?" Sheriff Hawkins asked.

"No. Not yet. But when they decide to pull out, they will. I've heard them talking about it. They plan to put them in a cave and blow the entrance closed. Let them die in there; doesn't make any difference how horribly. This is the scummiest bunch on the face of the earth."

"Desperate men do desperate things," Andy said.

Abby looked at the man. They were about the same age.

Abby couldn't figure out where Andy was coming from. He just didn't seem to fit with this bunch of tough men.

"But the cons haven't been making any plans to pull out?" Hawk asked.

"Not yet. I heard Karl say they've got to get rid of you people first. They can't afford to leave any of you alive to testify against them . . . or to somehow get out of the valley ahead of them."

"So it all boils down to us," Harry said.

"It sure does," Abby agreed. "Look, guys, I hate to be so bold, but do you have anything to eat? I'm really hungry. Those two rucksacks I've been lugging around are filled with bullets and other stuff . . . grenades, I think."

Harry smiled at her. "It's time for all of us to have a bite. Hand me those rucksacks Abby brought with her. Boys, we've got to come up with some sort of plan of action. . . ."

Randy cleared the valley simply by walking up to the sentry and telling him that Karl wanted to see him back at the caves, and not to use the radio. That's why, Randy explained, he was carrying a pack. He would take the man's place for a couple of days: give him a little break and a chance to get some pussy. As soon as the con was out of sight, Randy shouldered his pack and walked out and disappeared into the mist, smiling as he went.

The situation had turned into a standoff: Jack and his group could not get out of the valley, and Karl and his cons did not dare leave the valley with Jack and his people still alive.

"Problem is," Karl mused to Kathy just as dawn split

the sky, "we haven't hurt them at all, but they're taking a toll on us."

"Let's just pull out, Karl," Kathy suggested. "You and me. Just slip out and to hell with the rest of them."

"Can't do it, Baby. Oh, I've thought about it. But too many of them know what I'm going to do once we're out of this valley and know about us. They'd turn on us in a heartbeat if we tried to pull a fast one." He cut his eyes to her. "And don't forget about Dave."

She shrugged her indifference. "Dave goes down with the rest of the hostages, Karl. Nothing has happened to change that."

Treacherous bitch, Karl thought. *As coldblooded as a fish, and crazy as a road lizard. But I need her to help get us out of this country. Ole' Dave never knew he was marrying a real Looney Tunes when he hooked up with Kathy.* "I guess you want me to do the deed to Dave when the time comes, right, Sis?"

Again, she shrugged. "Doesn't make any difference to me. I've put up with the son of a bitch for years and hated every second of it. You tell me to shoot him, I'll do it."

Jesus God, Karl thought. *Kathy is as mean as a snake. And not right in the head . . . never has been.* He remembered things she had done when they were younger, weird things, cruel things. There was a word for what Kathy was, but he couldn't think of it. She was two or three people in one body. Goofy bitch.

"When the time comes, Kathy," he said drily, "you'll be the first to know."

"Thanks, lover."

Karl suppressed a sigh, thinking: *And when the time comes, Kathy, you'll be next, right after Ole' Dave. As soon as you help me get clear of this country, you go down for the long sleep. That's the way it has to be, Kid. Sorry about that.*

*   *   *

There were tourists camped on both the east and west sides of the valley, within five miles of the mini-battleground and the life and death struggle between the two factions. But because of the towering mountains that held the valley in a tiny cup, and the low-hanging mist that acted as a deadened agent, no sound reached out. It was as if the men and women in the valley were in another world. Alone. The campers outside the valley marveled at all the wonders of nature and the majesty of it all. They had no way of knowing they were only a few miles from pain and degradation and death.

In the valley, Jack and his group had come up with, discussed, and dismissed a dozen plans. They were as sty-mied as Karl and his people. The situation was truly a standoff.

Jack chanced a long-distance shot of several hundred yards and hit the man. He had overcompensated and the shot took the man high in the shoulder instead of the belly. But he had hit him, and the man went down.

"You got him!" Harry said, acting as Jack's spotter, watching the action through binoculars.

"Did you see where?"

"In the right shoulder."

"He's still alive, then."

"Yeah, he's flopping around on the ground. He's out of this game."

"The guy who was with him?"

"Went to cover. I can't see him."

Back at the caves, Karl heard the faint but still audible crash of the single high-powered shot and grimaced. He

didn't need a crystal ball to tell him what had happened:
the old bastards had put another of his men down.

"Who's on patrol this morning?" he asked Newton.

"Lofton and Burns. Was that a shot I just heard? Or
thought I heard."

"Yeah, it damn sure was." Karl looked around him at
the men sprawled in sleep on the cave floor. Something
was out of whack here. "Who's missing here, Newton?"

The con met Karl's eyes. "Barlow and Sims. They was
gone when I took a head count earlier. I thought they was
out on patrol."

Karl sighed in frustration and shook his head. "No. How
much gear did they take?"

"I don't know, Karl. I ain't checked."

"Well, check, Newton, and let me know."

"Okay, Karl. Will do."

Hawk and Dennis were too far from the caves for Hawk's
shots to be heard, but in less than two minutes Barlow
could no longer be counted among the living. Hawk's
7mm mag had sung its death song. Sims was out of it,
trying to get away from the snipers, doing his best to keep
from screaming, dragging a broken leg, the leg busted
high up, just below the groin. He struggled out of his pack
and rucksack and continued crawling away, back toward
the ridge and the caves.

"We just got some more supplies," Hawk said, working
the bolt and chambering another round.

Dennis lowered his binoculars. "How about the one
getting away?"

"Let him go. He's out of it."

"He damn sure is. That 7mm mag round knocked him
spinning, and busted his leg for sure."

"Lets get those packs and gear and switch locations

before the other cons can figure out where the shots came from."

Jack and Harry had already stripped their target of his gear and were hunting for the second man. The second man had dropped his pack and rucksack and was high-tailing it out of that area as fast as he could pick 'em up and put 'em down.

"Let him go," Jack said. "We keep on and we just might run into an ambush."

The men inspected the pack and rucksack: food packets, full magazines, and six grenades.

They exchanged smiles, knowing smiles. With the experience of years of combat behind them, both men sensed that the tide of this little war had turned in their favor. It was not something they could put into words . . . they just knew it. The little bloody campaign was far from over, and they both knew they might not make it out alive, but then, neither would the escaped cons.

Karl took a head count, and he wasn't happy with what he found. Two more men had slipped away that morning: Adams and Markham. And they had taken more than their share of food and grenades. Karl shook his head in disgust. They didn't have two weeks' supplies left. Jesus, everything was coming unglued. All the careful planning was for nothing.

"The stupid bastards. They may as well just give the supplies to those old men, 'cause they're damn sure going to get them . . . one way or the other."

"And put Adams and Markham down when they do," Newton added.

"You got that right," Karl agreed.

"So what are we gonna do, Karl?"

Karl sighed wearily. "Damned if I know."

Twenty-Four

Jack and his people, including Abby, moved across the valley floor at dusk and got into position facing the caves on the ridge. Lindsey, Judy, and Andy were left back at the camp with Max, Dennis with them as guard. Abby and Judy had drawn a crude map, pinpointing the caves where they knew hostages were being held.

"You boys are fully aware that the cons could kill the hostages during our attack, or use them for shields to make their escape?" Hawk had asked.

The men nodded in understanding, Ted saying, "We know."

"If they want to deal, we'll deal," Jack said. "Their freedom for the hostages' safety. However it goes, this has got to end. We've been running on luck for days. But luck can leave us as fast as it came."

"Let's face it and tell the truth," Dennis said. "We're tired, and tired people make mistakes. In this game, one mistake and we're dead. We've got to end this."

"One way or the other," Harry said softly, but with a grimness in his words.

Hawk cut his eyes to Bert. "You got anything to add, Bert?"

The guide shook his head. "I want to see my wife and assure her I'm all right. Then I want a hot meal and a bath. The sooner the better. Let's get this done and over with."

Before they left the group of men had all cut their eyes to Andy and the women. Andy had nodded his head in understanding of their silent gazes. "We'll be all right," Andy said. "I'll do what is necessary to stay alive and to keep the others alive. But I won't kill unless it's absolutely imperative."

Both Bert and the sheriff had sighed at that last bit. Ted had lowered his eyes and silently cursed his son's attitude. Harry had a disgusted expression on his face. "I'll stay back here," Dennis said. "Someone's got to do it."

"I know a little something about weapons," Abby had said. "My father was a hunter, and I used to fire his rifles. I can handle an M-sixteen . . . I think. I'll go with you guys. Believe me, I have a deeply personal score to settle with that bunch of perverted filth."

"I reckon you do, Abby," Bert said. "All right. Let's check you out with a weapon."

The men and Abby were now in position in the brush and ravines below the ridge and the caves, stationed thirty-five to forty yards apart. They would open fire as soon as targets presented themselves. Whoever spotted the first target could have him. And the first con to show himself was spotted by Abby.

"Bledsoe, you rotten bastard," Abby breathed, and pulled the M-16 to her shoulder. She had forgotten that the selector switch was on rapid fire, in bursts. She shot Bledsoe all over the place, several of the rounds taking him in the neck and face. He was finished before he hit the rocky ground.

Another ran out and Bert drilled him in the belly with his .30-30. A third, realizing what was happening, turned to beat it back into the cave. Harry plugged him low in the back, the slug knocking the man to his knees. Howling in rage and pain, the escaped con, for some reason turned to face his attackers, and Harry shot him in the neck.

Jack was using the high-powered bolt-action rifle on this assault, and he was deadly with it. On his first shot he put a round into the center of a con's chest. The second round slammed into a man's stomach.

After that, the rest of the escaped murderers, rapists, and child molesters elected to remain in the caves, safe from their attackers deadly aim.

"I never thought they'd pull something like this," Karl muttered. "The bastards are a gutsy bunch."

"Let's kill a couple of the hostages and toss their bodies out so the old farts can see them," Hobby suggested. "That'll show them we mean business."

Karl sighed with a patience he did not feel. "That wouldn't be smart, Hobby. These guys are tough. I underestimated them from the start."

Hobby didn't understand what Karl was talking about, but he nodded as if he did. "Ah . . . so what are we gonna do, Karl?"

"Wait. I got a hunch these guys will deal. But not if we harm the hostages."

"Oh. Right. Now I gotcha, Karl. Yeah. That's plenty smart of you, man."

Karl exhaled as he shook his head. An amazing number of cons were brilliant. Others were just average. The rest were like Hobby.

Karl walked to near the front of the cave, being careful to stay close to the wall, and hollered, "Okay, guys. You hear me?"

"Just barely," Jack yelled. "But clear enough. What's on your mind?"

"So you have us pinned down. It won't last long. Guards from the north and south ends of the valley will be here in a couple of hours." He cleared his throat. "But not all the guards. You get my drift?"

"Yeah. We get it. You think we can't handle them when they show up?"

"Not without losing some people, you won't."

"Not near as many as you're going to lose, Buster."

Karl smiled. The tough old bastard was right about that . . . that is, if he had called the guards in, which he hadn't done, not yet.

"But we can lose twice your number and still be way ahead of you guys, Pop. You'd better think about that. We got the high ground. And you don't have enough people to take it."

"It'll take your guards a while to get here, Buster," Jack called. "We can do a lot of damage before then. We know which caves the hostages are being held. We can avoid firing into those caves. But in the caves where just your cons are hiding . . . well, you ever seen what a bullet does when it starts ricocheting around rock walls?"

Karl smiled, but it was more a grimace. The old bastard was sure no dummy. He had been up and down the pike a few times, for a fact.

Abby wanted very much to call out and tell the cons that she was now armed and wanting desperately to kill the whole damn bunch of them. But she remained silent out of concern for her husband—a concern that she really did not feel all that strongly or deeply. he *was* still her husband, even though Abby knew that once this trip was over, providing any of them got out alive, the marriage was finished.

"You want to deal, Pop?" Karl called.

"We can talk about it, Sonny Boy," Jack replied. "What's on your mind? A trade, maybe?" He mentally crossed his fingers for good luck.

"No dice, Pops. We do something like that, then you hold all the cards. You're gonna have to come up with something better than that."

"What else is there?"

"That seems to be a problem, doesn't it?"

"Then we can trade for some of the hostages. The women and the kids, maybe?"

"And we keep the hairy legs, right?"

"That'll work. How about it?"

"I don't think so, Pop. We lose the women and the young cunts, we lose the upper hand."

Jack had known the suggestion would be rejected. He'd only made it in an attempt to bring some peace between Ted and his son. He could tell Andy that he did try to negotiate a trade. Ted could not hear what was being said; he was about a hundred yards away.

"So we continue to snipe away at you people," Jack called. "We've got enough supplies to last us a long time. If we don't make some contact with our families in a few days, they'll alert the authorities and this place will be swarming with cops—local, state, and federal, ground and air. Now what do you have to say, Buster?"

"My name's not Buster."

"I know. It's Karl Parsons," Jack called.

"Damn!" Karl muttered just as his sister came up to stand beside him.

"Good morning, Karl," Hawk called. "I'm Sheriff Hawkins. You probably have heard of me one time or another. I know your sister has. How you doing, Karl?"

"Jesus Christ," Karl said. "The new guy is a cop."

"And a good one, too," Kathy said. "I know all about Sheriff Hawkins. He runs one of the strictest law and order counties in the state. He don't deal, and he don't mess around with nobody. He don't care who you are. Rich or poor, you break the law, you're going to the bucket. How in the hell did he get into this valley? Why is he here?"

"He got in over the rocks and cliffs at the other end, Kathy," her brother told her. "Why? Hell, I don't know. Maybe he's on vacation. You can bet he didn't come in without telling someone where he was going. Goddamnit!"

Kathy looked around her. No one else was close enough to overhear what was being said between the brother and sister. "Let's stall until nightfall, Karl, then cut out of here. Just you and me—"

"I told you, Sis—some of these guys know my plans." He shook his head. "I cut out, and everything I so carefully worked out is blown to hell."

"Would you rather be dead or back in the joint?" she asked softly. "Those seem to be your only choices. I'd give that some thought."

Karl sighed. She was right. His choices were limited, and getting fewer and more difficult with each day that passed. "You may be right, Sis," he whispered. "Hell, you are right. No question about it. But we're going to be short on supplies. We won't be able to take much with us without alerting the others."

His sister smiled. "You think I came in here without a backup plan, brother? I've got three small caches of supplies between here and town. I can lead us right to the horses real easy."

Karl smiled. Maybe he would keep Kathy around. She was showing a lot of sense he didn't know she had. Yeah. The two of them could make Bonnie and Clyde look like kitty cats . . . and from everything Karl had read about that pair, they were nothing but a couple of simpleminded punks. Karl was well-read. In the bucket, he got that way. And if whatever they planned lasted six days or six years, they could go out in a blaze of glory, as the saying went. Yeah, by God. Karl liked the thought. He liked it a lot.

"What about it, Karl?" Kathy pressed a breast up against his arm.

"Yeah. I like it, Sis. I like your plan a lot. Come dusk, we're out of here, you and me."

"Good, Karl. That's great. I'll just ease around a little bit and put together some things. But I'll do it in such a way it won't alarm the others."

"Okay, Baby. We'll do it your way. But we've got to get through this day first."

"That's no sweat, Karl. We'll make it. Just stall those old farts."

"How old is Hawkins, anyway?"

"Oh . . . he's in his early fifties, I guess. But he looks like he's in good shape . . . last time I seen him, anyway. I wouldn't want to mess with him. He's been a cop for over thirty years. And has been involved in several pretty wild shoot-outs. He won them all," she added.

Karl moved closer to the mouth of the cave. "Hey, Hawkins? Can you hear me?"

"Yeah, I can hear you, Karl."

"I got to talk things over with my guys. Maybe we can work something out. I don't know. It's gonna take a while to hash it around."

"Okay, Karl. Now you're being smart." Hawk smiled knowingly and shook his head. He felt one hundred percent certain that Karl wasn't about to cut any deal. The no-good punk was up to something. Bet on that. "We'll wait," Hawk yelled. "But not for too long."

"Okay, Sheriff. I'll get back to you on this deal. Hang loose, man."

Hawk chuckled and did not reply.

"We've got nothing but time, Karl," Jack yelled.

"Yeah," Karl muttered low; only Kathy could hear him. "You have time. But time is something the rest of us don't have much of."

Kathy moved away, deeper back into the dimness of the cave. As she sat down beside her pack she pulled a small rucksack closer to her. The other cons in the cave paid no attention to her.

Hobby moved close to Karl. "What are we gonna do, Karl? We got to do something, man."

"I know, Hobby. I know. But for now, we're all safe in the caves."

"Not if they start bouncing lead around in here, we ain't."

"They won't do that, Hobby."

"How do you know that for sure and certain?"

"Because they don't know exactly where the hostages are being held, that's why."

"But that damn girl and that Abby what's-her-name cunt probably told 'em."

"But they don't know for sure. We might have moved them after Abby escaped. See what I mean?"

"Oh. Yeah. You're right, Karl. Sure. I see what you mean now."

Several hours passed with no shooting from either side. By that time Jack and his group knew that the guards at both ends of the pass had not been notified. The escaped cons could not take the chance of the campers escaping through either end of the unguarded passes. Karl and his group were trapped, at least for the moment. Jack and his people were also trapped—in a different way, but still trapped.

It was still a standoff.

Sheriff Hawkins had slipped over to talk with Jack. Neither man was happy about the situation. Hawk said, "I read Parsons's file before leaving the office the other day. He's a smart one. He got himself a pretty good education in the bucket. You can bet he's up to something, and it'll be tricky."

"Oh, I'm sure of that."

Hawk looked up at the brush in front of the caves. "This isn't worth a damn, Jack. It's still a standoff."

"You're reading my mind, Sheriff. But if we pull out . . . what happens, then?"

"Hell, I don't know. They won't kill the hostages, and we can't rescue them. The cons can't escape, but we aren't a large enough force to overrun them. That would be suicide on our part. The cons have become very cautious now. We're probably not going to get another target. I've been thinking. It'll be ten days or so before any of our friends and family on the outside begins to get worried about us, another couple of days before they report us missing, and another couple of days before help comes into this area to look for us."

"That's two weeks or better."

"You got it."

"We can't hold out another two weeks. Three or four days at the max for us."

"That's right. And that's with going to short rations. That in itself will soon take a toll on us. It's misty and cold at night. Body resistance is going to start to drop to low levels pretty damn quick in here." He looked at Jack. "Are any of you people on any type of medication?"

"Couple of the guys are on blood pressure medicine, but I know they brought a thirty day supply. Other than that, nothing that I know of."

Abby joined them and listened to the exchange for a moment. Both men paused and looked at the woman. "Any suggestions, Abby?" Hawk asked.

She shook her head. "No. I wouldn't trust any of those miserable excuses for human beings. Whatever they might come up with, it'll be a double cross. You can be sure of that. These guys aren't onetime losers and this isn't their first fall. They're all serving multiple life sentences. Some of them are looking at new charges—including murder—and they have absolutely nothing to lose."

"And here's something else," Jack said. "Come dark, I suspect those cons are going to try slipping out, taking the hostages with them . . . at least the women and the young people. The hostages will be gagged so they can't call out. And the cons just might kill one or two just to set an example for the others. And you can bet a large percentage of them will make it through our spread out lines. Then where will we be?"

"There is nothing else they can do to the women," Abby said, her voice filled with anger and bitterness. "Nothing. They've done it all. And the young boys, as well. They've double-teamed all the women, several times."

"Double-teamed?" Jack asked. "I'm not at all sure just what that means."

Abby explained and Jack's face paled.

"You understand now?" she asked.

"Unfortunately, yes," Jack said. "You actually *saw* them do that to women?"

"They did it to me," Abby said softly. "Several times. Why do you think I'm walking so strangely?"

"I thought your feet hurt."

"It's another part of my anatomy that hurts."

Hawk expelled a few seconds of very angry breath. His eyes held a mean glint. "Maybe we could ambush the bastards on their way out . . . and if it ever comes to a court of law, neither of you heard me say that."

"I'll say it was my idea," Jack said, glad the subject was changed. "That's a good idea, Hawk. If we can get them

out, that is. But if we tell them they can just leave, they'll
smell a rat right off."

"We have to make it sweet for them, then. How about
if they release one woman and one man, just to show good
faith on their part? They might go for that."

"It's worth a try. Okay. They might indeed go for it.
Abby, how about you?"

She shrugged her shoulders. "Sounds good to me. It's
sure worth a try. You want me to slip back and get some
opinions from the other guys?"

Jack shook his head. "I'm a hundred percent certain
they'll go along with it."

Hawk cut his eyes to the man. "Including the ambush
part?"

Jack smiled. "Especially that part."

Twenty-Five

Doris Fisher and her husband, Walt, were sent out by the cons in a show of good faith. Walt's face was puffy and bruised from several beatings he'd received, and Doris was nearly in a comatose state. She'd been raped and sodomized and forced to perform oral sex on the men so many times she was in shock.

"She quit speaking two days ago," Walt told the group. "I can't get her to say a word."

"I wish I could tell you she'll soon see a doctor," Jack said. "But I can't."

"I understand," Walt replied.

"How are the rest of the hostages?" Hawk asked as Abby led Doris away from the men and over to a small creek where she could clean up, with Abby's help.

"In bad shape." Walt sat down on the ground and rubbed his sore wrists. "But the boys and girls are in worse shape. One of the teenage boys, Paul Matthews, is dead, shot and killed while trying to escape. He just couldn't take being raped by those perverted sons of bitches any longer."

"They're raping the boys?" Bert asked.

"Some of the cons are, yes. Including our own son, Phil."

The others in the group, including Andy, had joined them, becoming worried as the day dragged on and Jack and his team had not returned. They had marched over to the caves, arriving just as the two hostages were being released.

"The dirty perverted bastards," Bert said.

Andy opened his mouth and quickly closed it when his father gave him a look that would bend a horseshoe.

"That knowledge will make the job ahead of us a damn sight easier," Bert said.

"What job?" Andy could no longer remain silent.

"You just stick around and you'll find out, boy," the guide told him.

"Stay out of it, Andy," his dad warned him. "Just stay out of it."

"We're comin' out!" the shout came from the ridges. "No funny stuff, now. You people start any shit, and the hostages get killed. You understand all that?"

"Come on out!" Jack yelled. "You've still got about five or six hours of daylight left. You head straight south down the valley floor and you can make the pass just before dark. And you leave the hostages there. Agreed?"

"Sure. We said we would, didn't we?" Karl yelled.

"Yeah, right," Hawk said sourly. "When pigs fly, you will."

"Give them a chance," Andy said.

"Kill them," Walt blurted. "Shoot every one of the rotten scum."

"You're just saying that in the heat of anger," Andy told the man.

"Who in the fuck are you?" Walt asked the younger man. "And who in the hell asked for your opinion?"

"Madness," Andy said. "This is madness. You've all reverted to savagery and barbarism."

Walt walked off in search of his wife. His back was stiff with anger, his swollen hands balled into fists.

"You're gonna get your ass whipped yet, Son," Ted told him. "And maybe that's what it's going to take to knock some of that stupidity out of you."

"You *would* think that," Andy retorted. "How typical of your type."

"I'm not believing any of this," Sheriff Hawkins muttered.

"I see them now," Jack called, as he adjusted his binoculars. "They're off the ridge and staying in the timber, close to the valley floor. Good God! There still must be three dozen cons."

"Just about that," Harry said, without lowering his binoculars. "They're stopping now."

"You guys step out where we can see you!" Karl shouted.

"No way," Jack shouted. "That wasn't part of the deal."

"What's the matter, don't you trust us?"

"Hell, no!"

Karl chuckled, a knowing smile creasing his lips. "They're not stupid, I'll give them that."

Kathy gave him a quick glance. Come nightfall, she and her brother would drift away from the others and go it alone. She knew the way.

"What do we do now?" a con called Lippy asked.

"Keep on walking," Karl told him. "What the hell else can we do?"

"They've left their wounded in the caves," Jack said. "I see just one man who appears to be wounded, either in the arm or shoulder."

"They must be in terrible agony," Andy said.

"If I have to listen to much more of this, I think I'm goin' to puke," Bert said.

Andy gave the guide a dirty look. But to the relief of all, he shut up for a moment.

"They're all the way clear of the ridges and the caves," Harry said. "The hostages are in the center of the column. They all appear to have their hands tied behind their backs. Some of them can just barely walk."

"All right, let's get ready to move out," Jack said. "Abby will stay at the rear of our column with Walt and his wife. And Andy," he added.

Abby rejoined the others and Jack handed her his binoculars. "Does that look like the whole bunch to you?"

She studied the line of men and women for a moment, then lowered the binoculars and nodded her head. "Yes. That's the whole bunch. Minus nearly all of the wounded. The man with his arm in a sling is called Lofton. They must have left the other wounded behind. Or killed them," she added.

"Oh, that's ridiculous. They wouldn't do that," Andy said. "They're all friends."

No one responded to Andy's remark. Abby returned Jack's binoculars to him. "Let's go," Jack said.

"I'll look after Mr. and Mrs. Fisher," Abby said. "Walt's a lot shakier than it appears, I think."

"Okay. Yeah. He's not in good shape. And keep an eye on Andy. Try to keep him from doing something stupid."

Abby rolled her eyes.

"If possible," Jack added.

"I heard that!" Andy said.

"Good," Jack told him. "Keep it in mind. It'll be a help to us all. Let's go, people."

As he was walking away Jack heard Andy ask, "What are the men planning, Abby? What is on their minds?"

Jack kept on walking, knowing that Abby would not reply.

If she did, she would profess not to have any knowledge of any plan. She didn't trust Andy, either. Abby was a changed woman in more ways than one. Especially in her views toward society's criminal element.

As Jack took the head of the short column, his smile was as savage as his thoughts. There was no way he and his people were going to allow the entire bunch of escaped convicts to leave the valley ... or even get close to the south pass with the hostages. Oh, some of the convicts would make it clear, maybe half a dozen, maybe a few more. Karl had deliberately made his column a long one, and Jack knew, or felt he knew, that it had been done to give the escaped cons a better chance of surviving in case of ambush.

But Karl's mistake had been in putting all the hostages in the center of the column. Getting the hostages clear was to be up to Sheriff Hawkins, Abby, and Bert. Dealing with the cons was up to Jack and his people.

Approximately halfway to the south pass, Jack dropped back and fell in beside Judy and Lindsey. "Stay close, kids," he said. Max was on a rope leash and walking easily along beside Judy, offering no resistance. "It's going to pop in about another twenty or thirty minutes."

"We'll be ready," Judy said. "What about Andy? I just don't trust that fellow."

"Yeah," Lindsey said, stepping closer. "I know fifteen-year-olds with more sense than he's got."

Jack smiled. The girls had matured quickly over the past few days ... or however long it had been. A week, ten days? Something like that. Hell, it was all a blur. But Jack knew, *knew*, that in most respects, the two girls had lost all vestiges of the innocence of youth at the hands of the cons. He was filled with sorrow at that thought.

"Andy's very naive, girls. This experience has tested him to the maximum."

"He failed the test," Lindsey said. "I think he's a jerk-off."

"He doesn't understand the real world, Kids." *If you* ARE *still kids,* he mentally amended. "He's never faced a real life and death test before. Sadly, there are millions just like him in America."

"Yeah," Judy said. "But it's people like him who have screwed up public schools ... among other things. Ah, what the hell do I know? I'm just a kid."

Jack chuckled. "I'll tell anybody you're a pretty sharp couple of kids, girls."

"Is it going to be over today, Jack?" Lindsey asked.

"For the most part, yes. In about a couple of hours, I would say."

"Yeah. One part of it," Judy said. "But after that comes meeting the press. when they find out we ambushed and killed in cold blood, then what happens to us?"

"The left-wingers might try to bring criminal charges against us. Others will encourage the families of the cons to sue in civil court. That's why I wanted you two to stay clear of this."

"No way," Judy said. "I've got a real grudge to settle with those slimy bastards. I'm in this all the way to the end. I don't really give a big rat's turd about public opinion when it's over. We're the ones who suffered at the hands of those creeps and crud."

"That's the way I feel about it, too," Lindsey stated. "That's the way it's going to be, Jack."

"All right, Girls. Stay loose."

Walking back to the head of the column, Jack said, "Get ready," as he passed each man.

He picked up the pace, moving the column along at quick step until they were just ahead of the convicts and their hostages. Jack and Harry were walking together now at the head of the column. Ted and Dennis had fallen back to the rear. Jack angled the column in toward the convicts, and then as they entered a stand of timber moved them to within a couple hundred yards of the cons and hostages.

"Why are we heading toward the convicts?" Andy asked. "I don't understand this."

No one responded.

Jack would lead them to the edge of the timber, and there they would be about fifty yards from the convicts.

"Where the hell did those old farts go, Karl?" Jans Pendley asked. "I can't see them no more."

"I don't know. But they wouldn't be stupid enough to try anything. They know we'd kill the hostages if they did something stupid."

"Damn right we would. But it makes me nervous 'cause I can't see where they are."

"Relax, Jans. They're on the other side of that stand of timber."

I think we're going to make it out of here, Karl thought.

"Look out!" The shout came from the timber.

"What the hell was that?" Nathan asked.

"It's a trap!" Andy shouted. "They're going to ambush you. Look out."

"Ambush?" Karl said, whirling around.

A rifle cracked and Mark Desmond grunted and grabbed at his chest, then fell face forward to the ground.

The hostages began awkwardly running in all directions, their hands tied behind their backs.

"The sons of bitches!" Karl shouted. "The dirty rotten bastards double crossed us."

"Kill them damn hostages!" a con named Hal yelled, and lifted his rifle.

Harry's rifle barked and Hal went down, the bullet entering his left side just below the armpit and exiting out the right side after blowing his heart apart.

Jack's bolt-action rifle boomed and another con went down, a bullet in his belly. He hit the ground screaming and cursing.

Karl and Kathy headed for the ridges and the timber as the hostages scattered.

"Get down on the ground!" Bert yelled to the hostages. "Hit the ground, all of you, belly down."

Jack and his people opened up on the convicts with everything they had.

The Valley of Death was about to start earning its name again.

Twenty-Six

Karl and Kathy made the timberline and disappeared from sight. About a dozen of the other cons were right behind them, running from the intense fire coming from Jack and his people. The hostages had heeded Bert's shout and hit the ground, hugging the earth as bullets whined above them. Some were sobbing from relief. Others appeared numb.

The dead and the howling, screaming dying littered the ambush site as Jack's entire group now opened up. The hostages were clear of the convicts now, and Jack and his bunch began tossing grenades. The lovely, isolated valley roared with explosions and the rattle of gunfire.

"I give up!" one con yelled.

"Screw you," Judy Post said, and shot him in the belly. "See how you like that foreign object jammed in you, you asshole!"

The convict called Doober ran toward the line of rescuers, yelling his rage and cursing. Four rifles found him and fired. The slugs stopped the man cold in his tracks, knocking him backward to the ground, forever stilling his unwarranted and lopsided outrage.

Dick and Joan Jamison crawled the few remaining yards and fell at Harry's feet.

"Stay down," Harry told the husband and wife. "You're safe now. I'll cut you loose as soon as I get a moment."

"Kill them all," Joan sobbed. "Cut my hands loose and give me a weapon. Goddamn them!"

Patti Matthews had managed to free her hands and had found one of her rapists. He was only slightly wounded when she crawled over to him, a rock in her hand.

"You got to help me, Baby," the rapist begged her. "I'm wounded."

"Oh, sure I will, you rotten son of a bitch," Patti said. Then she raised the rock and proceeded to beat the man's head and face into a bloody pulp. He was unrecognizable when she finally collapsed, exhausted and nearly hysterical, beside him. A torrent of tears, brought on by rage and nearly overwhelming relief, momentarily blinded her. Thoughts of her dead brother, his body rotting next to a dead con in a cave, filled her head.

Sheriff Hawkins lined up a con in his sights and blew him right out of the taxpayers' pocket and sent him to hell.

Abby stitched a con in the back with her M-16 and knocked the running man to his knees. He screamed for a few seconds, then fell over to die face down on the ground.

John Wilson and Sweet Boy made the timber and were safe, at least for the moment.

Hobby, Buster, and Burns had headed in the other direction, running straight north, and disappeared into a ravine.

Nathan, Billy Boy, Gunner, Big Un, and Don sprinted into the timber and vanished.

For many of the other escaped cons, the valley had turned into a raging death trap.

"Are you people the police?" Sandy Monroe asked, looking up at Dennis.

"No," Dennis told her, as the gunfire began to wane. "We're the old farts that have been giving the cons fits."

"You look like Robin Hoods to us," Sandy's husband said.

Dennis smiled. "Just stay down on the ground. It's just about over."

"It will never be over," Sandy muttered, her face pressed against the damp grass of the valley floor. "Not for most of us, it won't."

Another con, finding himself trapped with no escape, stood up and tried to surrender. Ted shot him.

"You murdered that man in cold blood!" Andy raged at his father.

Ted graphically summed up his feelings for Andy. "Oh, to hell with you! When we get out of here, I don't ever want to see or hear from you again."

"That suits me," the son told the father.

Ted turned around and popped his son on the mouth with a balled fist. Andy's feet flew out from under him and he landed on the ground, on his butt, his lips bloody.

"I should have done that a couple of times when you were a smart aleck teenager, boy," Ted told him. "Maybe things would have turned out different."

The gunfire had all but ceased.

"You've all turned into savages," Andy mouthed right back.

Shawn Hayes had crawled into the timber and looked at Andy for a few seconds, astonishment in his eyes. He cut his eyes to Ted. "Have you seen my wife?" he asked.

"She's with us," Ted told him. "She's all right."

"I don't mean to diminish what any of you have been

through," Andy told Shawn, working to free Shawn's swollen hands. "But you're alive. There was no excuse to slaughter the convicts in cold blood. We could have taken them prisoner for the courts to decide their punishment."

Ted looked at his son and shook his head in utter disbelief.

"Cease fire," Jack called. "It's over."

"Hello, old son," the guide Harden said as Bert was cutting the ropes that bound Harden's wrists. "Better late than never."

"Both of you look all right to me," Bert told his old friend. "You're not hurt, are you?"

"Only our pride," Claude told him. "How many of those crap heads got away?"

"About a dozen, I'd guess."

"Let me get my hands on a weapon," Harden said. "Then we'll make short work of any of that crud that's left."

"You guys get some rest first," Hawk said, walking up. "You look about all worn out."

"Hell with rest," Dave said, rubbing his wrists and trying to get some circulation back into his swollen hands. "I want to get that lyin' whore I married in gunsights. That's what I got on my mind."

"Settle down, Dave," Harden told him. "Kathy and that no-count brother of hers got clean away. And don't nobody know this country any better than Kathy. You know that well as the rest of us."

"Yeah," Dave reluctantly agreed. "I know." He looked at Hawk. "You come in here with no two-way, Sheriff?"

"Had one. It got busted somehow. Still can't figure out how it happened. Won't work a lick. Can't get a peep out of the damn thing."

"Don't forget," Jack said, "we've still got guards at both ends of the pass. And we've got a lot of people here who can hardly walk. Some need doctoring in a bad way. We'll do what we can with what we have, but we won't be able to pull out of this area until tomorrow . . . at the earliest."

"Yeah, you're right," Hawk agreed. "The hostages need rest and some food."

"Where is that sorry ass son of mine?" Ted asked. "I can't find him anywhere."

"I haven't seen him, Ted," Dennis said. "Not after you decked him."

"He disappeared right after cutting Shawn loose," Ted said. "At least I lost track of him about then."

"Let's start gathering up weapons and food," Harry suggested. "We're going to need all we can find. We've got quite a crowd now."

"All those dead and wounded have packs full of food and other gear," Dennis said. "I just checked some of them out. By the way, what about the wounded?"

"Piss on them," Bert said. "I'm not liftin' one damn finger to help none of them. Not now, not never. Tattoo that on your arm if you like."

"Me, too," Harden and Claude said as one.

"You can count me in on that," Dave said. "They damn sure get no help from me."

"Some of these men are still alive!" Andy called from the edge of the clearing. He was about seventy-five yards from the main group. "They need medical attention immediately."

"I might have known he'd be out there playing Boy Scout," Ted said.

No one made a move to assist the escaped cons. The newly freed hostages and their rescuers stood and looked at Andy. No one said anything.

"Are you just going to let them die?" Andy called.

"That sounds good to me," Dick Jamison said, limping

up. His face was bruised and swollen from a recent beating at the hands of the convicts.

"What the hell are we going to do with the wounded?" Dennis asked.

A hard silence greeted his question.

Dennis broke the silence. "Suits me."

Dave cleared his throat. "I know a place about two miles from here. It's got a spring and it would be easily guarded. Anybody interested?"

"Let's get a head count and start moving out," Jack said. "Your place sounds good to me, Dave." He smiled and stuck out a hand. "I'm Jack Bailey, by the way."

Dave returned the smile and took the hand. "You guys sure played hell with the convicts' plans."

"We sure tried," Jack replied.

The sound of crying reached the knot of survivors just as Don Stinson walked up.

"That's Mrs. Post," the man explained. "Her daughter's with her. They were both just told that her son was murdered late last night. A convict by the name of Jans Pendley cut his throat when he wouldn't be quiet. One of the other cons, I don't know for sure which one but I think it was John Wilson, had just raped the boy and hurt him pretty badly. The boy was weeping, both from pain and humiliation. They threw his body in a cave with the other dead, including the Matthews boy, Paul."

Ted lost it with that information. "That's it." He pushed the words through lips that had suddenly turned thin and bloodless. "That dots the i and crosses the t for me." He screamed at his son, "Get away from that bunch of trash, boy! I mean right now, right fucking now! Do what I tell you to do, or as God is my witness I'll shoot you myself and leave you for the buzzards and the ants."

Andy straightened up and stared at his father for a moment. The distance was too great to read his expression, but his father's words had struck home. After a few seconds, he began slowly walking back to the main group.

"Go help the decent people, boy," Ted told him. "And don't argue with me. Don't open your damn mouth to me. Just do what I tell you to do. Stay the hell away from that damn trash out in the meadow."

Andy looked at his father for a moment, read his feelings accurately, then slowly walked off toward where most of the recently rescued were gathered.

"Ain't you gonna do something for us?" one of the badly wounded cons yelled.

"Fuck you!" Bert told the man.

"We'll die out here!"

"Good," Harry said.

"Oh, lady!" one of the wounded cons shouted. "You can't do this to me. Please don't do this!"

The group turned and stared. No one made any move to stop Beth Post.

The woman was standing over one of the wounded convicts, a pistol in her right hand. Tears were streaming down her face.

"That's one of the men who raped her son," Harden said. "Forced him to suck him off every day. I don't know his name. Don't give a shit what it is. Mrs. Post is about to do what the courts should have done a long time ago."

Jack looked over at Judy Post. The teenager was standing motionless and expressionless a dozen or so yards from her mother. She held the malamute's leash in one hand. The big dog was sitting patiently on the ground beside her.

Andy stood with the group of rescued, looking at the scene being played out before him. He said nothing.

"I knew you wouldn't have the courage to kill me in cold blood," the wounded convict said.

"You damn filth!" Beth shouted.

"I'll give you odds she shoots him," Dave said.

"I won't take your bet," Hawk said, standing with the others and watching but making no attempt to interfere. "I think she will, too."

"I hope she does," Walt Fisher said, walking up. "The courts should have disposed of the whole damn bunch of them a long time ago."

"Dream on," Dave told the man. "The only way we'll ever return to true justice in this country is to overthrow the government and start all over."

"I'll agree with that," Jack said. "And I never thought those words would ever come out of my mouth."

The wounded con laughed at Beth Post.

Bad mistake on his part.

The pistol in Mrs. Post's hand cracked, the bullet punching a hole in the center of the con's forehead.

"One less," Bert said.

Andy finally found his voice. "My God, what has happened to us all?"

"When justice fails," Hawk said softly, speaking more to himself than to any particular person, "the citizens have a habit of taking over and straightening things out. It just usually takes them a long time to act."

Anne Chambers walked out into the clearing and gently took the pistol from Beth's hand. She led the sobbing woman away from the dead con.

"Well, we've finally done it," Andy said. "We have reverted to barbarism."

"I swear to God," Bert said. "I'm gonna shoot that guy before this is over."

The looks he received from the others silently asked why he hadn't done it before now.

"I don't think I would make any attempt to stop you," Ted said. He sighed and added, "My God, what a terrible thing for a father to say."

No one had anything to add to that.

The few cons who were still alive in the meadow were silent. They knew to a person the group of civilians had been pushed to the max. They did not want to join the con with the hole in his forehead. Living behind bars was a lousy existence, but it was better than being dead.

Jack broke the silence. "Gather up all the gear we can carry. Let's get ready to move out."

"Are we going to leave the cons behind?" Jack was asked. "We'd better settle that right now."

"We're not doctors and we're not guards," Jack replied. "If they live through the next few days we'll come back and do what we can for them. Other than that, I don't see that we're obligated to do anything. Hawk?"

Hawk shrugged his shoulders. "I'll catch hell about it when we get back . . . from some people and the liberal press. But I don't care. I'm in my last term in office. I'm retiring. I've had it with law enforcement. Leaving the wounded cons behind is the only practical thing to do far as I'm concerned. We can't take care of them."

"Andy can stay here and take care of that crap, if that's what he wants to do," Bert said.

"He'd about be dumb enough to do it," Ted replied. "Just about dumb enough. I don't think he'll choose to do that. But if he does?" Ted grimaced and held out his hands in a gesture which said, 'I won't try to stop him.' "He's a grown man," he added. "Physically, if not mentally."

"Well, we'll know in a few minutes," Jack said. "Let's get lined out and ready to march. Has all the gear been taken from the dead and wounded?"

"Almost," Dave said. "Another two or three minutes and we'll be ready to move out."

Most of the hostages were out in the meadow, stripping the bodies of backpacks, rucksacks, and weapons and ammo. None of the few cons still alive said a word to them. They did not dare utter a sound.

When all the gear was taken, Jack looked at Dave. He could clearly read cold revenge in the man's eyes. "We're ready," he said.

"Let's go," Dave said. "It isn't far. Easy walk. We'll be there about an hour 'fore dark."

"Lead the way," Jack said.

Twenty-Seven

The rescued hostages had gotten together after making camp and cleaning up and putting on some clean, if a bit mildewy, clothing and having a hot meal and some coffee—the first coffee they'd tasted since their capture. They'd come up with a number of convicts still on the loose.

"About twenty," Claude said. "Maybe a couple more than that. That's not counting the guards posted at the north and south ends of the pass."

"Say twenty-five cons still on the loose," Hawk said. "That's quite a force to be reckoned with."

"They scattered in all directions," Harry said. "But I suppose they could all get together."

"Even if they did they would be thinking on ways to escape," Jack said, "not attacking us. They would know that we're heavily armed now, and they would also find the bodies of the dead and dying in the meadow. But we'd still better stay on high alert and be ready for anything."

"You bet," Harden agreed. "At least two people on guard at all times. Four if we can do it. And we shoot any con we see on sight."

"I'll damn sure go along with that," Claude said. "No questions asked, and no offer of surrender. I'll be god-damned if I'll take any of that scum back to safety."

The men and several of the women nodded in agreement.

"This spot that Dave led us to is great," Dennis said. "We can all use the rest and a good clean up—something I'm sure looking forward to, and no smart ass remarks from any of you guys about that," he added with a grin. "But we've got to get out of this valley and back to town."

"Agreed," Jack said. "But surviving the cons still at large while we get out of this valley has got to be number one on our list."

"And that means walkin' out," Bert said. "Several days of hoofin' it and probably half a dozen or more firefights along the way." He frowned. "That means several days will be stretched into about five full days gettin' out of here."

"Yeah," Claude said. "We've got to be careful. I don't want to lose any people this close to bein' clear."

"So we head out at dawn," Jack said. "Which one of you guides want the first gig at point?"

"I'll take it," Harden said. "And I hope I get one of those cons who punched me around in gunsights. I really would like that."

"I'm fairly certain you'll get your wish," Hawk told him. "I'll make you a bet we'll meet up with them, probably in small bunches."

"That suits the hell out of me," Harden said.

"And me," his partner echoed. "I got some loose teeth right now from gettin' punched around by those bastards while my hands were tied behind my back. I got a score to even up. And I'm lookin' forward to it."

Jack looked at each person standing close by. They were primed and cocked and ready for a fight . . . wanting a fight. He sure couldn't blame them for wanting to settle the score. "I think we'll all get our wish about a fight. So, right now, let's get some sleep. We need rest," Jack said. "I'll post guards."

"That rest and sleep suggestion sure sounds good to me," Hawk said. "Wake me up whenever you want me to stand a guard shift. I'll be ready."

"One more thing," Harry said. "How is Mrs. Post?"

"She's better," Janet Stinson said. "If I could have gotten my hands on a gun I'd have done exactly what she did. And I still will if I get the chance."

"Mrs. Fisher?" Hawk asked.

"Still not talking. But she's alert and appears to be coming around slowly."

"She's led a very quiet and sheltered life," Anne Chambers said. "She just couldn't take this mentally, and she retreated behind a wall. She's going to need some professional help once we get out of here. Right now, I agree with Jack. Let's all get some much needed rest."

Karl and Kathy had reached the south pass and spoken with the two guards there, telling them about the ambush. Just as they finished talking, Sweet Boy, John Wilson, and Big Un showed up and flopped down on the ground, exhausted.

"What a fuck up," Big Un said. "Everything's gone to hell. And to make matters worse, I've had to put up with those two old fags for hours."

Sweet Boy gave him the Rigid Digit, and John Wilson giggled.

Big Un sighed. "You see what I mean? It's disgustin.'

We lost some good men back in the clearing and these two damned old queens make it without gettin' a scratch.''

"Life can sometimes be so unfair," Sweet Boy said. "I shall miss those young lads terribly."

"Oh, shit!" Big Un said. "See what I mean?"

"Knock it off," Karl ordered. "We've got to make up our minds about something right now. Do we cut and run and every man for himself, or stand and fight and keep those people penned up until we kill them all?"

"The horses broke loose and got away," one of the guards told him. "Me and Shorty seen them this morning."

"Yeah," Shorty said. "They wasn't goin' nowheres. They was just standin' around chomping on grass."

"So we're on foot," Big Un said. "Well, that tears it. For a fact, it does."

"What do you mean, Big Un?" the second guard asked.

"We can't get out of this damn place fast enough without horses. Them old farts and the sheriff and the others will either be just ahead of us or right behind us. There'll be ten thousand cops waitin' on us."

"Big Un's right," Kathy said. "We can't let those people get out ahead of us. We can't let them out, period. They've got to be killed. All of them."

"So we stay here and fight?" Shorty asked, doubt in his voice. "I don't know about that. I say we cut and run now. Least we'll have a chance of making it clear."

"Then cut and run," Karl told him. "No one is holding you here. If you want to be on your own, fine with me. Can you find your way out, Shorty?"

Shorty looked very uncomfortable for a few seconds. "Alone?" he asked.

"That's right."

He shook his head. "I guess not, Karl."

"Then we're in this together, all the way?"

"Sure, Karl," the other guard, Ned, quickly said. Ned

was from Chicago and had been hopelessly lost ever since the prison breakout.

Neither Karl nor Kathy made any mention of their original plan to bug out from the group before the ambush.

"They can't get out the north end," Kathy said. "I know that for a fact. So that means they've got to come this way."

"So we wait here and kill them," Karl said.

"I wish some of the others would join us," Shorty said. "I'd feel a whole lot better."

"Most of the others are dead," Karl informed him. "That valley floor is littered with the dead and dying. Those old farts know what they're doing."

"Most of them are *dead?*" Ned asked.

"Yes," Kathy told him. "We got shot all to pieces. I figure no more than fifteen to eighteen escaped from the ambush."

It was more like twenty-five. But they wouldn't all link up again . . . except perhaps in hell.

"Dead," Ned said softly. "Damn. I had a couple of real good buddies back there. We was in Joliet together. They was some nice guys, too."

"How touching," Sweet Boy said. "Do you want me to hold you and comfort you a little, Ned?"

"You put your fuckin' hands on me, Sweet Boy, and I'll kill you," Ned snarled.

Sweet Boy winked at the man and giggled.

"Disgusting," Shorty said. "Makes me sick at my stomach."

Sweet Boy blew kisses at Shorty.

Shorty walked away from the small group and looked out over the valley from his vantage point on the high ridges. He blinked a couple of times, then lifted his binoculars and stared for a moment. "Hey!" he shouted. "Here comes a bunch of our guys. 'Bout ten of them, looks like."

"Oh, I hope they brought that lovely boy Phil with

them," John Wilson said. "I've missed him. He has the cutest and tightest little booty."

"Goddamn!" Ned said. "You're as bad as Sweet Boy, John. And I didn't think anyone could be that bad."

Karl took the binoculars and studied the men below, then lowered the binoculars and smiled. "Some pretty tough ole' boys in that bunch. And it looks like they all managed to hold onto their weapons and packs. I think we might make it out of here."

"I just want to get back to Chicago," Ned said. "That's all I want. Just get me back home. I got friends there."

"They're all in the joint or dead," Karl told him. "Time passes, Ned. This is the first time in ten years you've been outside of the bucket."

Ned at first looked startled, then slowly shook his head. "I guess you're right, Karl. Time passes." He shrugged. "I still want to get back to Chicago."

"Well, maybe you will, Ned. I hope we all get out of this mess."

Sweet Boy looked at Karl, a sad smile on his lips. Sweet Boy was no fool. He knew the odds of getting out alive were slim to none.

"I want to get back to Los Angeles," John Wilson said wistfully. "I just love that city." Then he started softly singing "City of Angels."

No one else had anything to add. They fell silent, each with his own thoughts of freedom. Ned stood up on the edge of the ridge and waved his arms to attract the attention of the group below.

"They just made it here in time," Kathy broke the silence, as the new group began climbing up the rocks. "It'll be dark in a few minutes."

"We'll all get some rest and some food," Karl said. "Tomorrow will be the day that tells the rest of the story. One way or the other."

"And I don't believe it's going to have a happy ending for any of us," John Wilson muttered.

"Did you say something, John?" Karl asked.

"Nothing of any importance, Karl." He smiled. "Like us—nothing of any importance."

"Well, you can damn sure speak for yourself about that, faggy," Shorty told him. "I'm plenty important."

"To whom?" John asked.

Shorty thought about that for a few seconds, opened his mouth to speak, then thought better of it. He shook his head and gave John the finger. He looked over at Big Un, but the con was sound asleep, stretched out on the ground.

"That bastard can sleep anywhere, any time," Shorty said. "I never seen anyone like him."

"He realizes his importance," John said. "And sleeps the sleep of the totally useless. And if there was ever anyone totally useless, it's Big Un."

Karl looked over at John, studying the man for a moment. He didn't want to get in an argument with John Wilson. Karl was smart. John Wilson was borderline brilliant, but crazy as a road lizard. Read all the time, any thing he could get his hands on. Listened to really highbrow music whenever he could.

John met Karl's eyes. "You have anything to add to this vocal exercise in futility, Karl?"

"I probably could, John. But what would be the point?"

John Wilson laughed and stood up. "I think I shall join Big Un in slumber. I certainly have no inclination to greet anyone in that pack of cretins soon to join us."

"Why don't you take a flyin' leap off this ridge?" Shorty suggested. "That would sure make me happy."

"Oh, knock it off!" Kathy told them. "All of you. I'm tired of listening to your bullshit."

"Stupid cunt," John Wilson muttered, too low for anyone to hear . . . or so he thought. "The bull dykes will have a wonderful time with you in prison."

Kathy looked at him and grinned. "Men, women, don't make any difference to me. I can get off either way."

Ned had walked up and was listening. "That's the sound I heard back at the caves, wasn't it? You lickin' around on that Post girl. I thought maybe that was it."

"Disgusting," Shorty said.

Kathy shrugged off the criticism. It made no difference to her what anyone thought. She would take sex wherever she found it, and with whatever gender was readily available at the moment. There had been whispers about her in her community for years. Dave had never heard them.

Jans Pendley was the first one to climb up the ridge and flop down on the ground beside Karl.

"Glad you see you, Jans. Tough go back there, wasn't it?"

"We lost about half our boys and all the hostages," Jans replied, after taking several long drinks of water from his canteen.

"Any survivors among them?"

"Damn few. If there was, the old farts and the hostages finished them off."

"In cold blood?" Ned asked.

"Cold blood, hot blood, what difference does it make?" Jans asked.

"Straight folks don't usually act like that," Ned replied. "That's the difference. They're pissed off and they've got blood in their eyes. Don't expect mercy from any of them, 'cause you damn sure won't get it."

Big Un had sat up and was listening. When Ned finished, he said, "This time we kill them all, right off the bat. We don't jack around with any prisoners. We should have done that first thing, anyway. Then we wouldn't be in this mess."

"We wouldn't have had no pussy, either," Jans pointed out.

"I swear to God, Jans," Big Un said. "If anyone was to cut open your head, all they'd find is a bunch of little pussies, all workin' gapped open."

Jans grinned at him. "You're about right, Big Un. I do like my pussy."

"I have missed you, Baby," Kathy said, smiling at Jans.

"Well, we can sure do something about that."

Karl sighed. "Then go somewhere back behind those rocks and fuck. And don't make too damn much noise. I have to think."

"There ain't nothin' to think about, Karl," Big Un said. "We kill them all and be done with it."

Karl nodded his head. "Yeah. I do believe you're right, Big Un. We'll just kill them all."

Twenty-Eight

The clouds and mist that had been hanging low for days vanished the next morning, and the sun broke through. It couldn't have happened at a worse time. Visibility went from a few hundred yards to unlimited in a matter of a few minutes, catching Jack and his people and the freed hostages out in the open, near the mouth of the south pass.

"There they are!" one of the cons yelled from the rocks.

"Scatter!" Jack shouted. "Get behind whatever cover you can find."

The cons opened up from the high ground. Dennis went down, a bullet in his arm. Bert helped the man to cover, ripped open his left shirtsleeve, and began working on the bullet wound.

"I'll live," Dennis said through gritted teeth. "It doesn't look too bad."

"But it's gonna hurt like the devil," Bert told him as bullets howled around them.

Dennis forced a grin. "You're telling me?" he jokingly asked.

Hawk lined up a con in his sights and squeezed the trigger. He was shooting uphill and the shot went high, smacking Van in the center of his face. The 7mm slug opened his head up like a rotten cantaloupe and splattered Dick Gordon with blood and brains. Van tumbled down the slope, rolling over slowly and finally coming to rest near the bottom.

Dick was hollering in panic, working desperately to wipe Van's head off his face and jacket front. "Oh, shit!" he yelled. "I got his damn head all over me."

Jack got the con in cross hairs and smiled as he lined him up clean. The shot took Dick in the center of his chest and sat him back on his butt. Dick Gordon looked down at his chest for a few seconds, astonishment on his face. He cussed once, then fell over dead.

Karl and Kathy exchanged glances and both of them began slowly working their way backward into the rocks and brush. The returning fire from the campers below was so intense none of the cons on the ridge noticed that Karl and Kathy were gone.

Billy Boy's rifle jammed and he made the mistake of standing up as he tried to clear it. Claude drilled him clean in the belly, about two inches above the belt buckle. Billy Boy began screaming in pain. His screaming lasted only a few seconds as Harden lined him up and shot him in the neck. Billy Boy stumbled backward and died in the rocks.

Judy Post got off a good shot that struck Scott Craig in the chest and knocked him spinning. He dropped his rifle and stood up without thinking what he was doing. Judy shot him again, the slug striking him in the hip, sending him sprawling to the rocky ground.

Karl and Kathy had cleared the pass, putting The Valley of Death behind them as they quickly moved away.

* * *

Hundreds of miles to the west, Randy O'Donnell had located Jack Bailey's residence and was disappointed to find the house locked up. He drove on. He could wait. It had taken him several days and a lot of help from his organization to put together the whole story of the four ex-soldiers who had been friends for over forty years.

"I'll find you all," Randy muttered, as he drove past the home. "And when I do, I'll kill you. One by one."

He smiled and drove back to his safe house, provided him by the men and women in the United States-based part of his worldwide organization.

In Ireland, a man opened a hand-delivered packet. He looked at the plane tickets, then opened the sealed envelope. He read the message quickly, then burned it. He packed a suitcase, showered and dressed, and caught a bus to the airport. An hour later he was on his way to America.

Claude triggered off a round that caught Bruce in the upper chest, just a few inches below his neck. Shorty ran over to help him and four rifles barked, all four slugs finding their mark. Shorty went down, dead before he hit the rocky ground.

Rip stood up in a nearly blind panic and tried to make a run for it. Hawk's 7mm mag boomed and Rip fell forward on the ground, his spinal cord severed and his heart blown apart.

"Jesus Christ!" Buddy yelled. "We're gettin' slaughtered. I'm outta here." He turned and Claude's rifle cracked. Buddy went down, his blood staining the ground and the rocks.

John Wilson and Sweet Boy began crawling away. They made it into a line of huge jutting rocks and continued crawling until they were in thick brush. Only then did they get to their feet and start walking away as quickly as possible. But they got turned around in the rocks and came out on the valley floor, about fifty yards from where Walt Fisher was positioned.

Walt spotted them before they spotted him and opened up with his M-16. John Wilson went down first, his face, neck, and chest pocked with bloody holes.

Sweet Boy panicked at the sight and tried to run. Walt's rifle popped again, and Sweet Boy fell to his knees, his shoulder and right arm smashed by 5.56 rounds. He cursed the unknown assailant and tried to get up, staggering and falling against a jutting stone. Walt fired again, the round striking Sweet Boy in the center of his face and forever ending his span here on earth.

Dave began bouncing lead off the rocks behind the cons, and the results were terrible. One flattened ricochet slammed into the back of Newton Holmes's head and exited out his jaw. Newton died where he squatted without making a sound.

Buster, the con who hated dogs, lined up Beth Post in sights and was just applying a trigger squeeze when a grenade thrown by Don Stinson (who had gone to college on a baseball scholarship as a pitcher) exploded only a few yards behind him and splattered bits and pieces of Buster all over the rocks. Ted handed Don another grenade, and the younger man chunked it. The grenade landed between Gunner Monroe and Don and blew both men straight into the warm embrace of Satan.

Wayne and Bruce tried to run and half a dozen rifles began stuttering, the lead howling around the rocks and tearing into flesh. Both men were dead within minutes.

"That's it for me," Big Un said. "Those people are pissed off, and goin' to win this fight. I'm outta here." Big Un began inching slowly backward into the brush, staying on his belly. A few of the others looked around, saw what was happening, and began following him.

Gradually, the gunfire from the rocks began to diminish. Then it ceased altogether as the remaining cons made their careful way to safety.

By now, Karl and Kathy were a good mile and a half away from the mouth of the south pass and putting as much distance behind them as the terrain allowed.

Hawk was the first one to make a dash for the rocks, Jack following half a minute later. Ted was next, followed by Dave, Bert, Claude, and Harden. Dennis's arm was broken just above the elbow. He wanted very much to be in on what nearly all believed would be the final assault in the valley, but Beth and Lindsey held him back.

"Take it easy, Mr. Jackson," Lindsey told him. "You've got a broken arm, and we just got the bleeding stopped from that bullet wound."

"The same damn thing happened in Korea and in 'Nam," Dennis said.

"You were wounded?"

"Yes. Once in the leg, then in the side. They say the third time is the charm, but it must not apply to me."

"You're alive," Beth told him. "We all are, thanks to you people."

"I hope those guys are careful up there in the rocks."

"They will be," Lindsey said. "We've made it this far. They're not going to get careless now."

Hawk looked at the bodies sprawled among the rocks. There was blood splattered everywhere, and one of the men caught close to the grenade blast had lost an arm. Another one had lost part of his face.

"Quite a mess," Harden said, stepping into the rocks.

"You'll forgive me if I can't work up a lot of sympathy," Jack said.

"Help me," Scott Craig begged.

"Help you do what?" Ted asked. "You people started this crap. Not us."

"Man, I'm hurt bad!" Scott moaned.

"And we're days from civilization and hospitals," Claude told him. "With no way to transport you."

"Y'all could carry me," Scott suggested.

"Go to hell," Harden told him, then walked on to check out the rest of the dead and dying.

"Nice folks," Scott whispered.

"What the hell would you know about nice people?" Dave asked him.

A mean look drifted into Scott's eyes. "I bet your wife's fuckin' someone right about now. She managed to make it out of here alive. She might be fuckin' two at once. She likes it that much."

Dave smiled. "She can screw a grizzly if she wants to. And speaking of bears, that's just one of the things you'll have to worry about when we leave you. They can smell a blood scent miles away."

Panic suddenly replaced the ugly look in Scott's eyes. "You ain't gonna leave me behind, are you? Not really, I mean. That wouldn't be decent."

"Look who's talking about decent," Harry said, shaking his head in disbelief. "That's pretty much like a buzzard complaining about table manners."

The men made sure there was no weapon close to the wounded man and walked on. Scott cussed them as they moved away.

Two other cons were alive, but not for long. Jack and the others began gathering up all the food, water, weapons and other gear.

"Ain't you gonna leave me any water?" Buddy gasped.

Bert looked at him for a moment, then tossed a canteen to the ground and kept on walking.

"I hope the others kill you all!" Buddy called. "I hope

they gut shoot you and leave you to die. I hope it takes you days to die, you rotten bastard."

"Yeah, yeah," Bert said, and walked away.

"The others cleared out," Hawk said, as the group assembled near the mouth of the pass. I figure eight or ten of them."

"Let's get this gear distributed and get the hell out of here," Jack suggested. "We've got a long walk ahead of us."

"That's for sure," Bert said. "Oh, my achin' feet."

Claude looked at the guide and smiled. "Maybe we'll get lucky and find the horses."

"And maybe God will send a flamin' chariot down from the heavens to take us into town," Harden said. "But I wouldn't count on neither."

Everyone standing close by laughed at the expression on Harden's face.

"You're really going to leave the wounded behind?" Andy asked, to no one's surprise.

The group just looked at him.

"There are wounded men in the caves," Andy added.

"You want us to leave you some supplies?" Ted asked his son. "Then you could stay behind and play nursemaid to all these wonderful people. There should be some help back here in four/five days."

"That would be nice," Bert said. "Then I won't have to listen to your damn mouth anymore."

Andy turned away and found his pack. He had no more to say on the subject ... at least for the moment. But the silence wouldn't last long, and no one expected it to, especially Ted. The rift between father and son had widened with each day. Ted had reached the point where he didn't give a damn if he ever saw his son again.

Jack and Hawk looked around and carefully hid the surplus weapons and ammo in the timber. When they returned to the valley floor the group was ready to move out. Dennis's arm was in a sling and he was in pain, but no complaint passed his lips.

"I'll take the point," Hawk said. "Jack's volunteered to take the drag. Let's move out, people. Heads up all the time. There is still danger out there."

The group walked out of the valley. In only a few minutes, they could no longer hear the wild cursing of Scott Craig as he lay dying among the rocks.

The survivors saw no more of the escaped cons the rest of that day, and made good time as they began their march back toward civilization, covering about eight miles over some very rough country. That night, after a hot meal and coffee, Jack posted guards covering all four directions— each person would pull a two hour shift—and the men and women all got about eight hours of much needed rest.

They were up and moving the next day right after dawn, with everyone feeling much better. Doris Fisher had come full circle, and was talking once more. Her mind had just clicked off for a time to escape the harsh treatment at the hands of the cons. She said she'd first realized what was happening during the shoot-out near the rocks at the mouth of the valley.

"The horses have gone back to home pasture," Bert said, getting up from a squat after inspecting a number of hoofprints. He found a stick and poked at a pile of road apples. "They passed by here a couple of days ago. They should be back home by now. When they show up, there'll be folks all over the place looking for us."

"Maybe they'll send helicopters to pick us up?" Dick Jamison said wistfully. Both he and his wife were in the roughest shape of all. Neither of them had been in good physical condition when they started this trip.

"They probably will do just that as soon as we're spotted," Hawk said. Then he smiled and added, "When we get about five miles from town."

Everyone groaned and laughed and the group got wearily to their feet and moved out.

No one among them knew which direction the cons had taken when they slipped away from the mouth of the valley. None of the guides could pick up any signs of them heading toward town, at least by the route the survivors were taking. For the cons, it was good that they did take another route, for this bunch was ready for a fight, and mentally prepared to give a hell of a lot more than they got if that occurred.

Once, they all thought they heard shooting coming from the north. But the sounds were faint and none could be sure if was gunfire they'd heard.

In the middle of the afternoon of the second day after leaving the valley, several tiny black dots appeared in the western skies, preceded by the familiar *ka-whapping* sounds of huge helicopter blades.

The group paused and smiled as the dots grew larger and took shape. The choppers slowly circled as the survivors began waving.

For most of the survivors, the ordeal at the hands of the escaped convicts was over.

For others, the final deadly scene had yet to be played out.

And they all still had to meet the press.

Twenty-Nine

The survivors of the long ordeal were helicoptered into town and taken to a hospital, where they were examined. All spent their first night of freedom secluded in hospital rooms. Most of the men were released the next morning and escorted by federal marshals to a local motel, where rooms had been reserved for them. The women were kept at the hospital for further examinations, including tests for AIDS. Phil Fisher was scheduled for surgery to repair his torn anus. Federal marshals provided security for the survivors at the hospital and the motel.

Then the press—state, national, and international—descended on the Montana town like a swarm of locusts. Much to their chagrin, they were kept away from the survivors . . . for a time.

Federal marshals, FBI and ATF agents, and state police helicoptered into what the press was already calling The Valley of Death. The press was ordered to keep out for twenty-four hours. Many ignored that order, saying they didn't hear it, and hired private choppers to take them into the back country. Some even got very graphic shots, both still and tape, of the dozens of bodies.

There were three survivors among the cons, so far, and they made statements through their attorneys about the events that took place in The Valley of Death.

Most of the press treated the story in a neutral fashion: it was a sensational story, and they reported it as fairly as they knew how. But some left-wing members of the press (and a few national talk-show hosts—radio and TV), immediately began having public and very vocal snits about the rights of criminals. The attorneys representing the escaped cons gravitated to those types like metal shavings to a magnet.

Jack Bailey wadded up a newspaper and threw it across the motel room in disgust. "That makes me want to puke," he said.

"Well, we knew it was coming," Harry replied. "We talked about it."

"Yeah, but I never felt my own son would make such statements," Ted said. "He's painted us with a damn dark brush. According to Andy, we're all a bunch of slobbering, bloodthirsty savages."

Both Jack and Harry shrugged their shoulders in reply. Andy's statements to the press hadn't surprised either of them one little bit.

Dennis was being kept in the hospital for another day: his arm had become infected. It was nothing terribly serious, but the doctors wanted to keep an eye on him for a day or two.

The wives of the four old friends were sailing somewhere in the Greek isles, and the government had notified them about the ordeal, assuring the women that their husbands were okay and sent their love. No need to disrupt their vacation. Of course, that suggestion was something the women immediately ignored. They were on their way home.

"Maybe when they get here," Jack said, a smile playing on his lips, "we can all go camping?"

Ted looked at him for a moment, then said, "Where's my gun? I'm gonna shoot that man."

"Please do," Harry said.

Karl Parsons and his sister, Kathy, hid on the edge of the back country, about a mile from a privately owned ranch on the border of the park. They had successfully avoided dozens of police and federal agents for three days, and the searchers had moved on to another sector.

Only one of the escaped cons still at large had been captured, badly wounded. Burns had tried to shoot it out with the agents and had been shot several times. He was not expected to live. The rest were still at large and presumed to be still in the wild back country . . . somewhere in the thousands and thousands of acres of wilderness.

"No one there now except for old man Snyder and his wife," Kathy said.

"An old man runs this huge spread by himself?"

"There is no spread any longer. Just the few acres around the house. The government let him and his wife stay on until they die. All the rest is park."

"How far is town from here?"

"Twenty-five miles north, and thirty miles south. That's it. Straight west is more wilderness and mountains."

"And past that? I can't remember. It's been so damn long since I've been here."

"Take it easy, Karl. We're nearly home free, Baby."

"I'll believe that when I see it."

"Just past that is a major highway, and beyond that is

an Indian reservation. Past that is hundreds of miles of more wilderness.''

Karl was silent for a moment, thinking about the few options left him.

"We just saw the nurse from social service leave. They check on the Snyders every week—Make sure they have all their medicine and so forth. All their kids are long gone and moved away. All their friends their own age are either dead or in a damn old folks home somewhere. I doubt if anyone calls out here. We're home free, Brother.''

"Except for the old couple.''

"Yeah.''

Movement by the old barn caught their attention and they fell silent for a few heartbeats. Karl stared for a moment and then said, "What the hell was that?''

"I don't know. Wasn't a horse. Way too small for that.''

Two men suddenly burst from the far side of the barn, running toward the house. Both Karl and Kathy smiled.

"Jans Pendley,'' Karl said.

"And Big Un,'' Kathy added. She stared at the barn as more movement caught her eye. "Someone else, too, Brother.''

"I see them.''

They had lost their binoculars and most of their gear during the retreat from the valley. But they had held on to their weapons.

Several screams erupted from the house, followed by an angry shout. Karl and Kathy waited. There were no more screams and no more shouting.

"The old couple's had it,'' Karl said.

"Seems like it.''

"Two men by the barn.''

"I see them now. Looks like Hobby and Lippy.''

"I wonder how many more made it out of the valley.''

The question was not answered. Jans opened the back

door of the old house and called, "Come on in. It's clear now. We got food on the stove."

The brother and sister watched as Hobby and Libby began their walk from the barn.

"Let's go," Karl said, standing up. He called out, "Jans? Can you hear me?"

Jans brought up his rifle, hesitated, then recognized the voice and lowered the rifle. "Well, I'll be damned. Karl. Step out, man. You got anyone with you?"

Karl and Kathy stepped out of the timber and walked toward the house. Hobby and Lippy had paused between the barn and the house, waiting.

"Just the two of you?" Jans asked.

"That's it. There any coffee in that house?"

"Big Un's starting some now."

The group all shook hands and stood for a moment by the back door of the house.

"Got a TV and one of those satellite things here, Karl," Jans said. "We ought to be able to get some news on the things. But I don't know how to work it."

"We'll figure it out. What about the man and woman in the house?"

"We'll toss their bodies in the barn. They hadn't outta kicked up a fuss with me."

"Yeah? Well, hell with them."

"That's the way I see it, too."

"It was a fuckin' slaughter back yonder at the pass," Lippy said. "It was really bad. Them old bastards was really pissed off, I guess."

"They outsmarted us, that's all," Karl said. "Pure and simple. They outguessed us at every turn. Those old boys had combat experience, and they used it."

Hobby shook his head. "Yeah? Well, we'll see about their damned combat experience. I got me a score to settle with them old farts," Hobby said. "And I'm gonna settle it if it's the last thing I ever do. Bet on that."

"What you got on your mind?" Jans asked.

"Just what I said," Hobby told him.

"Hey, people," Jans called from the open back door. "Some of y'all come get these damn bodies outta here. This old woman's done shit her pants and it's stinkin'. Give me a break. I'm tryin' to cook in here."

"You men sure you're ready to face the press?" the FBI agent asked the four old friends. "It's going to be intense."

Dennis had been released from the hospital and was now with his friends at the motel. Andy had refused to stay in the same facility as his father.

"My son has sure been running off at the mouth," Ted said. "Every chance he gets, and to anyone who will listen."

The agent shrugged his understanding. "We couldn't stop him, Mr. Dawson."

"Oh, I'm not blaming any of you. I'm just sorry my own flesh and blood turned against us, that's all."

"It's not the press I'm worried about," Harry said. "It's the lawyers for those cons who survived the shoot-outs that irritate the hell out of me."

The agent made no comment about that, but he silently agreed with Harry. "You guys ready to meet the press?"

"Not really," Dennis said. "But they know who we are and where we live. What's the point in delaying it?"

"None, really," Jack said. "But I don't want our wives all mixed up in this thing."

"Tell you what I *can* do," the FBI agent said. "I can have someone meet them at the airport and give them a message from you. We can't tell you what to do about the press, but I can have someone there to meet your wives."

"That would be much appreciated," Harry said. He

looked at his friends. "Just have them check into a nice hotel and then call us here. We'll arrange something." He looked down at a stack of newspapers delivered to the room that morning . . . from all over the nation. The four of them were on the front page of every newspaper. "Lousy pictures," he added.

One headline read: "Several Dozen Die In Shoot-out With Campers."

Another headline read: "War Veterans Kill Dozens in Wild Shoot-out In Montana Wilderness."

"They mention the dead men killed in the shoot-out were escaped convicts about halfway down the column," Jack said, following his friend's eyes.

"At least they did mention that little fact," Ted said. "Very considerate of them."

Dennis had written down the names of their wives and the airline they were coming back to the states on, and the arrival time. He handed the motel letterhead paper to the FBI agent.

"I'll see your wives are notified," the agent said. "You can count on that."

"We appreciate it," Dennis said.

"Any more word on those cons that got away?" Jack asked, fixing himself a glass of ice water.

The agent shook his head. "Karl Parsons and his sister are still on the loose, as is Randy O'Donnell, along with nine or so others we know were in the back country area." He hesitated, then said, "Randy O'Donnell is a bad one, guys. He's an international terrorist. They kicked him out of the IRA years ago. He's a bloodthirsty bastard. Revengeful. He might decide to come after you people."

"We've talked about that," Harry said. "We think he might, and so will Karl."

"Hell, they all might," Ted said. "I think it would

behoove us to stay on our toes until those still on the loose are either caught or dead."

The FBI agent nodded. "I sure would, guys. Be real careful. You boys sure upset their plans, for a fact."

"And now they really have nothing to lose, right?" Harry asked.

"They're all facing either death or the rest of their lives in hard lockup. You guys keep a low profile until we either have them in custody or the morgue."

"I hope it's the latter," Jack said.

The agent smiled, and held up the paper with their wives' names and arrival time. "I'll get right on this, guys. By the way, there are two federal marshals posted in the hallway, and a couple more in the lobby, and two more outside. Hang loose." He left the motel room.

"Nice guy," Dennis said.

"Seems to be," Harry replied.

"Has anybody thought about how we're going to handle the press?" Jack asked.

"Hell, I guess tell the truth," Ted said. "What else can we do . . . should we do?"

"Some of them are sure to be crybaby left-wingers," Harry pointed out. "They'll be coming at us hard, trying to make us out to be right-wing monsters who picked on the poor unfortunate criminals."

"Why, Harry," Jack said, sarcasm dripping from his mouth. "How you talk. You know the press would never do anything like that."

"Oh, of course not," Dennis said, an equal amount of sarcasm in his tone. "Not if we had used rocks and sticks instead of guns, that is."

"That's right," Ted said. "We used those big ole' awful, terrible, nasty guns to defend ourselves. And that's a no no. Oh my, yes."

"Yeah, we're just a bunch of ole' meanies, that's what

we are," Jack added. "A gang of over-the-hill, right-wing gun nuts. Horseshit," he spat out the last.

Harry laughed. "Meeting with the press is going to be a fun experience."

"Oh, maybe it won't be that bad," Dennis said, a hopeful note in his voice. "We may be creating a problem where there really isn't one."

"You believe that, Denny?" Jack asked.

Dennis grinned. "Hell, no. But it sounded good when I said it, didn't it?" Then his smile faded as Ted mouthed some very obscene phrases.

"What's the matter, Ted?" Harry asked.

"I was just thinking about that damn son of mine. I can't believe he's said some of the things that have gotten back to us. But I know he did. I saw him on the television saying them. Damn that kid."

"Don't beat yourself up over him," Jack told his friend. "And he's not a kid. He's a grown man. But of a different era than us. He's had his head filled with crap ever since he was a kid, and believed every word of it. It isn't your fault. It's the times we live in, that's all."

"The people who really count in this country won't believe a word Andy has said," Harry told his friend. "And there will be some conservative editorial writers who will take our side in this mess."

"Yeah?" Ted questioned. "Okay. There'll be a few, probably. But the problem is, the newspapers and the TV don't allow that many conservatives to have a voice. At least that's the way it seems to me."

"I damn sure agree with you about that," Jack said. "Somebody ought to do a study on the absence of conservative voices in print and broadcast journalism. I know they're out there. There are millions of conservatives in America . . . so where in the hell are our voices?"

"Let's bring that up during the press conference," Dennis suggested. His friends laughed, and Dennis said, "No, I mean it. Let's bring it up and lay our feelings all out. If we're going to get creamed by the press during this thing, let's pour some cream out ourselves."

"I'm game for it," the others said together.

Ted said, "After what Andy has said about us it can't make things any worse, and our feelings about law and order will be out in the open."

"If we get a chance, let's do it," Jack said with a boyish, devilish grin.

"We tell the federal marshals to inform the press they can have at us in the morning," Harry suggested. "About nine o'clock okay with you guys?"

The others shrugged. "Suits me." Dennis spoke for them all. He added, "And a good time will be had by all."

Thirty

The first few questions the old friends were asked were easy ones. How long had the four men known each other? Did they go camping every year? Were they married? Did all of them have children?

Then the questions got tougher.

"Mr. Dawson," a reporter asked. "Your son, Andrew, says it wasn't necessary to kill the convicts. He told us the convicts made a bargain to turn the hostages loose in exchange for their freedom. He says you people ambushed the convicts and killed them in cold blood. How do you respond to that?"

Ted kept the lid on his temper . . . barely. But his friends standing beside him knew he was struggling. "I would say that my son still has a very vivid imagination. He always did have."

"Is that your reply?"

"It sure is."

"Those convicts still alive claim your son is telling the truth."

Jack stepped in quickly to field that question. "Sure they do. They have nothing to lose by stretching the truth."

"What do you mean?"

"If I have to explain that, then that makes you a bigger idiot than your questions indicate."

The questioning all went downhill from that point on, and it got verbally rough and personal.

Jack finally broke off the press conference by simply walking away, his friends with him. Federal marshals prevented the press from following the four men.

"Goddamn miserable sons of bitches!" Harry cussed the press. "They'll take the word of a bunch of rapists and murders and call us liars." He cut loose with a string of profanity that awed his friends.

"Watch your blood pressure, Harry," Jack cautioned him. "We expected this kind of treatment from some of the press, remember? And we sure got it," he added sourly.

"Doesn't mean I have to like it," Harry came right back. "And by God, I don't like it. If I catch that sorry little prick reporter who implied that we all were lying and nothing but coldblooded murderers I'm going to whip his sorry ass."

"That would just make things worse for all of us, Harry," Jack said.

Their wives had called earlier that morning and talked at length with their husbands, the men assuring the women they were all right.

"I don't care about that!" Harry snapped. "I won't take that kind of crap from anybody. Especially from some sorry ass little prick from some goddamn left-wing elitist magazine. Fuck that bastard."

The men had told their wives to stay in the city and enjoy themselves for a few days. All this would blow over by then. And then the eight of them would go to Montreal or Nome or Naples or Nairobi or Acapulco or some damn place.

"I agree with Harry," Dennis said. "Some of those reporters need a good ass whipping. Only a few, I'll admit. Most of them seemed like pretty nice people. But a good butt kicking would be just right for some of them."

Jack shrugged his shoulders. "I sure won't get in your way if that's what you decide to do. But you'd better understand something, boys. We've all squared off against other guys over the years, and we've all had our butts whipped. Most of the time we forget about it after a few days and go on about our business . . ." He sighed. "But left-wingers, liberals, whatever you want to call them, don't think the way we do. They'll take an ass whipping and then call the police and have you arrested and then hire a lawyer and sue you. In many quarters the days of *mano a mano* are fading fast. Think about that before you go off half-cocked and all pissed off and whip somebody's ass."

Harry stared at his longtime friend for a moment. "I'm gonna whip that smart mouth punk, Jack. Now I may get surprised. He may be some kung fu expert and tear me up bad, but I don't think so. I think he's just a smart aleck punk who believes that being a member of the press gives him the right to insult people, and this old man is going to teach that kid a hard lesson about life."

Jack smiled. "All right, Harry. I'm with you a hundred percent. He might have a couple of friends who jump in when the trouble starts."

"The more the merrier," Ted said. "I'm with you, Harry."

Dennis held up his broken arm, "You give me a shillelagh to take the place of this broken wing, and I'll be right there with you guys."

Harry's usual good nature broke through for a moment. "The Over-The-Hill Gang rides again!"

"We're-over-the hill for a fact, Harry," Ted told him. "And don't ever forget it. That punk is gonna have about thirty-five years on you. Good lungs and good muscle. If you fight him, finish it in a hurry, 'cause if it goes more than two or three minutes, you're gonna be in trouble."

"Ted's right about that," Jack said. "Sucker punch the punk if you have to, but get it done in a hurry."

Harry's smile faded. "I'll get it done," he said grimly. "I may take a few bumps and bruises along the way, but I'll finish it. Count on that."

The rough days in the back country had leaned and hardened the four men. They had all dropped most of the excess fat they'd accumulated over the softer, easier years, and muscles had toughened up. None of the four really looked their age. There was also a harsher, meaner look in their eyes now, a determined countenance that they had lost years ago, after returning from Vietnam.

Jack answered a knock on the door. The local attorney they had hired to handle matters until they could all get back home came in. The man wore an embarrassed expression. Jack waved him inside.

"This can't be good news," Dennis said. "I have this sinking feeling in my stomach."

"Well, you're right about that," the lawyer said. "It isn't good news. Sometimes I am very ashamed of my profession."

"Well, let's have it," Harry said. "Stalling won't make it any easier to take."

The attorney sighed. "The families of the dead convicts are suing you men . . . that's it in a nutshell."

"Suing us?" Ted questioned. "They're suing *us?*"

"Yes." He opened his briefcase and took out a folder. "It's all in here. The whole damn sad business. I'm really sorry about this, but as I told you men several days ago, a lawsuit was certainly possible."

"I don't believe it," Harry blurted. "The bastards try to kill us, we defend ourselves, and now their families are suing us for damages. What kind of fucked up judicial system do we have in this country?"

"Fucked up," the local attorney said. "You pegged it right, Mr. Michaels. In many cases, criminals have more rights than the law-abiding citizens. It's my personal belief that a judge will throw this out of court. But you're going to have some legal expenses. Get ready for that." He laid the folder down on a desk and turned to once more face the four men. "I'm really sorry about this . . . mess, guys. If you'll give me the names of your attorneys, I'll see they get copies of this."

"We'd appreciate that," Jack told the man. "Our people might as well get ready for court. Thanks for bringing this by . . . I guess," he added with a forced smile.

The local attorney nodded his head and then shuffled his feet on the carpet. He was clearly embarrassed by the whole thing. "Anything I can do to help you men, let me know. I'll certainly do it."

"Thanks," Dennis told the man. "We'll probably be calling on you."

"Any time, for anything. This lawsuit is a damn disgrace."

The attorney left the room and Harry exploded. He stomped around the room, cussing. The others listened in silence, letting him get it out of his system and wind down . . . and that took several minutes. Once Harry got wound up, it took some time for the spring to unwind.

Harry ran out of steam and flopped down on the couch, after pausing by the desk and picking up the file folder the attorney had left. He opened the file and quickly scanned it, then stared at the wall for a moment. He cut his eyes to his friends, one at a time. "I was in the trucking business for a good many years, boys," he said. "As you all well know. I still own a nice chunk of the firm I started. I do know some tough ole' boys, all of whom owe me a lot of markers. They would do anything I asked them to do. Believe it."

"What are you getting at, Harry?" Dennis asked.

Harry lifted the file folder. "I think these goddamn shyster lawyers might need a lesson taught them. And I'm just the boy who is ready to teach them that lesson."

"Whoa, Harry!" Jack said, holding up a hand. "Now just settle down for a minute. Get your head turned in the right direction and start thinking straight for a change. You—"

"My head's *on* straight, Jack," Harry cut him off. "I've been fucking around with lawyers all my life, and I'm sick of it." He held up the file folder. "This makes me want to puke. You know goddamn well what these scummy bastards want—they want us to settle for a nice piece of change in return for dropping the lawsuit. You know that as well as I do."

"What do you have in mind, Harry?" Ted asked. "Kill the attorneys?"

Harry stared at his friend. "Well, that thought entered my mind, I won't deny it. No. I don't want to do that. But I think I do know a way to discourage them from pursuing the lawsuit any further."

"Forget it, Harry," Jack said, a finality to his words. "We'll fight it out in court. As much as I would like to whip these lawyers asses, and they do deserve a good ass whipping for taking this case, just forget it."

"*You* forget it, Jack. I'm going to remember it for a long, long time. And if I ever get a chance to kick one these lawyers' asses, I'm going to do it." Harry stood up. "I'm gonna go back to my room and sit by myself and be pissed off for a time." He forced a smile. "And I mean what I said about those damn shysters, Jack. Every word of it."

When the motel room door closed behind Harry, Dennis said, "He means it, Jack. He wasn't kidding. Not one little bit."

"I know it," Jack said.

"I hope Harry doesn't run into some recruiter for a militia or survivalist group," Ted said. "The mood he's in right now, he'd sign up on the spot. Not that I have anything against those groups," he was quick to add. "I don't. Hell, if I knew where to join one, I'd probably sign up myself."

"Maybe we all ought to find a militia group and join," Dennis said softly.

"Are you serious, Denny?" Ted asked.

"Damn serious. The last couple of weeks have really opened my eyes about just how much justice has taken a beating in this country. Justice?" He snorted the one-word question contemptuously. "There is no justice in this country. Not any more. Every damn one of those cons we fought should have been put to death immediately after their last arrest and trial. God only knows how many lives they've ruined over the years. Or how many lives of the tourists they've scarred now, and ruined the last couple of weeks. Women and teenage girls raped and subjected to all sorts of perversion; young boys raped. All of them mentally scarred for the rest of their lives. Those goddamn cons— the bunch we tangled with—are savages, rabid animals. And you don't pet a rabid animal. You kill it. And now these fucking lawyers," he pointed to the file folder, "have sided with the families of the cons and are suing us. Join a militia group that wants a return to law and order in this country? You bet I would . . . in a heartbeat. And you can bet I'm going to find one and see if they'll have me . . . or if not, if I'm too old, the money I can give them for supplies and equipment. And I'll write them a check right now. This instant. I suggest we all give joining some militia group some damn serious thought, boys. Really think hard about it. Before it's too late, before this country sinks so low we can't pull it out of the sewer."

Dennis walked over to the table and fixed a glass of ice water. He stood for a moment in front of the big window that overlooked the mountains, snow-capped and majestic in the distance. "Look what has happened to young men like Andy," Dennis said softly. "Hundreds of thousands, maybe millions, just like him. God help us all."

"Your sentiments about Andy go double for me," Ted said. "In spades. And I agree with you about finding some militia or political group who have some definite ideas about what is wrong with this nation. Tell you the truth, I hadn't thought about it until you brought it up just now. I think it's a damn good idea." He smiled at his friend to lighten the moment. "Every now and then you do come up with a idea worth listening to. We might be a little old to join, and take an active role in training and so forth, but we can sure give money. And my checkbook is ready right now."

Jack sat down and his expression showed he was deep in thought. After a moment, he suddenly smiled and nodded his head in agreement. "Yeah. By God, I think that's a dandy idea, Denny. I really do. And I think we should tell the press what we plan to do and why we have reached that decision. Let's see what they do with it."

"Make us out to be ultra-right-wing monsters," Denny said. "Gun loving whackos. And you know they will. That's exactly what they'll do."

"Denny's right, Jack. But hell . . ." He shrugged his shoulders. "I agree it's a good idea. And what better spokesmen than us, after what we've been through? Let's do it."

Jack looked at his friends and then began laughing, and it was infectious. Soon the three men were all howling with laughter.

The rooms were adjoining and Harry opened the door and looked in, astonishment in his eyes. "What the hell is going on in here?" he demanded.

"We've all decided to join a militia!" Ted managed to gasp out.

Harry stared at Ted for a moment. "Your ass!" he said, then shook his head in disbelief and stepped back into his room and closed the door.

That set everybody off again.

After a moment, Harry jerked open the door and stepped into the room. He waited with an exasperated expression on his face until the laughter had subsided, and asked, "Are you guys serious?"

"Damn right," Dennis said.

"We're too old!"

"Who says we're too old?" Jack demanded.

"That's what I read somewhere," Harry told him. "But hell, if you guys know of a militia who'll have a bunch of a old farts like us," he shrugged, "I'm sure as hell game for it. We can give money, if nothing else."

"Now that is a real idea," Ted said. "I know three or four guys who are like us—retired fairly young, and pretty well fixed. Hell, we all have friends who are unhappy with the way government is going. Money just may be the way to go with this thing."

"Yeah," Dennis said. "I agree. Now who will get in contact with the militias?"

"We all will," Jack said. "We all live in different locales. So we start asking around . . . very discreetly, of course. Hell, we can get on the Internet and find some groups."

The four men smiled at each other. Retirement could be a bore. Now they had something to focus on.

Thirty-One

Karl and Kathy and the other cons took turns showering, washed and dried their clothes, and then had something to eat. The bodies of Mr. and Mrs. Snyder had been placed in the old barn, hidden under a stack of old hay. The barn had not been used to house animals in several years.

Jans had checked out both vehicles, a sedan and an old pickup truck, and both ran well. The cons would no longer have to hoof it.

"The roadblocks are down," Karl said. "Things are pretty well back to normal on the outside. But somebody who knows the old couple is bound to see us driving those vehicles and know we don't belong in them. So we're not home free . . . not yet."

"You know, Karl," Hobby said, almost a dreamy quality in his voice. "I don't much give a shit anymore. I want them old bastards in gunsights. We've all had it, and we all know it. Or should know it. Everyone of us here is looking at death row, and we're not going to have years of appeals. Not with all them campers testifying against us."

"So what's your point?" Jans asked.

"My point is this—I'm going out like they say in books, in a blaze of glory."

Karl had been thinking along those same lines—not to that extreme—but keeping his thoughts private.

Big Un nodded his head in agreement. "Yeah. That ain't a bad thought. I ain't goin' back in the bucket. I'm not gonna be locked down for twenty-three hours a day for the rest of my life. Whether we're facin' the needle or not."

Libby said, "I'm with you, Big Un. All the way. I want to kill me some cops, and I 'specially want to kill them old men. After that," he shrugged, "I don't give a big rat's ass what happens. But I want to go out knowin' I got my revenge. That's all I want."

"Jans?" Karl asked.

"It doesn't make any difference to me, one way or the other. I figure I'll find me some fine lookin' bitch, get me one last taste of pussy, and then . . ." He shook his head. "I don't give a damn what happens. I'm tired of runnin.' Tired of bein' tired all the time. But I'm not goin' back to hard lockdown. Not ever. That's firm and final."

Karl looked at his sister. "Sis?"

Kathy shrugged her indifference. "Whatever you say we do, Karl, we do. I'm with you all the way."

"All right," Karl said. "Well, maybe we have shot our wad. Hell I don't know. I know our pictures are all over the TV screen. And you guys are right about it being death row time for all of us. There won't be years of appeals for any of us. And I know from listening to newscasts on the radio the old boys are in town at a motel. They won't be hard to find. We just look for all the crowds out front.

That's where they'll be. But getting in and out of town is going to be very chancy."

"Who said anything about getting out?" Hobby asked. "I ain't plannin' on gettin' out of town. I plan on killin' them old bastards, that's all. Whatever happens after that, so be it." He shrugged.

Karl gave the man a long look. Then he, too, shrugged his shoulders. "Maybe you're right. If we get out, okay. If not? Well, we don't."

Kathy said, "I'm looking at the rest of my life in some women's prison. But hell, I knew that going into this thing. I just don't want to spend the rest of my life in prison. I don't mind another woman going down on me—as a matter of fact, I like it—but I do want it to be my choice. So I guess we're all in agreement. So . . . let's go in shooting, and the devil take the hind part."

"We'll all sleep in real beds tonight," Karl said. "Then make our final plans in the morning."

"Final," Hobby said. "That sure sounds real good to me."

When Karl and Kathy were alone, the others standing guard or napping, Kathy asked, "Are you serious about going out in a blaze of glory?"

"Hell, no," Karl replied. "I mean . . . we're gonna buy it sometime, yeah. But not tomorrow or the next day or the next month, and hopefully not the next year. I just said all that 'cause the others have made up their minds to die. I haven't. Not for a long time yet, I hope. You and me, Kid, we've got things to do and places to go and see before we crap out."

"But we're really going into town to kill those old dudes, right?"

"Sure we are, Baby. They're the ones who got us into this mess."

"Yeah. You're right about that."

"Okay. So that's settled. Are there any steaks in that freezer, Baby?"

"Sure. It's jam-packed full with all sorts of food. Steaks and chops."

"Why don't you thaw some out and cook 'em up for us? I think a steak would taste good about now."

"In a little while, Karl. I'm gonna go see Jans for a few minutes."

Karl laughed. "Okay, kid. Go hump in a real bed for a while."

After Kathy had left the kitchen Karl fixed a fresh cup of coffee and sat alone at the table. He had no intention of getting killed when they went into town. The others could get killed if that was their wish, and he supposed it was. He'd seen it happen to other cons. Something snapped in their heads, and they developed a death wish. Karl sure as hell had no such wish. He would go into town with the others, but then he planned on cutting out the first chance he got.

And Kathy? He smiled. This would be the perfect opportunity to get rid of her stupid ass. She was becoming a real drag. She was so hung up on Jans's cock it was getting on Karl's nerves. What he ought to do, if he could figure out a way to do it, was shoot them both . . . shoot them all . . . and leave them to rot, and cut out on his own. But at the first shot the others would be alerted and there would be one hell of a gun battle. Getting rid of them all was a good thought, but not practical . . . not at this time.

Karl looked up as Big Un came wandering into the kitchen, yawning hugely. "I be's hungry about my mouth," Big Un said.

The big stupid bastard, Karl thought. Sometimes, occasionally, Big Un behaved as though he had good sense. Other times, most of the time, he acted as though he didn't have a brain in his head.

"We'll sure get some headlines after we get done tomorrow, won't we, Karl?" Big Un asked.

"Yeah, we sure will, Big Un." *But you'll all be dead, you big dummy,* Karl thought. *Rotting in the grave. So what will you have accomplished? Other than committing suicide.*

Karl suddenly thought about Randy and carefully hid his quick smile. Randy O'Donnell. Randy would fit right in this whacky group.

Kathy started hollering just then, as Jans put the meat to her, both of them cussing and moaning and groaning. Sounded like a porn movie.

Karl sighed. His sister kept her brains between her legs most of the time. She'd been that way ever since Karl raped her back when they were kids. How old had she been? Ten or eleven, as he recalled. Something like that. Didn't take long for her to start really liking it.

Karl hoped all that hollering wouldn't wake up Hobby and Lippy. Big Un was bad enough by himself.

The small TV set in the kitchen was turned down low. Suddenly the announcement came on that there was a special bulletin concerning the escaped convicts. Karl reached over and turned up the volume just as Big Un sat down and the sight and sounds of helicopters filled the speaker and the screen.

The announcer said that this was the last of the escaped convicts believed to be hiding in the back country. Authorities had cornered the last four, and two had been killed during the shoot-out earlier that day.

He paused as the helicopters landed and two ambulances rolled out to the choppers, then said, "The two surviving escapees are James Moncel and Don Lemand, both of whom were wounded during the gunfight with authorities."

He went on to say there were about a dozen escapees still

unaccounted for. However, some of those were believed to be dead, their bodies as yet undiscovered in the valley.

"Moncel and Lemand were the guards at the north end of the valley," Karl said.

"Yeah." Big Un grunted. "That just about does it for the boys, then. I seen Ned and Nathan and Gorman slip off and get free during the fight in the rocks, but we got separated later. And I believe Randall and Oscar got loose. I don't know about none of the others."

"Be interesting if those ole' boys was to show up in town about the same time we did, wouldn't it?"

Big Un smiled. "Yeah, it would. That little burg would really rock and roll with all of us there. You reckon there's a chance of that happening?"

Karl shrugged. "Not much of one. But hell, stranger things have happened."

Jack woke up before dawn and could not get back to sleep. After rolling and tossing in the bed for half an hour, he finally said to hell with it and got up and dressed. He hesitated for a few seconds. Then, wondering why he felt he needed it, he tucked his 9mm pistol behind his belt, in the small of his back. He stepped out into the hall and spoke to the federal marshal stationed there, then walked to the lobby just as the night clerk and attendant were wheeling out the morning coffee urn. Jack pulled a cup of coffee, snagged a doughnut, and walked outside. He stood in the clear, cold air, clearing his head of the last few cobwebs of sleep.

He ate the doughnut and then sipped the nearly scalding hot coffee, almost burning his lips. He said a couple of cuss words and sat the cup on the bumper of a pickup truck—he would wait for it to cool.

Jack's eyes caught the faint shadow of movement off to

his left and he stared into the darkness for a moment. The movement, if that's really what it was, did not appear again. Jack picked up his coffee cup, blew on the brew for a few seconds, then took a sip. Still too damn hot.

He heard a whisper of sound off to his left and cut his eyes toward the faint noise. It was not repeated.

He knew he shouldn't, but he walked deeper into the darkness, toward the noise. *Might be a hurt animal,* he thought. As he slowly walked deeper into the shadows, Jack shifted his pistol from the small of his back to his side.

"Silly," he muttered. "You're acting like an old woman."

He paused, staring and listening intently. Nothing. The darkness greeted him silently. Jack looked around him. There was no one else in sight. Since the capture of the last cons in the valley, the feds had relaxed their guard of the survivors.

Jack walked on for about a dozen yards, then sat his coffee cup on the hood of a car and stood for a moment. Whatever had caused the noise, probably a dog or cat, was gone.

Jack turned to return to the more brightly lighted section of the parking lot. A voice sprang out of the darkness, the whisper low and menacing.

"You just stand still, mister, and you won't get hurt none. Lay your wallet on the hood of that car to your right. Do it, you son of a bitch!"

"I don't have my wallet with me," Jack lied. "It's in the motel room."

"You're a liar!"

"I'm telling you the truth, Buddy." Jack moved his hand slowly to the 9mm tucked behind his belt, at his right side. "I just came out for some air."

"That pisses me off, mister. And that's a stupid thing to do."

"Sorry. But it's the truth." Jack's hand closed around the butt of the autoloader.

"Put him down and let's get out of here," a second voice said.

I don't think I want you to do that, Jack thought, and threw himself to one side in the darkness, drawing the 9mm as he fell.

Thirty-Two

Jack landed in the damp cold grass just off the parking lot, rolling to one side and coming up with the autoloader just as the holdup man fired. The rounds from the unknown assailant's pistol tore up the grass just inches from Jack's head. Jack leveled his pistol and pulled the trigger three times. The sound of gunfire was enormous in the quiet moments of morning, ripping the peaceful setting and sending muzzle flashes leaping from Jack's 9mm.

The rounds from Jack's pistol all found their mark, and the gunman staggered backward several feet and then fell to the ground. The second man ran off into the darkness. Jack held his fire, not sure of a target.

"Where's it coming from?" Jack heard the question shouted from the front of the motel.

"Over here!" Jack called. "One guy ran off to the south. Watch it, he's armed." Jack didn't know that for sure, but it was a prudent assumption.

Within seconds, the floodlights in the parking lot snapped on, bathing the front and both sides of the motel complex in harsh light.

A federal marshal ran over to Jack just as he was getting up off the ground. Jack had the foresight to tuck his pistol behind his belt just a few seconds before the federal marshal came panting up. Jack glanced over at the would-be thief. The front of the man's shirt was covered with blood. He was alive, but just barely and not for long. Blood oozed out of the bullet wounds each time his heart beat.

"You just bad luck all the way around, you old son of a bitch!" the dying man said to Jack.

"Breaks of the game, Sonny Boy," Jack replied.

"Eddie Marshston," an FBI man said, looking down at the dying man.

Gunfire tore the early morning hours, coming from the south end of the parking lot.

"He's down!" someone called.

"You all right, sir?" another federal marshal asked Jack.

"I'm fine. Who are these people?"

"Some of the last of the escaped convicts," the federal marshal told him. "He's made his last break," he added.

"Fuck you!" Eddie gasped out.

"Hell of a thing to say when you're dying," the FBI man told Eddie.

"Fuck you, too!" Eddie told him.

The agent shrugged his reply.

Eddie started coughing, the blood spraying from his mouth, his hands tore up the ground as pain hit him. He stiffened, called out a few words that those standing around him could not understand, and then was still.

"This one caught a round in the side of the head. He's dead," a voice called out of the darkness.

Jack looked down at Eddie. The man's eyes were wide

open and staring at nothing but the darkness of death. "So is this one," he said softly.

Far in the distance, an over the road trucker blew his air horns.

Some members of the press had a field day with the latest shooting. Jack refused to meet with any of them, especially when several questioned on a national feed whether Jack had a permit to carry a pistol.

"Goddamn sons of bitches!" Jack cussed. "Never mention that the pistol saved my life. Never mind that I'm not a murderer, a rapist, a bank robber, a child molester, a thief. Never bring up the fact that I've obeyed the law all my life, fought in two wars, and paid more money in taxes than I care to think about. Oh, no. Don't mention that the son of a bitch was trying to rob me at gunpoint and was going to kill me . . . just question nationwide if I have a permit to carry a pistol. Those goddamn liberal cocksuckers!"

"The latter probably literally as well as figuratively," Harry added.

That brought a smile to Jack's lips and he nodded. "Yeah." Then he laughed. "Ah . . . to hell with it. I got an idea, guys. Let's get the hell out of here. Let's do it real quietly, and check into one of those individual cabin things on a lake somewhere. Close to a town, but far enough away so we can all do some fishing and some real relaxing. How about it?"

"Sounds great to me," Dennis said. "All our gear was brought back to us intact."

"Okay," Jack said. "There is a series of small lakes over west of here. I've been talking to our local attorney about them. That's where he goes to get away from it all and relax. He says the fishing is great. There are no hardtop roads leading directly to the lakes, but there are gravel and dirt roads. He says he can rent us a couple of four wheel drive vehicles on the Q.T., and we can be gone without anybody else knowing where we went."

"How about the FBI?" Ted asked.

"I talked to a couple of the agents. They said we can come and go anywhere, any time we please. We're certainly not under arrest, and we're not being detained for any reason. He didn't go so far as to say we didn't have to tell them where we're going, but I got that impression."

"Let's do it," Harry said. He smiled. "Of course, the cops took your pistol, Jack."

Jack laughed. "I have two more in my luggage. 9mm's I took from the dead out in the valley, and plenty of ammo."

"We do want to tell Lindsey where we're going," Dennis said.

"You bet. She's in good hands though, with social services, and under plenty of guard."

"Judy?"

"With her mom, in a secluded and well-guarded place."

"I believe it," Dennis said. "How about Max?"

"With Judy. Those two are inseparable. Some of the survivors are still in the hospital, but many of the others are out and back home. Okay, we're all in agreement. Let's call our wives and tell them we'll be out of pocket for a couple of days."

"They might want to join us, Jack," Harry said.

"Suits me. But I'll be surprised if they do."

"Great. Let's pack up our stuff and get in touch with that attorney. With any kind of luck we can be out of here tomorrow, before dawn."

After listening and watching several newscasts that morning concerning the shoot-out at the motel, Karl and the others agreed they had best delay their trip into town for another day.

"Somebody's out by the barn." Kathy spoke from the kitchen window.

The men grabbed weapons and moved into position. They waited tensely.

"It's Nathan!" Kathy said. "And he's got a couple of guys with him."

"Nathan?" Big Un blurted. "Yeah. He's from this area, ain't he?"

"Yes," Karl said, moving to the back door and looking out. "Shit!" he said. "Couple, my achin' ass. There's a whole gang with him. 'Bout half a dozen guys. Oh, well, what the hell." Karl opened the screen door and shouted, "Come on in, you guys. Hell, it's old home week here."

There were four men with Nathan: Ned, Gorman, Randall, and Oscar, all ragged and filthy and hungry. They had lost nearly all their equipment and supplies, but all had managed to hold onto their weapons.

"I remembered this old ranch from years back," Nathan said. "Wondered if it was still standin.' " He slurped at his mug of coffee and looked around him. "This all the boys that made it out?"

"I was going to ask you the same question," Karl said. "But I think I already know the answer."

"Yeah, you probably do. We're it, Karl. It was a slaughter back yonder in the valley. There was a couple of hundred of us when we broke out of the bucket. This is all that's left."

"We're gonna kill all them old farts," Libby said. "And anybody else who gets in the way. You boys wanna come along for the fun?"

The five men exchanged glances. Gorman shrugged and said, "Why the hell not?"

"I ain't goin' back to lockup," Oscar said. "None of us

are. We done talked about it and got it all settled. We're all lookin' at death row, and that ain't no choice at all. Hell with it. I'm goin' out shootin.' "

"You know where them old shits are?" Randall asked.

"We can find them easy enough," Karl said. "We know they're at a motel in town. There just aren't that many motels of any size. The reporters are hanging around like vultures. We'll find them."

"How about it?" Hobby asked.

Nathan nodded his head. "Suits me."

Karl looked at the other newcomers. They all nodded their heads in agreement.

"That's settled, then. Now, then. Something else. After you get cleaned up and get something to eat, somebody has to go into town and check around. I can't go. There are people who still remember me. Kathy can't go. She's from this area . . . somebody would be sure to spot her. Jans, Big Un, Libby, and Hobby have their pictures all over the damn TV. One of you guys will have to chance it."

"I'm out," Nathan said. "I'd be spotted in a heartbeat."

"Hell, I'll go," Ned said. "You got vehicles, I seen them."

Kathy came rushing into the room, carrying a small portable radio. "Listen to this! We got it made now." She turned up the volume and sat the radio down on the table.

Although the details were not aired, a reporter had paid a local to keep him informed. The local had watched the attorney renting two four-wheel drive vehicles and making arrangements to have them delivered to the rear of the motel. The local knew the attorney went to the lakes often to fish and relax. Didn't take a genius to put it all together. It was a lot of guesswork, but most of it turned out to be correct.

"You guys get cleaned up and get something to eat," Karl told the newcomers. "We'll carry out an old mattress and lay it in the back of the pickup. Couple of you can ride back there, covered with a tarp of something. I know those lakes. I've hid out there several times. I know a way around the town. We'll take that route. If we have any kind of luck at all, we'll make it. We'll knock off the old farts, take their money and rent cars, and split. It sure beats dyin.' "

"For a fact," Kathy said.

"Suits me," Nathan added. "Hell, we may have a chance of gettin' out of here after all."

"How many bathrooms in this house?" Oscar asked.

"Two," Karl told him.

"I got first dibs on one," Oscar said. "I got to take a bath, man." He scratched his belly. "I feel like I got bugs crawlin' around on me and I smell bad. Hell, I can smell myself, and when you can do that it's bad."

"Damn sure is," Big Un agreed, wrinkling up his nose. "You stink for a fact."

Oscar gave him a dirty look.

"I'll wash and dry your clothes while you guys are showering," Kathy said.

"Good deal," Nathan said. "I hope there's lots of hot water. We all can sure use a bath."

"Make it a quick one," Karl said.

Kathy looked at her brother. "We pulling out today?"

"Just as soon as everybody is ready to go. I don't see any point in delaying. Big Un, get out all those rods and reels and that fishing tackle we seen in the shed. We'll take it. Make us look like tourists. We'll all wear hats. There's plenty of them around here. Let's do it, boys. We got to keep our appointment for a killing."

"Well, what now?" Ted tossed the question out to his friends as they sat in the living area of the two room motel suite.

"What do you mean?" Jack asked.

"Is the trip still on? That's what I mean."

"Hell, yes, it's still on. That damn snoopy reporter doesn't know for sure where we're going. There are a half dozen lakes in that area. We'll slip out before dawn and go."

"We'll be followed, that's for sure," Dennis said. "You can bet on that."

"We can lose them," Ted said. "We've got the map the attorney gave us."

"Hell, this just might be just the excuse I need to kick some prick's ass," Harry said wistfully.

"Harry, for God's sake don't start with that kick ass stuff again," Jack told him. "I thought we agreed you would cool that crap."

"I didn't agree to a damn thing," Harry quickly replied. "I said I was going to kick that reporter's ass, and I fully intend to do just that. And if you doubt it, ole' buddy, just stick around and watch me."

Ted and Dennis groaned, Ted saying, "Let's get him out of here before he does something really stupid."

"You watch what I tell you," Harry replied. "I get me a chance, I'm gonna kick me some ass."

"Right now, go pack your stuff," Jack told him. "We're pulling out early in the morning."

"Yes, Sergeant Major!" Harry barked. "Whatever you say, Top Soldier. Right now!" He saluted smartly.

Jack gave him the finger and Harry jabbed two of them in the air. Then, laughing, he walked out of the room.

"I really hope that reporter who gave him a bad time doesn't get anywhere near Harry," Dennis said.

"So do I. Oh! By the way, social services said Lindsey could go with us if she wanted to, and she jumped at the chance. I'm supposed to pick her up this afternoon. I've got her a room here at the motel."

"Good deal!" Ted said. "I really like that kid."

"What does social services say about Lindsey coming to live with you and your wife?" Dennis asked.

"She said since Lindsey is sixteen and no one knows where her dad is, and Lindsey wants to come live with us, she doesn't see any big problem. She's contacting Lindsey's home state now. And speaking of wives, did anybody remember to jot down their arrival time in Kalispell?"

"I've got it," Ted said with a laugh.

"I wrote it down and stuck it somewhere and forgot where I put it," Jack said.

"A sure sign of advanced senility," Dennis said.

"I don't doubt it," Jack agreed. "By the way, where'd you put your glasses, Denny?"

"Huh? My glasses?"

"Yeah, your glasses. You're squinting. I noticed that. You better find them."

"Well ..." Dennis said, glancing around the room. "Well, hell, I put them around here somewhere. I know I did. I remember taking them off."

"Keep looking, boy," Jack urged. "Keep looking."

Ted was about to crack up laughing.

"You think this is funny, you old goat!" Dennis asked. "I just got those glasses yesterday. It was a special, hurry up job. Man was real nice about it, too. Now I've lost them. I don't need them except to read, but I sure need them then. Come on, you guys, help me look."

Ted was laughing so hard tears were forming in his eyes. Harry had overheard the conversation as he stood in the doorway of the adjoining room and was holding his sides laughing. Only Jack was managing to keep a straight face ... and that was becoming a real struggle for him.

"Assholes," Dennis muttered. "Bunch of damn laughing hyenas is what you are."

Jack finally burst out laughing, unable to contain himself

any longer. He pointed at Dennis. "You've got them on, dummy!" he yelled. "Gotcha again!"

Dennis put a hand to his face. Felt his glasses. Turned to glare for a moment at his friends who were all breaking up with laughter. Then a slow smile began working its way across his lips. He'd fallen for one of the oldest tricks around . . . again. His friends caught him with this stunt every couple of years. Dennis had been the first one of the four men to have to start wearing glasses, mainly for reading.

A knock on the door cooled the laughter. Ted opened it and waved the local attorney in. He stepped into the room and looked at the men, a smile playing around his lips. "I heard the laughing. Must have been quite a joke."

"It always is," Jack told him. "What's up?"

"I put a couple of rifles in one of the vehicles. Also several boxes of ammo. I don't think you'll need them . . ." He shrugged. "But you never know."

"We appreciate it," Harry said. "Some of those bastards are still on the loose."

"Yeah," Jack said. "They sure are. I found that out the hard way."

"Sorry about that reporter discovering your plans. The local who snitched on you got his ass chewed pretty good by the bureau . . . if that's any consolation."

"Every town has its jerks," Dennis said. "But the people here have been great toward us. Pass that word around, will you?"

"I sure will. The keys to the cabins and a map are in the vehicles. When are you guys pulling out for the lakes?"

"In the morning," Harry told him.

"You guys have fun and relax. I'll see you when you get back."

"Will do. Thanks for everything."

The attorney smiled at the quartet and left the room.

Jack turned to his friends and grinned. "You guys ready to go?"

"Been ready," Harry told him.

"Let's jump the gun and leave now. Lindsey's ready to go. Any reporters who follow us . . . we'll lead them on a goose chase."

Fifteen minutes later, the five of them were on the road, deliberately heading in the wrong direction.

Thirty-Three

Several carloads of reporters tried to follow, but after getting hopelessly turned around on the winding, twisting back roads the attorney had mapped out, most of them turned around and went back to town.

Four reporters, traveling in two vehicles, chose not to follow Jack and his friends. They headed straight for the lakes and staked out two of the entrances to the series of lakes. There was a chance that Jack and his friends might not come this way, but the odds were pretty good that they would. The four reporters, three men and one woman, had brought a couple of ice chests, ample food and water, blankets and tents, and changes of clothing. They were after a story, and they were determined to get one . . . and they didn't give a damn whose life they turned upside down to get that story.

These reporters were about to discover what it was like to be under the gun . . . literally.

Andy, to no one's surprise, had signed a contract to write a book about his experiences in The Valley of Death.

"That damn kid of mine'd better be careful what he says about us," Ted said. Then he sighed. "But he won't be."

The others said nothing. They were all certain that Ted was right. Andy was going to give them a bad time, verbally. They wondered if Andy would testify against his father if the lawsuits that were threatened ever came to be.

"Andy will testify against us all," Harry said to Jack as they rode along toward the lake. Lindsey was in the backseat, staying quiet, listening. "Andy is the new breed of American man . . . God help us all. All mouth and no guts. Hell, look who he voted for in the presidential race."

"And he's proud of it," Jack added. "Said the president is a fine man."

Even Lindsey groaned at that.

Jack and Harry smiled at the teenager's response. Lindsey said, "These snoopy reporters following us around and writing all those crappy things about you guys are liberals, aren't they, Jack?"

Jack had insisted she call him by his first name. "I'm sure most of them are, Baby. I think there is an unwritten rule against broadcast networks and major newspapers hiring conservatives."

"There ought to be a law against that," the teenager replied.

Both Jack and Harry laughed, Harry saying, "We agree with you, Lindsey."

"No, guys, I'm serious," the young woman responded. "Listen, there are millions of conservatives and moderates in America, right?"

"That's right," Jack said.

"Law-abiding and taxpaying, right?"

"Right again," Jack told her. "Most of us are, at least."

"But you, we, don't have a major voice in many newspapers or on TV, right?"

"It certainly seems that way," Harry replied. "Hell, it *is* that way."

"That isn't right. Fair, I mean," Lindsey said. "Seems to me newspapers should be balanced, with everybody's views presented equally. Shouldn't it be that way?"

"We think so," Jack told her. "But there is a little matter of infringing on the rights of a free press."

"How about infringing on the rights of Americans?" she replied. "Don't we have a right to have our views presented?"

"Doesn't seem to work that way." Jack told her.

"I think many in the press are crapheads," Lindsey said.

"You'll get no arguments from either of us on that," Harry replied.

"So what happens?" Lindsey questioned. "I've got nearly my whole life ahead of me. I can't say from where I sit it looks real good. What happens? How do we get our rights returned to us?"

"We may have to fight for them, Lindsey," Jack told her. "But only as a last resort. When working within the system is no longer a viable option."

"You really think it's coming to that?"

Jack hesitated, then nodded his head. "Yes, Baby. I really do."

"That's sad, Jack," she replied.

"Tragic and unnecessary," Harry said. He pointed. "There's the cut-off right up ahead, Jack."

"Only a few more miles to go and we can relax and start having a good time."

The body of Lindsey's mother—what was left of it—had finally been recovered. It would not be released for burial until the autopsy was complete, and that might take several more weeks. Lindsey did not speak of her mother very often. She was grieving in her own way. Jack had gotten the impression that mother and daughter were not that close.

"You think we lost all the reporters?" Harry asked.

Jack shook his head as he signaled for the turn. "I really doubt it. I think some of them will turn up here, aggravating the hell out of us."

"I know one I hope turns up," Harry said. "I really hope he does."

"It'll just make matters worse, Harry," Jack cautioned his friend.

"It'll be worth it just to see that bastard spitting out some teeth."

Lindsey laughed at that. "Can I charge admission and keep the money?"

Harry twisted in the front seat and grinned at her. "You got a deal, kid."

"Should be able to get a real crowd to see that," Lindsey replied.

Jack sighed. He really, really hoped that smart ass reporter who got on the wrong side of Harry stayed far, far away. Harry meant every word he said.

And while Harry was certainly no longer a young man, he was still tough as a boot, both mentally and physically. The highly decorated veteran of two wars had been in a rough business all his adult life, dealing with some very rough people, and he had come out on top over the years.

Neither of the men nor Lindsey paid any attention to the car parked by the side of the combination service station/cafe; it was just one of several there.

Nor did they pay any attention to the old pickup truck parked on the other side of the large building, two men sitting in the cab. The two men exchanged glances and smiled at each other.

* * *

Hundreds of miles away, in Southern California, a man
parked his car in front of a motel on the outskirts of a
small town just north of Los Angeles and looked carefully
all around him. He had been parked across the street,
waiting while the maids finished their work cleaning the
rooms. Only one room in this section was occupied this
early in the day, and Randy O'Donnell was in that one
room.

Billy Moody touched the butt of the pistol tucked behind
his belt, on his left side, and got out of the car. It was
uncomfortable carrying the pistol with the sound suppressor screwed on. But he wouldn't be carrying it long. He
walked swiftly to the motel room and knocked on the door.

"Management, sir," he called. "I would like to talk with
you, please."

The door swung inward and Billy slammed a shoulder
against it, knocking Randy backward and sending him tum-
bling to the floor. Billy stepped quickly into the room and
closed the door. He drew the small caliber pistol from
behind his belt and thumbed the hammer back. He stood
for a moment, smiling as Randy struggled to get to his
feet, the side of Randy's face reddening from impacting
against the heavy motel room door.

"You son of a bitch!" Randy cursed.

"Now, now, Randy," Billy said. "No need for that. You
knew this day was coming."

"It doesn't mean I have to like it. Or you, for that matter.
And I don't like you. Never have. You were always a strange
duck, Billy."

Billy laughed at the man.

"Bastard!"

"Oh, now, now, Randy. No need for all that. You know
you've been a very bad boy," Billy said. "You really should

have stayed in prison. It might not be much of a life, but it is a continuation of life."

"And mine is about to end, right, Billy?"

The two men had known each other since childhood, growing up in the same small village in Northern Ireland.

"Correct, Randy."

"The committee put the word out on me? I don't believe that for a second."

"Oh, but they did, Randy. Yes, indeed, they certainly did just that. As long as you stayed behind bars, you were safe. But now . . ." He shrugged. "You're a loose cannon, so to speak, Randy. A liability."

"You'll never leave the States alive. My people will kill you."

"Don't be silly. Peace talks are underway even as we speak. That's the way it is. We've got to bring peace to our land. Your day has come and gone." Billy smiled sadly. "And mine, too, I have to say."

Randy started to get up and Billy lifted the silenced autoloader. "Now, now. Do it very slowly, Randy. No sudden moves."

Randy smiled. "Why not? You're going to kill me regardless, aren't you?"

"Yes. But a few more moments of life would be nice, wouldn't they?"

"I really don't care anymore. What the hell is the point?"

Billy nodded his head. "Yes. That is probably quite true. You just don't care anymore. No one in your group does. That's why they have to go."

Randy blinked a couple of times. "You? . . ." He fell silent.

"Yes. Me, Randy. I have quite the task ahead of me, don't I?"

"You'll never get it done, you bastard."

"Oh, I think I will. Most of it is concluded already."

"Then I am not the first?"

"Oh my, no. I stopped off for a couple of days in New York City. What a marvelous place. I walked for hours, just seeing the sights, so to speak. Have you ever been to the top of the Empire State Building? What a magnificent view. It literally takes one's breath away."

"Fuck the Empire State Building."

Billy sighed. "You always were so crude, Randy. Even as a boy, you were profane."

"Fuck New York City. And fuck you too, Billy. Jimmy O'Grady?"

"He's dead, I'm afraid. I must say, with a great deal of regret I might add, he was quite the disappointment. Begged for his life and all that sort of nonsense. I always figured him to be a man of courage and vision. It was really shocking to see him groveling."

"You won't see me begging you for a goddamn thing."

"Have you been to confession lately, Randy?"

"Fuck the Church, too."

Billy sighed and shook his head. "You'll face eternal damnation for your sacrilige, Randy. I'll call a priest for you in a moment."

"You know what you can do with a priest, too, don't you? Get this over with, you traitorous bastard."

"As you wish, Randy."

Billy squeezed the trigger twice. Both rounds took his childhood friend in the face, one above the other, in the center of his forehead. Randy fell back on the carpet and died without making a sound.

Billy unscrewed the sound suppressor and placed it in one pocket of his jacket and securely tucked the pistol behind his belt. He picked up the dead man and placed him on the freshly made bed, his head on the pillow and his back to the door. He carefully placed a blanket over him, then cleaned up the few spots of blood on the carpet.

He cracked the drapes and peered out. There was no one in sight.

Billy stepped out, making sure the motel room door locked behind him, and walked to his car and drove off. His business in America was finished.

Thirty-Four

At a store closer to the gravel road that would take them to the small lake and their cabins—which were still about eight miles away—Jack pulled in at a small convenience store and the men bought supplies to last for several days, including lamp oil and a couple of dozen candles, for the cabins had no electricity.

"Almost like camping out," Harry said to Lindsey. "But this way we'll have a roof over our heads." It was accompanied by a grin and a wink.

She screwed up her face and managed a wink of sorts. The girl just could not wink.

None of them paid any attention to the old pickup truck and the car that pulled off the road and parked several hundred yards from the store. Nor did any of them pay any attention when the car and truck pulled out and followed some distance behind them as Jack led the way to the cabins by the lake.

"Boy," Lindsey said, getting out and looking around.

"That guy who lined up these places sure wasn't kidding when he said we didn't have any neighbors to worry about."

"I believe he said the closest cabin was about four miles away," Ted said, walking up.

"That is sure some pretty lake," Dennis said. "I'm surprised there aren't more cabins around it."

"There used to be," Jack replied. "So I was told. But the lake got over-fished, and pretty soon nobody came here at all. Many of the cabins either fell down or burned or were torn down. The lake was restocked several years ago and people are just now returning."

"That's right about the nearest neighbor being four miles away?" Ted asked.

"The closest cabin, yes. But the guy who owns it only comes up here a couple of weekends a month. We're pretty much alone here."

"Suits me," Dennis said.

"Well, let's get this stuff unloaded and then take a stroll down to the lake. Maybe wet a hook."

Harry opened the rear door and reached inside just as a rifle cracked. Ted yelled, grabbed at his shoulder, and went down, his face white from shock.

"Under the car, Lindsey!" Jack yelled, pushing the girl down.

None of the men said a word or went into a panic. No need. They knew the remaining cons had found them, followed them from town, probably. Now they had a fight on their hands.

Jack reached into the rear compartment and pulled out a rifle case, unzipping it as he crouched behind the Explorer. Two boxes of cartridges fell out. He ripped open a box of ammo, hurriedly loaded up the .270, and stowed the boxes of ammo in his jacket pocket.

Harry had crawled over to the other vehicle and gotten the second rifle. It was just the two of them now. Dennis had a broken arm and couldn't handle a rifle, and Ted was down with a bullet wound in the shoulder.

Jack slid a pistol to Lindsey. "It's loaded up full, Baby," he told her. "You handled one like it in the valley. Use it only if you get a clear target. Other than that, keep your head down. Okay?"

"Okay, Jack."

A bullet slammed into the Explorer and Jack snapped a shot with the rifle into the bushes where he thought the gunman was hiding. Someone screamed and pitched face forward out of the bushes, face and neck red with blood.

"Lucky shot," Jack muttered.

"Who got hit?" a voice called.

"Oscar," a second voice called. "Bullet blowed his lower jaw off."

Harry fired three quick rounds from his clip-fed, semi-auto rifle and another man screamed in pain.

"I'm hit, I'm hit! Oh, shit, I got one in the belly!"

Harry put two more rounds into the brush and the man stopped yelling . . . abruptly.

"Is that Randall?" Karl yelled.

"Yeah," Gorman said. "Gut shot. And I'm out of here."

"You get your ass back here!"

"Fuck you, Karl. I'm gone. These old bastards got all the luck, man."

"I'm with you, Tony," Ned called. "Let's go."

"Goddamn you boys!" Kathy screamed at the pair.

"We're takin' the truck," Gorman said. "Bye."

"Shit!" Big Un shouted. "You come back here, you yellow bastards!"

Harry, Jack, Lindsey, and Dennis, who was firing a pistol, all fired at the sound of Big Un's cursing. The cursing stopped abruptly and there was a crashing, thudding sound from the weeds and brush by the side of the cabin. Big

Un sprawled onto the clearing, his face and chest bloody. He did not move.

"Goddamn you old farts!" Jans Pendley screamed.

The four crouched behind the two vehicles all fired at once. They didn't hit anything, but they sure lit a fire under Jans's feet.

"I'm out of here!" Jans hollered. "Hell with this crap!"

"You coward!" Kathy screamed. "You dirty coward!"

Lindsey emptied her pistol at the sound of Kathy's voice. The woman staggered out of the brush, half a dozen bullet wounds in her chest and neck and face, due to the rise of the pistol. She sank to her knees in the clearing, tried to speak, then fell forward on her face and was still.

"Bitch!" Lindsey said, remembering what some of the other women had said Kathy had forced them to do while being held captive.

Hobby, Lippy, Nathan, and Karl hauled their ashes out of there without firing another shot or shouting another obscenity. They had had quite enough of the 'old farts'.

After a few moments Jack stood up from his crouch and tore open Ted's shirt, carefully looking at Ted's shoulder. It was oozing blood, not gushing.

"It hurts like fire, but I'll be all right," Ted said. "I was hit worse than this in 'Nam and we walked out of that damn swamp, remember?"

"Vividly," Jack said. He looked at the others and said, a note of distinct weariness in his tone, "Harry, you and Dennis take Ted into town to a doctor. Flag down a deputy or state officer if you see one, and they'll clear the way for you. I'll stay out here with Lindsey and make sure no animals get to the bodies."

"Okay, Jack," Harry said. "You two sure you want to stay out here by yourselves? I mean . . ."

He paused and held up a hand. They all listened. The

sound of sirens was faint in the distance, and getting louder.

"Well, either the Bureau was following us, or somebody heard the shots and called it in," Jack said.

"I have just one thing to say, Jack," Harry said.

"Oh? What's that?"

Harry smiled. "It's been a hell of a vacation!"

Thirty-Five

The truck Gorman and Ned were in ran out of gas a mile from the cabins and about a hundred yards from where the reporters were parked. Gorman didn't give the reporters a chance to voluntarily give up their car. He shot the man in the head and took the woman. The men took turns driving and humping the reporter in the back-seat. She would be tossed out of the car the next day, alive and the worse for wear but with a decidedly different view of criminals than she had held for years. Gorman and Ned would tangle with police at a roadblock a few hours later, and the taxpayers would be spared further expense.

Nathan surrendered to police an hour after leaving the cabins.

Hobby and Lippy disappeared for several weeks. They were both shot to death by a farmer and his son in Nebraska after trying to steal the farmer's car.

Both Karl and Jans would die in a hail of bullets about a month after the shoot-out at the cabins.

Of the several hundred men who escaped from the federal lockup, not one managed to stay free for any length of time. Dozens were killed or badly wounded.

After much thought, Andy turned down the book contract and decided to keep his mouth shut about the events in The Valley of Death. Andy and his father have not spoken a word to each other since the ordeal.

Sheriff Hawkins retired, and fishes a lot.

Both Dennis and Ted recovered from their wounds.

Luckily, the reporter and Harry never came face-to-face again. But Harry has a long memory.

Lindsey lives with Jack and his wife in California.

The four old friends are making plans for another camping trip . . . next year.

WILLIAM W. JOHNSTONE
THE ASHES SERIES